2ND TIME AROUND

2ND TIME AROUND

by

James Earl Hardy

ALYSON PUBLICATIONS
LOS ANGELES

Manufactured in the United States of America.
Printed on acid-free paper.

This trade paperback original is published by Alyson Publications Inc.,
P.O. Box 4371, Los Angeles, California 90078.
Distribution in the United Kingdom by Turnaround Publisher Services Ltd.,
Unit 3, Olympia Trading Estate, Coburg Road, Wood Green,
London N22 6TZ, England.

First edition: October 1996

5 4 3

ISBN 1-55583-372-1

Library of Congress Cataloging-in-Publication Data
Hardy, James Earl.
    2nd time around / by James Earl Hardy. — 1st ed.
    Sequel to: B-boy blues.
    ISBN 1-55583-372-1
    I. Title.
PS3558.A62375A613 1996
813'.54—dc20   96-21100
                                                CIP

"A House Is Not a Home" by Burt Bacharach and Hal David. Copyright
© 1964 by Largo Music Inc. o/b/o Diplomat Music Corp. All rights
reserved. Used by permission.

IN LOVING MEMORY

Essex Charles Hemphill
Warrior of the Word
Thanks 4 Lighting the Fire
(1957–1995)

&

Steven Franklin Lester Carroll
A Golden Guy Who May Be Gone
but His Spirit Lives On
as Oleta Sings... *We Will Meet Again*
(1965–1996)

J.E.H. WOULD LIKE 2 SEND SHOUT-OUTS 2:

GOD, Who Has Been Mighty Jood 2 Me. Thank U...4 Blessin Me...2 B Myself...Again.

My Mother, Brenda Hannah, Who Gave Me Life So That I Could Touch the Lives of Others. I Pray I've Done U Proud.

My Families—the Saunders (Aunt Sheila; "my sisters," Renie and Inacent; and Michelle Hannah, a homegirl with heart); the Lees (My Father and #1 Fan, James Albert; Glo; Roz; Will and Michelle; and A.D.L.); the Boyces (Aunt Muriel, Chip, and Dee); and the Hardys (2 many 2 mention). Thanks 4 supporting and loving me unconditionally.

The Reids—Earl (a.k.a. Fox), Andrea Jackson, and my beautiful godson, Andre Eli Vincent (a.k.a. Bamm Bamm)—who give new meaning 2 the phrases "good neighbor" and "extended family." Thanks 4 "adopting" me.

Michelle "Sheba" Booker and Cassandra Sellers-Johnson, my Big Sisters. U Go, Divas!

Gordon Eric Easley, K Maurice Jones, and Andre Sydnor. Thanks once 4 the friendship, twice 4 the brotherhood.

The 2 Courtneys, "Love" and Harris. Welcome 2 the Club.

James "Belasco" Tucker, 4 bringing Pooquie and Little Bit 2 life. U R just 2-tuff!

My literary family. Your cards and letters (keep 'em comin!), your words of encouragement and empowerment R gifts I will always treasure. I hope it's jood 2 & 4 U all the *2nd Time Around*.

The bookstores, libraries, clubs, community groups, and schools (a very loud "Hay!" 2 Harvey Milk High in NYC!) that invited me 2 visit. Hope we can do it again the *2nd Time Around*.

Bernard "Pooquie" Henderson and Arnold "Babyface" Burk, 2 of the *phynest*, funniest men I've ever met. I guess life *does* imitate art, huh?

Thomas J. Bevel and Melvin Parks. Those inspired illustrations of the *B-Boy Blues* cast R da Bomb!

Dennis Holmes (a.k.a. Dr. Legs) and Blacks Assisting Blacks

Against AIDS (BABAA/St. Louis). That *B-Boy Blues* festival in the park was *most* festive!

Franklin Alford, Kevin Brown (Will U B *My Bodyguard* the *2nd Time Around?*), Brent Dorian Carpenter, Craig Cobb and Jonathan Clemmons (Black-on-Black Luv 2 THE MAX!), Diversity of Ohio (Columbus), Gay Men of African Descent (GMAD/NYC), Gentlemen Inc. (NYC), E. Lynn Harris, Ernest Horton, Mark Johnson, Anderson Jones, Doug Jones, Dr. Elias Farajaje-Jones, William Jones, Heather Keets, Grant Lewis Jr., Dale Madison, Other Countries (NYC), Larry Sanders, Sisters and Brothers in the Life (SABIL/Albany), Carlton Smith, Albert Sneed and the House of Charles (Go, Motor City!), Gregory Eugene Travis, Linda Villarosa, Anthony Williams, Rich Williams, and Charles S. Wilson Jr. Thank U all 4 being Black & Beautiful.

Stanley Bennett Clay (*SBC*), the *Colours* Organization, Charlene Cothran (*Venus*), John Bernard Jones (*JFY—Just For You, Millennium*), Curtis Lipscomb (*Kick!*), and Gregory Victorianne (*Buti Voxx*). Thanks 4 Giving Same Gender Loving People of African Descent a Press We Can Be Proud Of—& That Makes Us Proud of Ourselves.

New Youth Connections. My 2nd home, always.

Brother Yao, 4 giving me the notebook that *2nd Time Around* was born in. Write On, My Brother.

Charlotte Sheedy, 4 Representin with a c-a-p-i-t-a-l *R*.

Sasha Alyson, 4 taking a chance on me.

& last but not least,

Mitchell, Raheim, & Junior, 4 allowing me 2 come in-2 their lives and share their stories with U. I pray they keep confiding in me, so the *2nd Time* won't be the last.

REWIND '81

Home.

Most folk know how ta spell tha word. And most think they livin in one when they really livin in a house.

Tha first time I learned about tha diff'rence was when I was nine.

I was listenin ta tha radio; I know it had ta be WBLS, "tha-Black-is-Black-and-all-that-and-if-you-can't-hang-get-tha-fuck-back" station, cuz that was all my moms 'n' me listened ta. She was in love wit' that Frankie Crocker wit' tha superdeep voice. He start talkin, and she just be swoonin at tha fuckin radio. I liked his voice too—I wanted one just like it when I grew up and I got one (but mine, I gotta say, is better).

It was August, and we was havin one of them serious heat waves. It was so hot they was talkin about a drought and shit, ain't enuff H-2-0 ta go around. Man, it was so hot, you could fry a fuckin egg on tha sidewalk. Anyway, it was like close ta midnite, and I was s'pose ta be asleep. I ain't like goin ta sleep durin tha summer, cuz I felt like, yo, this my vacation and I don't wanna miss none of it. I would try stayin up as late as I could—and that was usually like one o'clock.

"Boy, what you doin up?" my moms would always ask, watchin me creep inta tha livin room. Well, it wasn't just a livin room. It was, you know, one of them livin room/family room/TV room/dinin room/guest room/party room-type deals, all-in-fuckin-one. Yeah, that room was a lot, but there wasn't that much room ta move around in. You know, you take six, seven steps and ya can't take no mo'? I always said I woulda liked ta have met tha mutha-fuckas that designed that shit so I could knock 'em upside they heads. I mean, just who they think was gonna be livin in tha shit? They was prob'ly white. Like my moms said, "They think we multiply like roaches anyway, so we must live like 'em too, right?"

Anyway, on that nite, Moms was where she always was: sittin on tha couch. And she was doin what she always did: readin a book. I don't remember tha title. Moms loved ta read, and I guess that's where I get it from. It was dark in tha room—it was dark in tha whole house—except fuh tha little lamp on tha dinin room table.

"I ain't sleepy, Ma," I would always say, and she'd have me come on over. She let me lay my head on her shoulder, and I would curl up next ta her.

As soon as I found my spot, Frankie said he was about ta play a new artist, singin a song that we might know but ain't never heard sung like this. I could tell by tha intro that Moms knew it right off tha bat—her breathin got heavier, and she started hummin along.

And then came Tha Voice. *I tell ya, ain't never been one like it, and there ain't never gonna be another one like it. First time I heard it, I just* knew *this brotha was gonna be big. Tha Voice was even smoother than Frankie's. And those lyrics...*

> *A chair is still a chair*
> *even when there's no one*
> *sit-tin there*

A'ight, *I thought,* I can go along wit' that. *I mean, even at nine, that shit made perfect sense ta me. Just cuz you ain't sittin in no chair don't mean it ain't one, right? But then tha brotha really dropped some science....*

> *But a chair is not a house*
> *and a house is not a home*
> *when there's no one there*
> *to hold you tight*
> *and no one there*
> *you can kiss*
> *good-night*

I put my left thumb in my mouth, and Moms dropped tha book in her lap. We was both...I don't know. Hyp-no-tized? By tha time tha song went off—tha brotha was beggin, "Say you're gonna be in love with me...I want you, I need you to be..." *—she was cryin.*

I got scared. "Ma, ma, what's wrong, what's wrong?" *I was wipin away her tears.*

She didn't even look at me. "Oh, nothin, baby, nothin."

She had been like this befo', and those times it was cuz of my pops. She cried too much and too long over him leavin, and she always did it sittin in tha same spot she was in. But it couldn't be him this time...could it? I ain't know it then, but I know now that somebody don't hafta be in yo' life fuh 'em ta touch ya like that, fuh 'em ta have an effect like that on ya. Till this day she ain't tell me if it was him she was cryin about, but I know it was. I just know that song meant somethin ta him, ta her. That was tha first time I saw how a song can move somebody ta cryin.

Long after that song played she still cried and, cuz I ain't know why she was crying, I cried too. And we just sat there, cryin. And I remember thinkin about that song. "A House Is Not a Home." Ain't that it? And I started addin shit up (yeah, I was a smart mutha-fuckin kid): if she cryin about Pops, is she sad cuz our house ain't no home cuz he ain't here?

I fell asleep, prob'ly as soon as tha clock hit one. I was almost gone when I felt her pull me closer and hold me. But she ain't wake me up ta tell me ta go inta my room like she always do. She settled next ta me, and we just stayed like that. And she began hummin tha song. And as she hummed, I could hear it as I went ta sleep and even when I was sleepin. It was just fillin up my head and goin thru me. And, I don't know…I think I knew right then and there that I was gonna make my mom's house a home. Ain't nuthin that said I couldn't do it. If it made her happy, I had ta try, cuz I ain't wanna see her cry like that again.

And I also knew that I ain't wanna feel like my moms did. I ain't wanna be cryin over nobody like that. And tha best way ta do that was ta not let nobody get close ta me. I could make a home out of a house fuh myself wit'out nobody else.

But then I met Little Bit.

FROM THA JUMP

Ain't love a bitch?

Now, don't get me wrong—I love feelin this way, cuz I feel jood. How jood do I feel? Well, tha shit is gonna sound corny, but I feel so jood about Little Bit, about us, that I would give him tha world. I ain't never thought I say that shit, cuz I never knew what tha fuck it meant. Well, I ain't know what it mean but I sure as hell knew it made no fuckin sense. *If this world were mine, I'd give you anything.* Ain't that how Marvin 'n' Tammi sang it? "I'd give the flowers, the birds, and the bees." Yeah-fuckin-right. I always saw that shit as a joke. You *can't* give nobody no birds or bees, and even if ya could, why would you?

But now that I got Little Bit, I think I know tha deal. I *do* wish I could give him tha birds, tha bees, tha flowers, tha trees, tha sky, tha sun, tha moon, all that shit, ya know, cuz I *can't* do it, cuz it can't be done, but I wanna make tha impossible possible fuh him, *to* him, wit' him. And if that means killin fire or movin tha fuckin mountains, so be it, I do it. Uh-huh, that's how much he means ta me. It took me some time ta realize it, ta see I felt that way. I don't know when it started...tha first time I saw him, tha first time he sang ta me, tha first time I held him, tha first time we kissed, tha first time I tasted him (and he is tasty, too), tha first time he gave it up (and that shit was on point and Jood wit' a capital *J*, G). It coulda been when we was just tagetha, ya know, just bein wit' each other, doin nuthin but layin up or loungin around. I don't know when it went down, but it got me.

But I hate feelin this way cuz I ain't never felt like this befo'. I mean, there's a whole lota shit goin on in me—I can *feel* them emotions just jumpin around, ya know?—and it's somethin I can't control and it ain't somethin I wanted. Shit, I ain't even *think* it could happen ta me. I always saw this love thang as bein fuh suckers. All that mushy-mushy shit ain't never been fuh Tha Kid. Gettin all wrapped up in somebody, always thinkin about what they doin, thinkin, feelin, dreamin, havin 'em on yo' mind *all* tha fuckin time, knowin you can't be wit'out 'em, live wit'out 'em? That shit is just straight-up *wacked*, it drives you cray-zee. I know cuz I seen people go thru it—and most of 'em been in love wit' me. I was trippin on that shit, and I wasn't tha one feelin it. But now, I *really* know how they felt. And it ain't cute.

It's just so strange, ya know: I mean, one day, you just mindin yo' bizness, not botherin nobody, and then *bam!* It just slams inta you, like you just got hit by a car or a bus or a truck or an Amtrak train and shit. I mean, it just comes outa nowhere and makes sure you *know* it's there. And it don't let up. It keeps at ya, all tha time, till you ain't got no choice but ta call it out and claim it. It pushes, and pushes, and pushes, till you can't take it anymore. It weighs on ya heart; sometimes it felt like my heart was comin outa my chest and shit, it was beatin so fast, so hard. I couldn't sleep, I couldn't eat, I ain't even wanna fuck or jerk off. Shit, I *knew* somethin was wrong when I wasn't even horny. Man, I was startin ta walk around like one of them zombies in *Night of the Living Dead,* talkin ta myself and shit, tellin whatever this shit was ta leave me tha fuck alone. I was tryin ta shake it off, get rid of it, ignore it, but it wouldn't go away. It just ate at me, makin it clear as fuckin day that this was somethin I couldn't deny.

But what tha *fuck* was it?

So, I was mopin around tha house, not wantin ta do nuthin, and my moms was like, 'What the hell is wrong with you, lookin all pitiful? You in love or somethin?" I freaked out. Love? In love? Could it really be *that?* I was tryin ta fuhget Little Bit; I ain't hate him or nuthin, but I just wanted ta get him outa my mind cuz I felt guilty about what I did, not callin ta see if he was a'ight, just steppin, leavin him high 'n' dry. But it ain't work. I mean, I loved bein around Little Bit, but did that mean I loved *him?*

It made me wanna punch a fuckin wall, knowin I felt like this and I couldn't do nuthin about it. I was mad at myself. Why? Cuz I fucked up, *big time.* I blew tha best thing that ever happened ta me. I thought about how *stoo*pid I was while waxin sentimental, listenin over and over and over again ta that song Little Bit sang ta me that nite we met (I don't know why since it just made me feel worse about what went down). Then I came across another Lalah Hathaway jam, "I'm Coming Back"—and it really hit home. I had ta come back...*home.* And that's when I just knew I *had* ta try and get him back. I couldn't give it up ta nobody but him, ya know what I'm sayin? (And, yeah, I been waitin a *long* time ta give it up.) He's Tha One. And if it was really love and he loved me too, then I wouldn't hafta go thru this by myself.

So I got up tha courage ta go back and tell him I loved him. And, yeah, I took my Li'l Brotha Man, cuz I knew Little Bit wasn't gonna slam no do' in *his* face. I think Li'l Brotha Man loves Little Bit just as much as I do—when I told him who we was gonna see, his whole face was shinin and shit, beams of light just bouncin off it. I ain't never seen him get so happy over goin ta see somebody befo'. I was just as happy as he was, but I was mo' scared than happy. I mean, I ain't wanna say "I love you" ta his face cuz I ain't wanna get *my* face broke. That's why I was glad we was sittin down on tha couch when I told him and he couldn't look me in my eyes. But I was still afraid of his answer. After all I had put Little Bit thru…why would he love a mutha-fucka like me? I know *I* wouldn't. All that shit I said, all that shit I did, and all tha shit I ain't say and do but shoulda done and said…? *He don't want you,* I said ta myself, waitin fuh him ta answer me. *You ain't nuthin but a sorry-ass nigga. He can do better than yo' ass.* He would have ev'ry right ta say *fuck* I love you and *fuck* you too. But—and I know this is gonna sound *stoo*pid considerin how I hurt him—I ain't wanna get hurt neither. (Yeah, there I go, thinkin about me again, right?) But I remember tha look on all tha faces of them females and them niggaz who told me they love me and shit and I ain't say tha same. I mean, it *is* jood lovin somebody and somebody loves you back, ya know? And ta know you feel that way fuh somebody and it ain't mutual, that's like…like…I don't know. Fuh some, I guess it would be like dyin. And that's tha way those folks who said they loved me looked when I ain't make it ditto.

So, I was ready fuh defeat. I just knew Little Bit was gonna say, "No, Pooquie, I don't love you," and kick my ass *to* and *off* tha curb. But when he squeezed my hand and I felt him smile, I knew he was gonna say it—and he did. And it was like, right then, I had tha world in the palm of my hands. Them three words was all I needed ta hear, and I coulda just died right there. Little Bit made my nite. He made my life.

But that, little did I know, was tha *easy* part. Sayin it is one thing; showin it, bein it, *livin* it is another. I just knew that bein tagetha was gonna be better this time. And it was. But tha shit just don't stay that way. It takes a lota hard fuckin work ta love somebody, and I ain't had no experience wit' this. I mean, lovin Little Bit ain't like lovin Li'l Brotha Man, my moms, or Brotha Man. I don't know how ta explain it, but it's almost like learnin ta ride a bicycle. Ya know, I can work them wheels, burn some serious rubber on a ten-speed. But at first it was awkward; I felt clumsy and dumb, 'specially when I fell off tha fuckin bike like a dozen times. Ya gotta be on point, on balance, tha straight 'n' narrow, lookin at tha road and not ya feet, trustin ya hands ta do tha steerin, ya feet ta do tha pedalin, and ya legs ta do tha pushin. This love thang is kinda like that, chartin unknown territory and shit, takin a trip, a ride that you know is gonna be excitin but is gonna hold a whole lota surprises fuh yo' ass. It's gonna make you see and feel things you might not wanna. Sometimes you gonna be ridin like tha wind, smooth mutha-fuckin sailin and shit. And sometimes it's gonna be bumpy, you gonna tumble, may even crumble, just fall flat on yo' mutha-fuckin face. But no matter what tha fuck goes down, you gonna be better fuh it, cuz it teaches you somethin new about yo'self, what ya can and can't handle.

And that's what's happenin ta me right now. I feel a serious love fuh Little Bit, and I know he loves me. But can I *really* love him? Do I know how ta do it? Can I learn how ta do it? Little Bit says I can. It ain't gonna happen overnite, and it ain't gonna be as cool as I want it ta be. Am I afraid? *Hell*-fuckin-yeah. But that's natural, ain't it? But somethin he said really got me: "You can't be afraid or ashamed of who you are."

Hunh?

Now, I had ta think about *that* shit. And tha more I thought about it tha more it was obvious that…I *don't* know who I am. Or do I? I mean, I know who I am, but do I *really* know who I am? This is some *cray-zee* shit ta be dealin wit', ya know? It's like I'm discoverin things about me—*tryin* ta discover things about me—and askin questions about me I ain't never asked befo'. You know, like, who I am…what I am…why I am…how I am…where I am…where I came from…where I wanna go…. It's like that silly shit you hear folks say on tha *Ricki Flake* show, but is deep as a mutha-fuckin ocean.

And it all scares tha *shit* outa me.

MAKIN WAVES

"Little Bit?"

"Mmm, yeah?"

"You fallin asleep."

"I am not."

"You is too, I can tell."

"How? You ain't hear me snorin, so don't even say you did."

"You was droolin."

"Droolin?"

"Yeah."

"I was not!"

"You was too. You do it when you about ta doze off. *Then* you start snorin."

"We are in a tub, Pooquie. That's water you feel."

"No it ain't. I know when my Baby is droolin on me like a baby."

"I'm sorry."

"Don't be. I love it."

"You do?"

"Yeah."

"Why?"

"Cuz...I don't know. It's just one thing that makes you you."

"Well, I guess I can't help but fall asleep. It's so relaxing, lying back in the arms of the man I love."

"Say that again."

"Say what again?"

"You know."

"Lying back...in the arms...of the man...I love."

"Mmm, I like tha way that sound."

"I do too. That's why I said it twice."

"You can say it a third time."

"You would like that, wouldn't you?"

"Nah...I would *love* it."

"OK...*l*ying back in the arms of the man I *l-o-v-e*."

"Thank you."

"You're more than welcome."

And I'm mo' than happy ta get that juicy kiss.

"Baby?"

"Yes?"

"How long you think we been in here?"

"I don't know. I guess maybe a half hour. Why?"

"That would explain it."

"Explain what?"

"Why all tha bubbles are gone."

"Yeah. And why the water isn't exactly hot anymore."

"Uh-huh, tha shit is cold!"

"Well, do you wanna make it hot?"

"It don't hafta be, cuz I am."

"Funny, very funny."

"I ain't tryin ta be. I'm serious."

"I know, I know. You don't have to tell me you're hot...I can *feel* it."

Uh-huh, tag my tongue, why don't ya.

"Mmm, I can *taste* it too. You could definitely spoil me, Pooquie."

"Huh?"

"Spoil me."

"Whatcha mean?"

"Well, I'm getting a little too used to this."

"Useta what?"

"These bubble baths, the massages, you servin me breakfast in bed..."

"So? What's wrong wit' that?"

"What's wrong is that we can't take a bath together every night and—"

"Who says we can't?"

"Nothing says we *can't*, but it can't be that way all the time."

"Baby, it can be any way we want it ta be."

"What I mean is, it's something we *have* to do every day, but there ain't no guarantee we can always do it *together*."

"We *can*."

"And besides, we don't have enough bubble bath!"

"Then we make our own bubbles."

"Oh, really?"

"Yeah. Come on, Baby. You *spoilin* tha mood."

"I'm just—"

"—I know, I know, you just tryin ta be re-al-is-tic, right? That's been yo' *fav'*rite word tha past five days...*and* nites."

"Well, I think that—"

"—it's important fuh us ta be. Yeah, I know. I know it is. And, like I said, I think we bein realistic about things."

"I never said we weren't. I just want us to—"

"—keep level heads about how we feel and what we want, yeah, I know. Baby, it's all jood. Do we hafta go over *that* again?"

"No, no, we don't. I'm sorry."

"Baby, all I wanna do is hold you like this ev'ry nite. I don't think that's a lot ta ask. Ya know?"

"Yeah. No, it isn't a lot to ask. I guess it all is just too *jood* to be true."

"Who *you* tellin? I ain't never thought I'd be wit' somebody like this."

"Yeah?"

"Yeah."

"So, why do you wanna be?"

"Cuz."

" 'Cause what?"

"Cuz I love you."

"Mmm, I *love* the way that sounds. Say it again."

"I l-o-v-e you."

"Three times!"

"Little Bit, you cray-zee!"

"Come on, three's the charm. And I did it for you. *Please?*"

"A'ight, a'ight. I...love...you."

"Thank you."

"Nah, thank *you,* Baby."

"Pooquie?"

"Yeah?"

"I hate to say this, but...not even you can keep me warm in this water."

"A'ight...let's drain it and fill it back up."

"Fill it back up?"

"Yeah."

"What for?"

"So we can chill a little bit longer."

"Pooquie, we'll get too wrinkled."

"I don't care."

"And I still have to do your hair."

"Ain't even no hair up there, Baby."

"And I—"

Just shut up and gimme them honeysuckle lips.

"OK, Pooquie, OK…five more minutes."

"Fifteen, Baby, c'mon…"

"Ten. Ten and *only* ten. All right?"

"A'ight, a'ight. And put some bubble stuff in."

"I thought you said we could make our own?"

"I did, but, you know, it was just a, a—"

"A *lie?*"

"Nah, Baby, it wasn't no lie.…"

"Well, that's what it was." He broke away from me. "I thought you said you would never lie to me."

"C'mon, Baby, it was a sweet nuthin.…"

"Uh-huh. It *sounded* sweet and it meant absolutely *nothin.*"

"I *meant* it cuz I *said* it."

"Oh, yeah?"

"*Yeah.*"

"*Well*…you got any other sweet nothings you'd like to share?"

"*Yeah.*"

"*What?*"

"I don't *need* no H-2-O ta take a bath wit' you."

"Why not?"

"Cuz all I gotta do is dive in-to *you.*"

"Oh, *really?*"

"Yeah, *really.*"

"Mmm…would you, uh, like to dip your toe in it now?"

"Yeah…but it ain't my toe that's gonna do tha dippin."

And it wasn't.

REWIND '81

"Girl, I tell ya, it's hard out here."

"Yeah, I know."

"Well, if you know, how come you ain't doin nothin to make it easy on you."

"What you talkin about, Francie?"

"I'm talkin about you workin two jobs when you don't have to."

"I don't?"

"No, you don't."

"Why don't I?"

"You know why. There ain't nothin like havin somebody around to help out."

"Havin somebody around?"

"Girl, what is with you? It's been four years since that nigger left."

"Francie, don't call him that, all right?"

"What would you call him, runnin out on his wife and kid? When you gonna stop makin excuses for him? What you doin, waitin for him to come back?"

"No, no, I'm not."

"For all you know, he dead. He may as well be."

"You let me worry about that, OK?"

"Well, you shouldn't be worryin about him in any way."

"He may not be here, but I am still a married woman."

"Girl, you really foolin yourself. That piece of paper ain't mean a damn thing to him, or he wouldn't have left. The bottom line is that he ain't here but you are, and your life has to go on."

"Meaning?"

"Meanin, who you savin yourself for? You need some company. When was the last time you fucked?"

"Francie, that ain't none of your business!"

"That long, hunh? You need it, I need it, we all need it, and four years is too fuckin long to be goin without it."

"I can't be bringin no strange man up into this apartment."

"Why not? Don't you pay the rent? The bills?"

"Francie, I do *have a son."*

"I know, and that's another reason why you need to have a man up in here."

"What?"

"He need a man around here too. You can't be no daddy to him."

"Who says I can't?"

"C'mon, girl, he at that age when he don't just need his mama. How you gonna teach him how to be a man?"

"I been doin fine. We been doin fine."

"Fine ain't gonna cut it. I'm tellin you, you just can't do it. You want him turnin out funny? He got to have some men, a man, around him. If all he around is girls and women, that's what he gonna end up bein."

"Francie, that's silly."

"No it ain't. Look at Winnie. One day her Melvin is playin baseball, the next thing you know she comes home and finds him in one of her dresses."

"That ain't gonna happen to Junior."

"You dreamin, girl. I'm tellin you, it can happen."

"If it does happen, it ain't gonna be because his daddy ain't around."

"Well, I ain't takin that chance. Yeah, some of these niggers ain't worth shit, but at least D is seein what he's supposed to grow up to be. You should see how Raheim acts when Trey or Flint stops by and they take him and D out for a drive or somethin. I'm tellin you, Raheim sees it, and don't think he don't be wonderin why his mama don't be entertainin like his Aunt Francie."

"You still seein Trey? I thought it was over between y'all."

"Yeah, it is, but he be droppin by sometime, just to see how we doin. You want him?"

"Excuse me?"

"You heard. Do you want him?"

"Why would I want him?"

"Why not? He available, and you ain't exactly been in play. And he wants you."

"He wants me*?"*

"He always been wantin you, even though he ain't gonna admit it. Every time Raheim come over, he always ask him, 'How that fine mama of yours doin?' "

"No, I don't want him."

"Well, you want me to ask him about any friends?"

"No. I'm just not ready to do somethin like that. I don't know…I might not ever be ready."

"Grace?"

"Yeah?"

"He ain't comin back. And even if he did, why would you want him?"*

"*This ain't about* him. *This is about* me."

"*OK, whatever you say. But I'm tellin you—you and Raheim gonna be much better off if you just forget about* him."

"*Well, I don't need a man to take care of me and my son. And Junior is the only man I need in this house.*"

"*He* ain't *no man.*"

"*He's the man of* this *house.*"

"*Fine, fine. But I'm tellin ya: he may be the only man you* need *in this house, but he ain't gonna be the only one you'll* want."

TRUST & HONESTY

"No?"

"Yes, Raheim…no."

"Why not?"

"Because it's too early to be thinking about something like that—"

"Too early? Baby, whatcha talkin 'bout? We *livin* tagetha."

"Well, we might be but we really aren't."

"Hunh?"

"What I mean is that, while you are here almost seven days a week, you do have another home outside of this apartment, another life outside of me."

"So?"

"Well, we don't live together in the sense that this is *our* place. You don't pay rent—"

"Is that whatcha want me ta do? Pay rent? I do it, I ain't got no problem wit' that."

"No, Raheim, that's not what I want you to do. You hold your own. We already talked about that. It's that we just got back together and we're starting to get to know each other again. And there will be times when you'll need your space and I'll need mine."

"Space?"

"Yes. You come and go when you want, Raheim. And you have another place to go to. And that's fine. And it's important that…knowing I have the option of telling you I need time for myself is very important."

"A'ight, a'ight. I know whatcha sayin. You sayin you wanna be able ta tell me ta get tha *fuck* out if you feel like it, and I can't say a *God*-day-am thang cuz this yo' place."

"You don't have to put it like that."

"That's what you mean."

"It is not."

"It is too."

"It is *not.*"

"Don't even try it, Baby. You know it's true."

"OK, OK, fine…I don't feel that way, because I would hope I would never have to *tell* you to get the fuck out, I don't wanna be bothered. But since you put it that way…I *should* have the right to say that if I want and not expect to see you until I want to."

"Listen up, Baby, listen up, a'ight? We tagetha, right?"

"Yes."

"And we a couple, right?"

"Yes."

"So what's tha problem?"

"The problem is that we are not ready for that type of commitment."

"We ain't?"

"No, we're not."

"Maybe you ain't, but I am."

"No, you're not, Raheim."

"How tha *fuck* you gonna tell me what I'm ready fuh?"

"You don't have to get all upset—"

"Then don't be actin like you *know* ev'ry mutha-fuckin thang."

"OK, OK…you *might* be ready for that step but I am not, and I don't think we should do it if we're not both there."

"So when you think you gonna be there?"

"I don't know."

"So, what, I'm s'pose ta wait fuh you ta decide when you ready?"

"This is not about me making you wait for me."

"It is too, Baby. This don't hafta be no big deal, but you makin it one."

"It *is* a big deal, Pooquie. I just want us to do this slow. We have the time. There is no rush. I don't see why this one thing is so important."

"You don't, hunh? Little Bit, I love you."

"I know, Pooquie, I love you too."

"Well then, what's holdin you back?"

"Nothing is holding me back."

"C'mon, Baby, be straight wit' me…I know, I know. It's cuz I fucked up, right?"

"What?"

"It's cuz I *fucked* up."

"What do you mean?"

"You don't trust me."

"Pooquie, it's not that I don't trust you—"

"If you did, Baby, we wouldn't be talkin about this."

"I trust you. If I didn't, I would not have taken you back. But—"

"*Yeah?*"

"Raheim, will you...this is not easy to talk about."

"Go on, say it: I fucked up and you punishin me."

"Raheim, please. Just listen to me—"

"I'm listenin, I'm listenin, go ahead."

"You...you did hurt me, and—"

"Little Bit, I know—"

"No, you *don't* know, Pooquie. You *don't* know...will you just let me..."

"C'mon, Baby, don't—don't cry."

"It's hard...to talk about, but we have to. Just...just let me try to get this out, Pooquie."

"A'ight, Baby, a'ight. C'mon, let's sit down on tha couch."

We did.

"Pooquie...when you hit me, I...I hated you."

"You did?"

"Yes, I did. But after time I saw that hating you...it wasn't a good thing. It isn't good to hate...it takes a lot out of you. I came to a point where I stopped hating you because I had to go on and it wasn't healthy for me. But I *haven't* stopped hating what you did."

"I said I was sorry, Baby."

"I know."

"And I said I ain't never gonna do it again."

"Yes, I know, Pooquie, I know. You've told me so many times. You only have to tell me once. But because it happened...I don't know...there's...fear."

"You...you afraid of me?"

"No, I'm not afraid of *you*. I feel safe with you. And I don't think I would feel that way if that time didn't pass. I'm just afraid it might happen again."

"But Baby, I—"

"Pooquie, you can say you won't do it again, you can say it won't happen again, and I believe you when you say it, I know you really mean it...I can *feel* it...but...we just don't know...they say you *will* do it again."

"*They?* Who they? Nobody but Gene, right?"

"No, no, I'm talking about the people who...deal with this kind of thing."

"Whatcha mean, Baby?"

"I just, you know, read up on it. People don't think it can happen to us, but it does."

"C'mon, Baby, it...it wasn't like that."

"But it was, Pooquie. You abused me."

"But it was a mistake, Baby. I ain't never do that ta nobody I love."

"How about to somebody you hate?"

"Whatcha sayin?"

"I'm saying that that's what I saw in your eyes...just before you hit me."

"I was angry, Baby. I ain't hate you. I ain't like that, you should—"

"I should know? How could I? That's just it, Pooquie. We were together for two months, and I knew more about Junior than I did about you."

"Uh...yeah...yeah...I guess so."

"One thing I *did* learn that I do not like is your temper. You do get angry too quick. Like that night at the party—"

"You gotta bring up that?"

"Yes, I do, because I haven't before and we have to talk about it."

"A'ight, a'ight. What about it?"

"Pooquie, you can't let your emotions...I still don't understand why you became so enraged. Well, I *do* know."

"You do?"

"Yes."

"Whatcha think it is?"

"Why don't you tell me. You know."

"Uh, uh...I...if uh...if things don't go my way, I just go off and sometimes I don't care what I say...I guess...I don't know...I guess I just wanna..."

"Control?"

"Uh...I...I don't know. I guess."

"Well, it can't be like that, Pooquie. It's not a jood thing to be with me or with anyone else. And what about Junior?"

"What about Li'l Brotha Man?"

"That day in the kitchen. The look on his face when you cursed at him, yelled at him. You can't keep on doing that, going off on people like that. If you treat him like that, he'll grow up thinking that that's the way to deal with things, by striking out."

"But, Baby, I was just dealin wit' a whole lot, and—"

"That's no excuse, Pooquie. If you got a lot on your mind, a lot to handle, you can't take it out on others. And the only person you can control is *you*. You can't control me, treating me like I'm your property."

"I don't treat you like that."

"You don't right now, but you did. Trying to tell me what I can wear, who I can dance with—"

"Baby, that ain't really tha way it was—"

"Yes it was, Pooquie. You get jealous and you don't see anything but red. Things ain't the way you want them to be and you throw a tantrum. Instead of dealing with it, you use words...and your hands to hurt."

"But, Baby, you makin it seem like I ain't do nuthin but...but abuse you, all tha time."

"No, I am not saying that. But you can't deny that it all happened."

"I ain't."

"In a way, you are. You're trying to explain it away, to couch it.... Even if you called me names once, it happened.... Even if you only hit me once, it happened...and it shouldn't happen at all."

"But I ain't like that anymore."

"Well, you can say that, Pooquie. But are you saying that because you've changed or because it's what you want me to hear?"

"Baby...I...I hurt you bad...and I hurt myself...I don't never wanna feel that again...I don't never want ya ta, neither...and I don't want ya ta be afraid...."

"I don't want to be. But it's there. I...I just have to be sure. It's not about making you suffer or getting back at you. I have to feel that...that I can let you in my life...completely."

"A'ight."

"I'm taking a chance."

"I ain't gonna let you down, Baby."

"I don't want you to let *yourself* down, Pooquie, the same way I don't wanna let *myself* down. The biggest chance we're taking is on ourselves, not on each other."

"I'm sorry, Baby."

"What are you sorry about this time?"

"Fuh puttin you thru this. It's all my fault."

"I'm not gonna argue with you, 'cause it is. I'm kinda sorry too."

"Why?"

" 'Cause I didn't say anything before...I guess I didn't want to push you away. But I know you're sorry. Like I said, I do forgive you for what you did...it's just that I can't forget."

"You think you ever gonna fuhget?"

"I probably never will. But I hope one day...it won't be right there, right in front of me. But I don't know when that day is gonna come."

"But what can I *do*, Baby?"

"Just keep on doin what you doin...assuring me...and working on *you*. I mean, it's OK to be angry. Hell, to be a Black man in America, you *have* to be angry just to keep your sanity!"

"You got *that* right, Baby!"

"Yeah. But it's a different story when you let the anger control you. You have to know what to do with it, you have to learn how to express it the right way, so that it doesn't hurt anyone...including yourself."

"Well, I'm gonna work on it, Baby. And I ain't gonna do it fuh you. I'm gonna do it fuh *me*."

"*Jood*. 'Cause if you do, then *we'll* be all right."

Lip lock time.

"And Pooquie?"

"Yeah?"

"Don't worry about not having a key to the house, 'cause you already have the key to my heart."

2 ALL MY TRICKS 'N' TREATS

"Hey...long time no *feel*."

Ah, *shit*. Me 'n' Little Bit was at this Halloween party Uptown. I ain't wanna go. I hate Halloween. Tha shit just spooks me tha fuck out. I don't see how mutha-fuckas can get inta celebratin ghouls, goblins 'n' gremlins. Li'l Brotha Man, he likes ta go trickin 'n' treatin, but that's tha only thing I'll do (this year he went as Blackman—you know, dressed up like Batman, minus that wack-ass mask). But since we ain't been doin nuthin but knockin boots since we got back tagetha (and knockin 'em *day*-am jood), Little Bit wanted ta get out tha house. Wasn't nobody dressed up in no costumes—this ain't that kinda jam, ya know what I'm sayin? But I just knew half tha mutha-fuckas up in tha place was just itchin ta put on a dress and high heels.

Anyway, I got on tha drink line. Little Bit 'n' Angel was in tha other room, catchin up. They ain't seen each other since Brotha Man made his exit. I was just mindin my own bizness, ya know, I wasn't botherin nobody, groovin ta "Love Is the Message" (there *ain't* no party wit'out that jam), wishin somebody would tell these voguin queens that Paris done burned, when I felt this hand goin up tha back of my left thigh. My body froze, my head turned around, and there was tha *last* person I needed ta see, wit' Little Bit around.

David.

I could just *see* a fight happenin, but this time it wasn't gonna be me throwin down. I know Little Bit danced wit' that greazy nigga that nite at tha brotha-boy bash cuz of David. Brotha Man said I was *stoo*pid ta be flauntin David up in his face like that. But, yo, I wasn't flauntin; I ain't think Little Bit would mind if I danced wit' him. A'ight, a'ight: so I prob'ly danced a little too long and a little too close wit' him. I wasn't gonna stay wit' him all nite. I guess I shoulda told Little Bit who David was, but then you know there woulda been some *serious* static. But that mutha-fucka Little Bit was dancin wit', he was just tryin ta move in on my Baby. I guess Little Bit figured that what's jood fuh you is jood fuh me. And that's why I jumped that mutha-fucka.

I tried blamin my bloody nose on Little Bit, David, and that sorry-ass nigga, but I ain't really had nobody ta blame but me. I really fucked up. Well, history *ain't* repeatin itself. I ain't gettin inta nuthin wit' David. I know David don't like Little Bit—he told me. I could see him tryin ta start some shit—like he was doin right then. I recognize that hand any-place. He know how that shit useta turn me on. That's right, *useta*. It don't get ta me unless Little Bit do it now.

But he *was* makin me nervous. So I tried ta be cool, I tried ta smile, keepin an eye out fuh Little Bit. "Ha, yeah."

He still held on. "I missed seeing you…and feeling you."

I moved his hand. "Yeah, I bet you do."

"What's wrong? You don't like being fondled no more?"

Tha line moved, and we did too. "Yeah, but not by you."

"You wasn't sayin that the last time I had my hand there in August."

Yeah, we did tha nasty—and it *was* nasty. But… "That was then, this is now."

"And what's so different about now?"

"You know. I got my Baby, that's what's diff'rent now."

"Uh-huh…" He turned. He spotted Little Bit. He frowned.

I did too. "You got a problem?"

"Uh, no, no…so, how are things?" He gave me that fake smile.

I shrugged. "They a'ight."

"Well?"

"Well…?"

"Aren't you going to ask me?"

"Ask you what?"

"How things are going with me?"

"You know you wanna tell me, so go ahead."

"Yeah, you're right, I do. Things are fine. They could be better."

I moved up. He had that *Aren't you going to ask me why?* look. But he knew I wasn't, so he did.

I still played dumb. "Ask you what?"

He punched my arm. "*You* know. *Why* they could be better."

"Why we gotta play this game?"

"Play a game? I ain't playin no game—"

"You is too."

"What I'm doing is trying to make you guess the obvious: that things could be better if we were together."

"Better fuh who?"

"Better for the both of us."

I laughed. Tha line moved again. "You think so, huh?"

"Yeah, I do."

"Ha, you think wrong."

"Snuggles, I know you—"

"You *don't* know me, and *don't* call me that, a'ight?"

"Why?"

"Cuz I ain't yo' *fuckin* Snuggles, a'ight?"

He grinned. "You always will be, to me."

I really felt like punchin tha shit outa him, but I ain't need ta be thrown outa no party again. Anyway, it was my turn on line. I turned ta tha brotha pourin tha liquid. "Yeah, my man, gimme a orange juice, straight."

David sucked his teeth. "Orange juice? Since when you get so soft?"

"It ain't fuh me, a'ight?"

"Uh-huh...why don't you just get him a milk shake?"

I frowned. I took tha juice and nodded at tha brotha.

It was his turn. "Sex on the Beach, please."

He smiled. I didn't.

I bent over ta get a beer outa this big garbage can filled wit' ice. He decided ta pinch me on tha ass.

I found my Bud. I turned ta him. "You just askin fuh it, ain't ya?"

"Uh-huh. And I *want* it."

I started walkin away, and he grabbed my arm. "Wait."

I sighed. "What?"

"You gonna save a dance for me?"

"Nah."

"Why not?"

"You know why not. You just don't get it. It's over."

"You say that now...but just like before, you'll be back."

"Why you even wanna play yo'self?"

"I'm not."

"Uh-huh. Well, you just hold on ta that, cuz that's all you got."

He got real close; we was almost eye ta eye. "What I *got* is a treat for *you.*"

I grinned. "A *treat?* Ha, comin from you, it be a *trick.* Now, pardon me, but my Baby's waitin."

His face was cracked, but he tried ta put it back tagetha. "Uh-huh, that's all right. *I'll* be waiting too."

Uh-huh, and you gonna be waitin. Why don't he just get over it? I mean, I know it's hard ta fuhget Tha Kid...like Little Bit say, I'm just a too p-h-y-n-e brotha. But David actin like Glenn Close in *Fatal Attraction* and shit. He trippin cuz he know, he can see it in my eyes. And he heard me say it, too: that last time he gave me some, I called out fuh Little Bit. He ain't say nuthin about it, but I know he was hurt. So he know I'm talkin about somethin real, not artificial like it was wit' him. Yeah, tha sex was jood, but that's all it was. This about love, and ain't no way he can love me like Little Bit.

But even tho' I knew all this, I got smoochy (that's what Li'l Brotha Man calls it when me 'n' Sunshine be huggin up sometimes) wit' Little Bit. Yeah, Little Bit was surprised. It's one thing ta get on tha flo' and work that groove; it's another ta hold my Baby's hand and kiss him and squeeze him up. In tha apartment? No prob. But all out in fronta ev'rybody? You *gots* ta be cray-zee. Yeah, I know—I was doin it cuz I felt I had somethin ta prove. But David got tha message. It fucked wit' him; he gave us some dirty looks, but he ain't come up ta me fuh tha rest of tha nite.

Angel said Little Bit saw me 'n' David and he ain't look too happy. So when we was in bed fuh tha nite, I asked him about it.

"I'm not angry at you because you talked to him, Pooquie."

"You ain't?"

"No, I ain't. Should I be?"

"Nah, I guess not. I mean, I ain't know he was gonna be there."

"I'm not that pleased about the way he acts around me, though."

"Whatcha mean, Baby? He don't be botherin you."

"Well, he *does* bother me. He doesn't have to talk to me, he doesn't have to hold a conversation with me. But the least he could do is acknowledge that I exist. His ignoring me, acting like you are still available...it's so childish. I'm sure he would be very happy if I confronted him so we could fight over you."

"Fight over me?"

"Yes, fight over you. And don't even make it seem like *that* never crossed your mind."

Yeah, it did.

He sighed. "But I have a lot more class and integrity than that. He doesn't."

"You mean, you wouldn't fight over me?"

"No."

"Why not?"

"Why should I?"

"Cuz I'm yo' man."

"Right. And if you my man then I shouldn't have to fight anybody *for* you. I know you mine. And if somebody turns your head, then that means *you* didn't want to be *my* man."

Hmm...jood point.

"Maybe if he respected me, respected *us,* I wouldn't have a problem with him."

"If you felt like that, Baby, you shoulda told me."

"Why should I have to tell you? It should bother you that he acts that way."

"Well, it do, and I ain't gonna talk ta him again. It ain't like I talk ta him anyway. I mean, he came up ta me. He still sweatin me. He was tryin ta start some shit, and I just told him ta stay tha fuck away from me."

"Fine. But this is something we'll probably see again."

"Whatcha mean?"

"Well, there are men in my past I'm sure you might not want me to talk to or have anything to do with—"

Yeah...like ev'rybody.

"—and they may pop up one day and we'll have to deal with it. And speaking of men in our past: how many have there been in yours?"

"Huh?"

"You already told me about Crystal and the girls you've been with. But what about the men?"

Uh-oh.

"Whatcha mean, Baby?"

"Come on, Pooquie, you know exactly what I mean. I know I'm the first man you've ever been in love with, but I don't know how many other men you've *been* with."

"Uh, uh..." I was searchin, tryin ta stretch it. "Uh, when you say 'been wit'' ..."

"I mean *been* with...be with, like me."

"I...I...I don't know, Baby."

"You don't know?"

"Nah. I mean, I ain't never thought about it."

"Do you...know how many?"

"I...I don't know, Baby. I ain't never count 'em."

I watched him out tha corner of my eye. He ain't look happy.

He sighed. "Can you...name any of them?"

"Uh...David."

"I know about him. The others."

Roll Call:

Brotha Man: me 'n' him was kickin it since we was ten.

Angel. Yeah, Angel. I gotta admit I ain't like him at first. When me 'n' Brotha Man fell out fuh awhile, they started hangin, and I got jealous cuz it seemed like I was bein replaced. It felt like he was his boy. But when I gave him a chance, he turned out ta be a real cool brotha (I mean, that rica *in Puerto Rican is from Africa, ain't it?). Anyway, we was playin a mean game of tha* dozens one day, and Angel got me so jood ("Yo Mama so stoopid, she got on tha bus and tried ta pay wit' food stamps!") that I could only come back wit' "Nigga, suck my dick." He just grinned and said, "Whip that shit out and I will." He shouldn'ta said that. I whipped it out, and he showed me he ain't no angel by goin ta town on it. And befo' I knew it, Brotha Man joined in, waxin his ass. Now, that shit made me bug tha fuck out, cuz I ain't never even seen Brotha Man use his piece on nobody. I thought he just gave it up. After Brotha Man made Angel scream, we switched places: I fucked Angel and Angel fucked Brotha Man. Day-am, that shit was too fuckin jood. Angel knew how ta give it up and how ta turn ya tha fuck on, cursin at ya in Spanish and shit, callin ya "Papi." We had three mo' sessions like that, and then they just stopped. I don't know why, they just did.

Cedric 'n' Timmy: I met 'em both at Harry's, like David 'n' Little Bit. They gave it up when I wanted it. But when they wanted mo', I stepped.

I ain't wanna tell Little Bit about none of 'em, 'specially Brotha Man 'n' Angel. So I just dropped Cedric 'n' Timmy on him. If there was anybody we was gonna run inta, they would be tha ones. And they'd be tha only ones I'd recognize, cuz I couldn't remember nobody else's name. Shit, half tha time I ain't even ask their name....

I kicked it wit' at least five niggaz on tha train, twice durin tha day (yeah, it was risky, but that tension just made it jooda). I dicked one conductor down while he was announcin stops and shit.

I was bustin most booty as a security guard at the Gap on tha weekdays, a office buildin on Tuesday and Thursday nites, and a co-op not far from my house called Harlem Towers on tha weekend. During them two years, there had ta be at least three brothas I could count on, wit' two stand-bys comin and goin dependin on tha season. Folks do some cray-zee shit in storage rooms, stairwells, on rooftops, and terraces. I know.

There's tha two times I did it in tha park (no, it was in tha daylight), that one time in tha laun-dro-mat (cuz he was always starin me down, I took tha queen who owned tha place on a spin cycle), and that nite I borrowed Brotha Man's Jeep outside Hector's cuz this one nigga couldn't wait ta get back ta his place.

And while I knew I wasn't s'pose ta be dippin while on duty, I did drop a load while droppin off a package on one of my rounds. That ass was tha best tip I ever got.

And then there was Heaven. Day-am, I miss that spot. It was tha joint. It's been closed like two years. It was just three blocks from my house. Whether it was boxer nite, G-string nite, or "Blatino" nite (you know, Black and Latino), there wasn't nuthin but wall-2-wall niggaz—no punks, perps, or pussies allowed, G—packed front-2-back, in ev'ry size 'n' shape, just fuh tha takin. And yeah, Tha Kid did a whole lota takin. She-it, I had ta fight off them niggaz, they was *all over me. I be tappin somebody's ass and got niggaz nibblin, suckin, feelin, kissin me on my face, my neck, my chest, my nipples, my back, my arms, my legs, and my thighs. And yeah, somebody was always tryin to tap me (but we wasn't havin that, cuz I wasn't open fuh bizness, ya know what I'm sayin?). But Heaven? It was open fuh bizness like five months, and when it was open, it was the place. I baked me a whole lota cakes up in that mutha-fucka. If there's a real heaven, I hope it's like that one.*

I couldn't tell Little Bit about any of this — 'specially since I ain't always use a condom. But he wasn't gonna let me slide.

"You mean, besides David, it was just those other two men, Pooquie?"

Now, play this right, mutha-fucka. "Yeah, yeah, Baby. There was a few others, but they ain't important."

"A few others? How many is a few?"

"Uh, like, five, six."

"Why weren't they important?"

"Cuz they ain't mean nuthin. It was just a dick thang."

"Are you sure?"

"Yeah. Why? You don't believe me?"

"Yes, yes, I do. It's just that…I just don't want you to be afraid to tell me anything about your past. I mean, I'm not going to hold whatever you did then against you now, no matter how bad you might think it is."

"Baby…I…there's some people I was wit' I…I can't remember they names. But it ain't like I was knockin boots wit' ev'rybody I ever met."

"Even if you did…that's nothing you have to be ashamed of. I guess I made you feel uncomfortable, putting you on the spot like that. I didn't mean to."

"Nah, Baby, you had a right ta ask me that. I mean, you gotta know where I been ta understand where I'm at."

"And you have that right, too."

And that's when he broke it down about him and all them brothas that had they chance wit' him but fucked up. Tha thing that really got me was him kickin it wit' his gymnastics coach. Can you imagine that shit? I guess that's one way ta make sure you gonna pass yo' class, hunh?

When he was done, he had named like six people. He was prob'ly holdin back, but that was a'ight. I was doin it too. Knowin what he told me made me see why he ain't want us ta rush.

"If those past experiences taught me anything, it's that you gotta let love do its own thing. Just sit back…*lay* back…and let it work on you."

I nodded. "I hear that."

"I was hurt many times before, but I've learned my lessons. And going through all that is gonna make it easier for me to let myself go with you."

"Now, I *really* hear that."

Lip-lock time.

"This my first time, Baby...I guess I'm gonna be trippin us up a whole lot."

"That's OK. I'm sure there was something you learned in all of those experiences you had that will help you and help us."

"Uh...uh, yeah, there is."

"Yeah? What is it?"

"Yo, wit' all that testin 'n' teasin 'n' tastin, I learned what it takes ta make ya feel Jood wit' a *cap*ital *J*, Baby."

"Oh, really?"

I squeezed his bubblin brown booty. *"Oh, yeah."*

He giggled. "Mmm...I didn't think that came from experience."

"Huh?"

"You know...I thought that was a natural thing."

"Oh, it is, Baby, it is...but only when it comes ta you."

REWIND '84

"*Good movie, huh?*"

"*Nah, man, it ain't good. It was* jood. *What's tha name of it again?*"

"*How many times I gotta* tell *you?* Cooley High."

"*Yeah. It was cooley.*"

"*Ain't it? I told ya. It's too fresh.*"

"*Dag, I wish it ain't come on so late. It's like almost three in tha mornin, and we gotta go ta church.*"

"*So? It was worth stayin up, man.*"

"*Yeah, it was. But, man, you was just* too *loud. I just knew my moms was gonna tell us ta turn it off.*"

"*I can't help it. It's just too funny. Anyway, she saw what we was lookin at. She knew it was a fresh movie.*"

"*Yeah. She wanted ta stay and watch some of it...and now I see where you get all that shit from.*"

"*What?*"

"*Fakin that bloody nose so we can get outa class and cut tha rest of tha period.*"

"*I told you, man, that's where I got it from.*"

"*That guy...what's his name?*"

"*Cochise?*"

"*Yeah? What kinda name is that?*"

"*I don't know.*"

"*I mean, he was cool, real cool, but that name. Day-am!*"

"*But he and Preach was havin much fun.*"

"*Yeah. Why they call* him *that?*"

"*Preach?*"

"*Yeah.*"

"*Man, they gotta call him somethin. And why you askin so many questions? Day-am, it's just a movie.*"

"*Man, it* ain't *just no movie. That shit they went thru, it's real, man. Like what happened ta Cochise at tha end—*"

"Yeah."

"I mean, he was goin off ta make it big playin ball. That's why ya gotta keep yo' nose clean, man. Hangin wit' tha wrong crew, it can take you out."

"Yeah. Ev'ry time I see Preach find him, man—"

"Man, I know. I saw ya cryin."

"Huh?"

"I saw you."

"Man, I wasn't cryin."

"Ha, that wasn't no Visine drippin outa yo' eyes!"

"Yeah, well, I saw you, too."

"Me?"

"Yeah, you. I saw how you was blinkin a lot, tryin ta hold back. Man, you can't fool me."

"Yeah...I guess we was both inta it."

"Yeah."

"But what tha fuck Preach po' that beer on Cochise grave fuh?"

"Day-am, nigga, don't you know nuthin? He was givin him his respect."

"Respect? By doin that?"

"Yeah. We talkin 'bout his homez, his main man. And I wantcha ta do that fuh me, too."

"Huh?"

"I wantcha ta do it fuh me."

"Man, you cray-zee?"

"Nah, I ain't crazy. If I die befo' you, I wantcha ta do it. Promise?"

"Promise?"

"Yeah, promise. And I want y'all ta play that song."

"What song?"

"You know, tha song at tha end, 'Say Good-bye to Yesterday.' Yo, that song is fresh."

"Uh, a'ight, a'ight, I promise, I promise. Now, can we stop talkin about dyin?"

"Whatcha wanna talk about?"

"Somethin else that happened in tha movie."

"What?"

"How Cochise moved in on Preach's girl. That was ruff."

"Yeah."

"You do somethin like that ta me?"

"Man, how you gonna ask me that?"

"Just askin."

"You know I ain't gonna do nuthin like that ta you."

"Yeah, you better not, cuz you know I pound yo' ass."

"Ain't no girl, ain't no nigga gonna get up in between us like that."

"I bet that's what Cochise 'n' Preach thought too."

"Man, Cochise was always huntin. Anyway, if one of us should be lookin over they shoulder, it's me."

"You?"

"Yeah, me. Man, all you gotta do is snap yo' fingers and them girls just be all over you. And you just be huntin like Cochise. Man, I gotta watch out fuh you."

"Nah, nah, man. I might always be huntin, but I ain't goin after nuthin my homez got his eye on. Man, you my Brotha. My Brotha Man."

"Brotha Man...man, I like that. It's fresh."

"Man, we better go ta sleep."

"Yeah."

"Man, get yo' funky feet outa my face!"

"Yo, my feet ain't funky."

"You ain't down here smellin 'em, so how you know?"

"Yo' feet don't smell that jood neither, ya know?"

"Man, shut up."

"And at least I ain't got feet like Big Bird."

"I said, shut up."

"Yo, man, don't be ticklin my feet!"

"Then go ta sleep, already."

"A'ight, a'ight."

"G'nite, Brotha Man."

"G'nite, Cochise."

"You funny, you real funny...."

LUV JONZ IN MY BONZ

CAN U KEEP A SECRET?

When I'm itchin 4 a scratch
I know what 2 do
I just call on Little Bit
and he pulls it on thru

But I ain't gotta say a word
See, my Baby knows tha T
He can tell when tha time comes
2 turn in-2 my Little G

Let's get warmed up, now
Uh-huh, here we go
Just a few preliminaries
B 4 we start tha show

Ya wanna taste
Ya wanna taste
Come and get it
Ya wanna taste
Ya wanna taste
Ain't nuthin like it

Oh, pleeze, Baby, pleeze, Baby
pleeze, pleeze, pleeze
Wet it, wash it, wipe it, wop it up
And bring me 2 my knees

Drink me up, Baby
Just don't take no sips
Drink me up, Baby
I got somethin 4 yo' lips

Ain't it juicy
Ain't it sweet
Ain't it just
A 1 of a kind jood treat?

I know it's just like Lay's
Ya can't just have 1
But we just gettin started, Baby
We ain't even begun

Just gimme 1 mo' lickin
And make that shit jood
Day-am, Baby!
Ya did it like I knew ya would

Now that's outa tha way
U can go 4 that slam dunk
Uh-huh, U guessed it
It's time 2 knock off a chunk

This hunger I can't deny
It's on U I'm hooked
What mo' can I say, Baby?
U got Tha Kid whooped

Turn me in, turn me out
And put me thru tha loop
Just get on up in it, Baby
and make me wanna *Shoop*

Just dive in, Baby
My water is fine
Just dive right on in
U ain't gotta take yo' time

I got a jonz in my bonz
And a boogie in my butt
I know ya wanna house me
So come on in my hut

Let me get ya situated
Let me suit U up 4 play
I'll put this raincoat on ya
So we can do this tha right way

Now, just pull up 2 my bumper, Baby
Wit' that long Black limousine
Pull up 2 that bumper, Baby
And make Tha Kid scream

Cuz ya got my booty callin:

Come Baby, Come Baby, Baby Come Come
Ya Gotta Gimme Lovin
Ya Gotta Gimme Some

So let it be, you always creep
So let it be, you always creep
CreepCreepCreepCreep
All up in my Stream

Ahhh, yeah!!!

Welcome back, Mack
You know tha drill
It's been lonely wit'out ya
So let's crank on up that hill

It's a tight fit
Tight fit
Ooh, yeah
It's tha right kinda fit

They say it's tha motion of tha ocean
Not tha size of tha boat
But U gotta pack somethin mean
If U plan on stayin afloat

U got tha tool, Baby
Now work it like a 9 - 2 - 5
Put ya whole body in it
U know how 2 drop that dime

Oh, yeah, U just tha right size
And tha feelin is phat
Just claim ev'ry inch, Baby
Ya know I lust it like that

Day-am, U livin large
Just keep growin strong
Wit' a piece like that
U can't go wrong

Cuz U got tha right one, Baby
Uh-huh!

And tha shit be on
and on
and on
and on
and on
tha beat don't stop till tha break of dawn

And ya *don't* stop!

Baby, Baby, Bay-bay
I got so much luv in me
Baby, Baby, Bay-bay
U know if U gonna get me off
Ya *got* 2 luv me
got 2 luv me
got 2 luv me…*deep*

Here we go—here we go—here we go now
here we go—here we go—here we go now
here we go—here we go—here we go now
Get Buzy

Uh-huh this is tha way
            this is tha way
            this is tha way we rock

            This is tha way
            this is tha way
            this is tha way we roll

So just roll on wit' it, Baby!

Just go on and work
Just go on and work it...I'm talkin overtime
Work it...2 tha bone
            2 tha bonebone
            2 tha bonebonebone

Day-am, this shit is Da Bomb
U know I can't get enuff
Bump 'n' Grind or Jump 'n' Jack
Don't matter, long as it's *ruff*

Cuz it don't mean a thang
If it ain't got that swang
So go on and hit that switch
And make my booty sang

Oh, I don't wanna be a freak
    I don't wanna be a freak
    I don't wanna be a freak
But I can't help myself!

U got me fallin
        fallin 2 ya,
        fallin 4 ya,
        fallin wit' ya,
        fallin thru ya,
        fallin after ya,
        fallin *ovah* ya,
        fallin under ya,
        fallin around ya,

Just f
     a
       l
         l
           i
              n

Now take it
2 tha left
Now take it
2 tha right
And dip Baby, dip Baby, dip Baby, dip
Now slide Baby, slide Baby, slide Baby, slide

Dig that trench, and go 4 yours
Dig that trench, and go 4 yours
Dig that trench, and go 4 yours
Cuz there's lots of room
4 U 2

Take it all
Take it all
Take all
of my Honey Dip
Just soak it up
Just soak it up
Don't ya leave
a single drip

Day-am Baby
Day-am Baby
Day-am Baby
She-it!

Now bring it on home
We almost there
Bring it on home
Never U mind tha wear 'n' tear

Yeah, Little Bit, all up against tha wall
Yeah, Little Bit, all up against tha do'
Yeah, Little Bit, sprawl that shit out on tha flo'
Just bust it till ya get 2 tha core

Cuz…this is it,
     this is it
     this is
     I
     T
     it

Mmm…

…Ahhh, yeeeaaah

Now…

…just bring it on down
     bring it on down
          it on down
               on down
                    down
               on down…*low*

Uh-huh…

…just…like…that

E-Z…

…like Sunday mornin

But hold on, Baby
Don't make yo' exit yet
I wanna make this last
I wanna take all I can get

Is it, is it
is it still jood 2 ya?
Is it, is it
is it still jood 4 ya?
I know it is…4 me

But don't tell nobody
        don't tell nobody
        it is

A'IGHT?

OUR HONEYMOON IS OVER

Me 'n' Little Bit was in bed. I was layin on my stomach and Little Bit was sittin on my back, givin me a massage. Them magic hands were doin a job on Tha Kid, and I really needed it—we was watchin tha results from tha mayor's race in tha city. It was really close fuh most of tha nite, but that Fool-iani won. And Tha Kid was pissed.

"I can't be*lieve* this shit. That mutha-fucka pulled it out. Fifty thousand votes, Baby. I betcha Dinkins woulda won if all them mutha-fuckas got up off their lazy asses and went ta tha fuckin polls."

"Pooquie, be cool...."

"Fuck that bein cool, Baby. Ain't no way that mutha-fucka shoulda won. Two million fuckin Black folks in tha city and shit? It just don't make no sense."

"Well, maybe some of those folks liked what Giuliani had to say."

"C'mon, Baby. All that mutha-fucka wanna do is lock us all up."

"Maybe some of them didn't like the job Dinkins did."

"Hunh?"

"I've heard some Black folks say they weren't gonna vote for him because in his quest to be the mayor of all the people, they feel he forgot about his own people."

"That shit is tired, Little Bit, and you know it. What tha fuck they expect tha brotha ta do? He got all these crackers just workin ta get him out, and we help 'em?"

"So, what—you think that every single Black person in the city should have voted for Dinkins?"

"*Hell-fuckin-yeah!* White folks say they liberal, Baby, but you know they ain't. They give Koch twelve fuckin years ta run tha city inta tha mutha-fuckin ground and expect Dinkins ta just turn shit around like that. And cuz he couldn't keep tha niggers in line—"

He noogied my head wit' his elbow. "Pooquie!"

I turned ta look up at him. "Sorry, Baby, but be*lieve* me, there wasn't no other way ta say it."

He chuckled. "Uh-huh." We kissed.

I punched tha pillow I was layin on. "I mean, if tha brotha can't count on his own, who can he count on?"

"Well, maybe some people, Black, white, and otherwise, didn't like what either one of them said and decided not to vote."

"Now, *that's* cray-zee."

"What's so crazy about that?"

I turned over on my left side; he still sat on me. "You got tha right ta vote and you ain't gonna use it?"

"That's right. Having that right comes with responsibility, Pooquie, and that means using it correctly. And if you are presented with candidates who do not speak to you, why waste your vote on them?"

"Ev'ry vote counts, Baby, so how you gonna call it a waste?"

"It *is* a waste if you feel you have no choice, if you feel neither one of them deserves it. Some folks don't wanna choose from the lesser of two evils."

"C'mon, Baby, that's just an excuse."

"No, it's not, Pooquie. You have to vote with confidence, and if you don't have that, how can you pull that lever?"

"A'ight, a'ight, then check this out...let's say you ain't like either one of 'em...you mean you would stay home?"

"Yes, I would."

"Baby, that's *stoo*pid."

He got off me. "No, it isn't."

I rolled outa bed, followin him inta tha bathroom. "It is too. Think about whatcha sayin, Little Bit."

"I know exactly what I'm sayin. It is my right to exercise my right to vote any way I please—and if that means *not* voting, so be it."

I still ain't believe what I was hearin. "That's bullshit. After all we been thru ta get tha right ta vote? Baby, I remember all them stories my moms and my grandmoms told me...about us havin ta guess how many bubbles was in a bar of soap and say the Bill of Rights backwards and shit...yo, people *died* so we can vote. When you don't vote, you takin all that fuh granted."

He washed his hands. "Pooquie, I know all about that...I mean, my parents and grandparents lived through it too. But I certainly am not honoring them if I don't vote with integrity. It's a personal thing, and neither you nor anyone else has the right to tell somebody that they're supposed to do it, or *how* they're supposed to."

"Baby, you fuckin trippin. I guess workin fuh them white folks really got ta you."

"And what is *that* supposed to mean?"

"What tha *fuck* I just say? You soundin like one of them Republi*klan* mutha-fuckas. They tell us we gotta get outa this group-thinkin mode when they all conspirin ta bury our asses. I bet you ain't even vote fuh Dinkins."

"*That* ain't none of your business."

"Uh-huh, you ain't vote fuh him. See, we get a little money and a little position, and we think we got it made, like we white and shit."

"Pooquie, why don't you just leave it alone?" he said, dryin his hands.

"Why? Cuz I'm sayin shit that's true?"

He rolled his eyes and pushed his way pass me. "No, 'cause you makin yourself look like a fuckin fool, that's why. You gettin all bent out of shape over something so trivial. If we can't disagree without you cursing at me and insulting me just because you're upset that we didn't come and support Dinkins the way you think we should have, then this conversation is over."

I followed him. "Little Bit—"

"I don't want to hear it, Raheim."

"Whatcha mean, you 'don't wanna hear it'?"

"What part of that statement do you *not* understand?"

"That's right, just be a smart-ass, a'ight?"

"See, there you go again. I'm just supposed to want to listen because you say so, talk because you want to, right? I *don't* think so. *I'm* going to sleep." He climbed in bed.

"So, that's how you gonna be? Now you doin whatcha say I always do."

"And that is?"

"Runnin away."

He sat up on his side and grinned. "And what exactly am I *running* away from, Raheim?"

"From what we talkin about."

He turned off tha TV. "I am not running away from anything. What I am doing is trying to end this ridiculous discussion."

"*Ridiculous?*" I pointed at him. "*You* tha one bein ridiculous."

"Raheim, why are you so mad?"

"Yo, *dogs* get mad, a'ight?"

He put his hands up. "Fine, Raheim, fine. I just don't want to argue anymore, OK? Good-night."

And wit' that, he turned off tha light.

"Little Bit? Little Bit? Why you wanna be like that?" I moved from tha foot of tha bed, closer ta him.

"Raheim, please, don't touch...just leave me alone."

"*Just leave you alone?* A'ight, a'ight. *Fuck* you then!"

I stormed out inta tha livin room and, fuh tha first (and not tha last) time, slept on tha couch.

Well, I ain't really sleep. I stayed up fuh most of tha nite, angry. And I finally fell asleep when I realized that I ain't had no reason ta be angry. Little Bit was right. There I go again, thinkin it's all about me. I took my frustration over Dinkins losin out on him. I don't know where tha fuck that shit I said about him came from and why I said it. Now, if I had just kept on, he mighta asked me ta leave. We was almost there— he ain't want me ta touch him, he wanted me ta leave him alone. We already talked about that—things gettin so tense we gotta have some space (We also said we would never go ta bed angry, but I could see it wasn't gonna be easy fuh me ta follow *that* rule). But ta think that somethin silly like this could make that happen—and that married folks break up over *stoo*pid shit like this—just fucked wit' me fuh tha rest of tha nite.

In tha mornin, I heard Little Bit go inta tha bathroom and tha shower come on.

"Raheim..." he said, as I pulled tha curtain back. He was already all soaped up.

I ain't give him tha chance ta say nuthin else. I just took him in my arms and kissed him. I tell ya, that's all I had ta do. He dropped tha soap and wash rag. We washed, then dried, then got all wet again. Like my girl Miss Janet would say, we can do it *anytime, anyplace,* but *this* was becomin our place ta get busy (Little Bit musta realized that too, cuz he had a box of Zulus on tha windowsill). He worked me so fuckin jood I knocked tha tub rack down, bringin tha shampoo, body oil, and scrub brush wit' it. He laughed cuz most of that shit fell on my head. But he wasn't laughin when it was his turn. He sat on it and I rocked him, makin him give up that ass like it was goin outa style.

We went ta bed and maxed. I was gonna be late fuh work, but I ain't care.

"Little Bit?"

"Yes?" He lifted his head; he was layin on top me. I just loved hearin his heartbeat against mine.

"You angry at me?"

"No, Pooquie."

"I'm sorry, Baby."

"I know."

"Me and my big fuckin mouth."

"I know."

"I always gotta have shit my way."

"I know."

I slapped him on tha ass. "Baby, you ain't gotta agree wit' ev'rythang I say."

"Why not? You tellin the truth!"

We cracked up. We kissed.

I sighed. "I wanna say it ain't never gonna happen again—"

"—but we both know that it probably will."

Yeah, we do.

"But that doesn't mean it's the end of the world, Pooquie. You're just a very passionate man. It's one of the things I love about you."

"It is?"

He tapped my nose. "Yes, it is. You just get a little too fired up about things. It's not like it's something we can't work on."

"I love you, Little Bit."

"I know. Oh, and just for the record: I voted for the brother."

We giggled.

REWIND '85

"Raheim?"
"Yeah?"
"You sleep?"
"If I was sleep, how I be talkin ta you?"
"I don't know, you could be talkin in yo' sleep. My moms do that."
"I ain't talkin in my sleep. I'm up."
"Can I ask you somethin?"
"Go 'head."
"What's goin on wit' yo' cousin?"
"Who?"
"Diana."
"Whatcha mean?"
"I heard yo' aunt done threw her outa tha house."
"I...I don't know."
"Come on, man, you do know."
"I don't wanna say nuthin."
"Hey, I'm yo' boy. You can tell me. I ain't gonna tell nobody."
"You ain't?"
"No, I ain't."
"Uh, a'ight, a'ight...you can't tell nobody, not even yo' moms."
"I ain't gonna tell nobody."
"A'ight...my aunt did throw her out."
"Why?"
"Cuz."
"Yeah, cuz why?"
"Cuz she...she caught her doin somethin."
"Man, what she catch her doin?"
"She...she was..."
"Man, tell me already."
"Man, don't be talkin so loud, a'ight? My moms gonna hear."
"She know?"

"Yeah, she know, stoopid. How she not gonna know?"

"Just askin. Man, tell me already."

"She was in bed...wit' somebody."

"She was in bed wit' somebody?"

"Will you cut it, man? You talkin too loud."

"Man, I'm almost whisperin. Who was he? We know him?"

"It ain't no him."

"I betcha it was that Tyrone. He a old, nasty *mutha-fucka. Remember when he wanted ta pay us if we let him see our dicks? He ain't nuthin but—"*

"Man, you ain't even hear what I say."

"Huh? You say somethin? I ain't know—"

"That's cuz you busy runnin yo' mouth. I said...and don't get loud or nuthin when I say it again, a'ight?"

"A'ight."

"It wasn't no him her moms caught her in bed wit'."

*"It wasn't no him...*man...*"*

"I told *you not ta be all loud, my moms gonna come in here, man. Now I'm gonna take my hand off yo' mouth...you gonna be quiet?... A'ight..."*

"Man...man, you lyin."

"I ain't."

"Who told you that?"

"Diana."

"Nah, man, nah, that ain't true."

"It is too. I heard my moms talkin about it on tha phone wit' somebody—I guess it was my Aunt Hope."

"Well, what she say? What Diana say?"

"They said tha same thang...how Aunt Hope had come home early from work and found Diana and this girl in bed tagetha."

"Nah, man. What was they doin?"

"Man, you *know what they was doin."*

"I don't know."

"You do too, cuz we be doin it."

"We be doin it*?"*

"Yeah, dummy."

"Man...man, they can't be doin that*."*

"Whatcha mean?"

"They ain't got what we got."

"They don't need *what we got."*

"Man, you...you sayin they was...they was..."

"Uh-huh, bumpin pussy."

"Naaahhh."

"Man, will you keep it tha fuck *down already."*

"*Sorry, man, sorry. They was…they was…*"

"*You heard, bumpin pussy.*"

"*I heard you tha first time, man, you ain't had ta say it again.*"

"*Well, you ain't act like it.*"

"*Day-am. Why they wanna do that?*"

"*Why you and me be bumpin uglies?*"

"*Cuz tha shit feels* jood.*"*

"*There ya go.*"

"*Man, you ever bump pussy?*"

"Hunh?"

"*You know. You ever do it wit' a girl?*"

"*Nah. But I ate pussy befo'.*"

"*Nah!*"

"*Yeah.*"

"*Yeah?*"

"*Yeah.*"

"Get *tha fuck outa here! Who pussy?*"

"*Man, I ain't gonna tell you again ta be quiet.*"

"*Sorry, man, sorry…who pussy?*"

"*Don't worry about it.*"

"*C'mon, man, tell me, tell me.*"

"*I ain't tellin.*"

"*Let me guess, let me guess…Bonita?*"

"*Nah.*"

"*Uh, Felecia?*"

"*Nah.*"

"*Then it's gotta be Wendy. She always on you, man.*"

"*Nah, it ain't none of them, man, so stop tryin ta guess, cuz I ain't gonna tell.*"

"*A'ight then, a'ight, be like that, man.*"

"*I will.*"

"*But can I ask somethin else?*"

"*Just as long as it ain't who it is.*"

"*It ain't gonna be that…what's it like?*"

"*What's it like?*"

"*Yeah.*"

"*I don't know.*"

"*Whatcha mean? So, you ain't do it, huh?*"

"*Yeah, I did, but I don't know what it's* like.*"*

"*Well…how it taste?*"

"*I…I guess it taste a'ight.*"

"*What it taste like?*"

"I don't know, man. I ain't never taste nuthin like it, so I don't know what I can say it taste like."

"Uh, is it sweet?"

"Uh...yeah...yeah, I guess it is."

"Is it real soft?"

"Yeah."

"Is it milky?"

"Milky?"

"Yeah, milky...you know, like our stuff."

"Uh...yeah...in a way."

"You like it?"

"Yeah, I guess. She liked it."

"Yeah?"

"Yeah, she was pushin my face all up in it. Man, I could hardly breathe."

"That's like I be sayin sometime, when I'm suckin you, huh?"

"Yeah, like you."

"It was Diana, hunh?"

"What?"

"You ate Diana's pussy."

"I ain't sayin."

"You just did, man."

"Man, shut up."

"Uh, where she at?"

"Diana?"

"Yeah."

"Why you wanna know? She ain't givin you none."

"Man, I'm just askin a question. I don't want her pussy."

"Man, you do too."

"I do not."

"Man, you been on her ever since she useta baby-sit us years back. But ya wouldn't know what ta do if she put it all up in yo' face, any-ol'-way."

"Man, shut up."

"But last time we talked, she said she was gonna stay wit' that girl her moms caught her wit'."

"So, what, she ain't inta suckin dick?"

"Man, I told you she ain't gonna want you. Anyway, you ain't got no dick."

"Man, shut up."

"I'm just jokin, man...look at ya, actin like a pussy."

"I ain't actin like no pussy."

"You is too. Gettin all pouty and rollin yo' eyes. If you stop, I let you suck me."

"I can suck you?"

"Yeah, but you can't be loud."

"I ain't gonna be loud. I ain't. You gonna stick it in me?"

"Nah, nah, we ain't doin that. You be too loud."

"I ain't, I ain't."

"Let's just do this, a'ight? I can stick it in after my moms leave fuh work in tha mornin."

"OK."

"And maybe I eat yo' pussy."

"Huh? Man, what you talkin 'bout?"

"You heard."

"Man, I ain't got no pussy."

"I'm holdin on ta it now."

"Man, that's my butt."

"I know what it is."

"No you don't, cuz you callin it a pussy."

"That's cuz I wanna call it that."

"I ain't got one, and I ain't one."

"Man, don't get all upset about it, a'ight? Don't worry, don't worry, you gonna see in tha mornin, you gonna see...."

STRANGE DOIN'S IN THA PARK

There he is again.

I ain't tell Little Bit about him, cuz I knew he'd wanna come down and read him like he read that other white boy in tha Village. Besides, I'm useta folks scopin me out. I ain't got ta do nuthin but stand around and look jood, and folks be all in my shit. They be runnin inta people and trees and poles and shit, tryin ta get a jood look. And they say some *stoo*pid shit just so they can get up in my face. You know:

"Don't I know you?"

"Haven't we met?"

"Didn't you go to *fill in the blank* High/College?"

"Didn't I see you at *fill in the place and the day?*"

"Aren't you *blah blah's* brother, cousin, ex?"

Of course, tha answer is always no (unless I got Li'l Brotha Man and they wanna know if he mine), but I can't really blame 'em fuh tryin. Yo, Tha Kid just got it goin on, ya know what I'm sayin?

But this one white boy, he just been all *in* my mutha-fuckin face. I mean, he don't just be starin—he be studyin me like I'm a book and shit and he gotta take a test on me tha next day. It's been like this a whole week. I come out here in Washington Square Park ta chill on my lunch break, and there he is, always sittin on a bench across from me. He reminds me of Woody Allen, all dorky-lookin and shit. I thought he was him at first, but then I nixed that. I don't think Woody be hangin out in this park, and I ain't never seen him talkin ta no brothas or sistas or even lookin in our direction. It's fucked up how he can do all them movies about New York and there ain't no Black people in 'em. And they always wanna know if my man Spike got any white friends?

Anyway, I just knew it was a matter of time befo' he made his way on over. And he did.

He gave me one of them *I'm doing this because I know you know I been scopin you out* smiles. He snapped his suspenders. His whole ensemble said one thing: mo' money. "Uh, excuse me?"

I turned off my Walkman (I was listenin ta "Gangsta Lean" by DRS; yeah, it reminds me of Brotha Man). I took off my headphones.

"Uh...could I, uh, speak with you for a moment?"

I nodded.

He sat next ta me on tha bench. "Let me introduce myself. My name is Thomas Grayson."

"Raheim." I usually don't give out my real name—I usually settle on somethin wack like "Bubba"—but somethin told me not ta perpetrate this time.

I shook his hand; it was a limp, sweaty shake. I wiped my hand on tha back of my spandex when he wasn't lookin.

"It is nice to meet you, Raheim.... You are, uh, a very handsome young man."

Uh-oh. Where was *this* goin? Was this mutha-fucka gonna offer ta take care of me if I agree ta be his "boy from the hood" and let him sample a little bit of *this* Harlem? Wouldn't be tha first time. I decided ta play along. "Yeah, I heard that befo'."

"Well, I do mean it. But I guess I should say why your good looks interest me."

This was gonna be jood, and I just couldn't wait ta hear it. "I'm listenin, G."

"G? Uh, my name is Thomas."

I chuckled. "It's just a...whatcha call it...a term of en*dear*ment."

"Oh. *Oh,* ha, yes, I see." He got that look all white folks get when they just been schooled about somethin they don't know nuthin about. I knew what was comin next: he would try playin it off by graspin my arm, my shoulder, or my elbow (why do these white mutha-fuckas feel they got tha right ta touch you five seconds after meetin you and shit?). But he not only touched my shoulder, he started pattin it like I was his pet and shit. When I frowned, he stopped and moved his hand.

He tried smilin. "Uh...uh, I'm the vice president of image relations for All-American apparel...have you heard of it?"

Yeah, I heard of it. It's one of them no-frill, No-Name wit' *two* capital *N*'s, wanna-be-all-that jean companies. You know, they can't hang at Macy's or Bloomie's, so they gotta stake out their claim at Woolworth and Walgreens. Last time I ever saw a pair was on Sunshine in high school. They was whatcha bought when you ain't had no green fuh what was in style. I ain't had that prob: Tha Kid wouldn't be caught dead in a pair.

But I decided ta fuck wit' Tommy Boy. "All-American? You kiddin? Man, I wore them in high school."

His face lit up. "You did?"

"Yeah."

"Well, I'm surprised."

"Surprised? Why?"

"Well, I didn't think that...well...our clothes are not normally worn by the, uh, hip-hop crowd."

Hip-hop crowd. Uh-huh. *Say it, mutha-fucka...the niggers.*

I shrugged. "Yeah, man, you be surprised what da boyz wear in da hood."

"Well, I am glad you said that. It just so happens that we are hoping to expand our base, increase our audience. We've done a little research and believe that targeting that group might be a good idea."

Might be a good idea? Mutha-fucka, pleeze! Who sets tha stylez? Who sets tha trendz? Ya know we do. If we wearin it, ya know it's da bomb.

I raised my eyebrows. "Oh, yeah?"

"Yes. As a matter of fact, for the past several months, we have been searching for the right individual who personifies that audience, who, when they look at his face, they will know that he is speaking their language, that he is walking their walk, that he knows where they come from, where they are at, and where they want to go."

"So, what this gotta do wit' me?"

"Well, I believe *you* have what we want."

What tha fuck is he talkin about? "Hunh?"

"I—or rather, we, All-American—would like for you to be our newest model."

I just knew he was outa his fuckin mind. *"A model? Me?"*

"Yes."

I brushed him off. "Man, you gotta be jokin."

"No, I'm not."

"But I ain't never modeled befo'."

"Well, that's fine, because we want a fresh face, just an average guy. Besides, there aren't that many black male models for us to choose from, and the few that are out there do not have that—uh, how do I say it?—street look we need."

I knew I shoulda been ticked off by what he said, but he was right on two points. I can't really think of no brothas makin bank like tha white boys in tha trade, and those that are, they pretty boys. You know, they so light bright, day-am near white that they ain't gonna scare white folks. Shit, half tha time you open up a magazine and see a brotha or sista you gotta do a double take cuz they *look* like one but you ain't exactly sure, even in *Ebony* and *Jet.*

"We tried to get a few names in the rap music field," he continued, "but none of them were interested. I guess they didn't think we were right for their image."

"And you think *I* am?"

"I'm not really sure, but we are willing to give you a tryout and see."

"A tryout?"

"Yes. We'll have a photographer take some photos of you, and if the board likes what they see, you will see your face and body in newspapers and magazines."

"Tha board?"

"Oh, sorry, the board of directors."

I just knew he was fuckin wit' me. It just couldn't be on tha up-'n'-ups. I mean, *me*, modelin jeans and shit?

"I know this is a lot to spring on you at once," Tommy Boy said, reachin in his suit jacket pocket. "Here's my card. Please call me tomorrow so we can talk further. Maybe we can have lunch if you're not busy. If this is something you're willing to try, we'd like to move on it as soon as possible."

I took it from him. "Uh, a'ight. Cool. I'll call you."

"Great. It was certainly nice meeting you."

"Yeah, you too." I ain't wanna shake his hand again, but I did.

He walked off. I checked out his card; it was gold (could it be real?) wit' that Old English–type letterin. Huh, All-American may not be Levi's, but they got tha bills ta make it *look* like they are.

I couldn't believe it. I just stood there, lookin at tha card, and I couldn't help but grin up a storm. Why?

Cuz I was just, as they say in tha bizness, "discovered."

2 TELL THA (WHOLE) TRUTH

Little Bit had Babyface come by tha house and look at tha modelin contract. He wanted ta make sure I wasn't bein ripped off. He ain't think this whole thing was legit ("One day, you're sitting in the park, minding your own business, and the next thing you know, somebody is offering you money to wear jeans?"). I had ta agree wit' one thing Little Bit said: these All-American folks was just a little *too* anxious. Tommy Boy steps ta me on Monday, we have lunch on Tuesday, I meet Tha Good Ol' (and they was *old,* too) White Boys on Wednesday, and they give me a contract on Thursday? Ev'rything was happenin too fuckin fast, and Little Bit thought we was gonna find tha reasons why between tha lines.

Babyface parked it on tha couch, took off his tie, and went over it as Little Bit made some tea. I was in tha easy chair. He was done in five minutes.

"From what I can see, just about everything seems all right. But there are a few things you should consider first before you sign."

"Like what?"

"Listen to this...quote: 'The model will receive no payment for items sold with his/her image/likeness.' "

"What does that mean?"

"That means you don't receive a dime if they decide to put your face on a poster, postcard, T-shirt—you know, things like that."

"Why would they wanna do that?"

"Believe you me, if we start buying those jeans, their stock is gonna shoot through the roof and they'll be no question as to why. And you a fine brother; the ladies and the gents are gonna want to hang you up in their bedrooms."

I blushed. Little Bit, standin in tha kitchen, sucked his teeth. "Please, Babyface, he don't need no more buttering up."

"Leave tha brotha be, Baby. He got jood taste."

Babyface winked at me.

Little Bit tapped my head. "Uh-huh…*any*way, as you were saying, Babyface…"

Babyface giggled. "If folks start goin crazy over you, they're gonna use every avenue available to make money."

Little Bit put Babyface's tea on tha coffee table. "So you think he should ask for a piece of that?"

"Definitely. And this part here: 'Said model is not to entertain or accept other offers from other firms/companies during his/her tenure with All-American.' "

Little Bit sat on tha arm of tha easy chair. "That seems fair. What's wrong with it?"

"What's wrong is that this contract says you are their man for two years. Now, what if this whole thing falls through after six months, or six weeks? Now, I could see them not wanting you to work for another company that sells jeans. But what if—and we just gonna go all out—a rep from Pepsi or Gatorade wanted you for a commercial?"

He got my attention. "Gatorade?"

"Yeah. Or what about a Reebok or a Payless—"

I knew he *had* ta be jokin. "*Payless?* Man, ain't no way—"

"Hey, the shoes might be cheap and cheesy, but if they came to you with the right kind of money, you'd wear 'em. What I'm sayin is that, after you do this, those doors are gonna start openin up for you to do other things."

Little Bit rubbed my head. "But he can't do that if All-American has him tied up for two years?"

"Yeah. This contract says you are with them for two years but does not say that you will be *working* for two years. They could just take one photo of you and use it that whole time. Then what do you do?"

I knew all that stuff was important, but I was most int'rested in tha dollar sign. "Well, then, should I ask fuh mo' money?"

He sipped his tea. "They're not going to give you more money, I can tell you that. To be honest, forty thou a year is a rather large sum for someone who isn't a professional model. Add in the perks you'll probably get, maybe a few trips and gifts, it's really a six-figure deal when you think about it. That is a serious investment; it ain't nothin' to sneeze at. They really are counting on you to deliver. But it's not going to hurt to try and renegotiate on some of these other points. You may as well try and milk this for everything you can. They see you as their ticket, so you gotta see them as yours."

Little Bit asked him ta go down wit' me ta tha office ta work ev'rything out. I was a'ight wit' it; I mean, he was doin it fuh free, and I just couldn't wait ta see tha look on Tommy Boy and all them white folks' faces when Babyface fell up in there wit' me. Yeah, there's white boys walkin around wit' dreds, but white folks can't take Tha Real Thang, 'specially when they can't *be* Tha Real Thang.

I really appreciated him helpin me; I really did. But all I could think, while we was all talkin about tha contract, was what my man Keith Sweat useta say: *something just ain't right.* And it all came out when me 'n' Little Bit was sittin up in bed readin tha next nite.

"So he got them to change all of that stuff?" he asked.

"Yeah. Babyface knows his shit, Baby. I mean, you shoulda seen him. He had them white folks just hangin on ev'ry fuckin word he said, bustin 'em out wit' that legalese. I gotta get tha brotha somethin, just ta say thanks."

"That's a jood idea.... Pooquie?"

"Yeah?"

"Um...we're being honest about everything, right?"

"Yeah."

"Well, I have something to tell you. I don't want you to find out later on and think I was tryin to hide it from you."

I ain't say a word. I ain't even look up from my magazine.

"It's about me...and Babyface.... Uh, when you left, I was lonely and...I...I needed someone...and...and we slept together."

He was lookin straight at me, waitin fuh some reaction. But I still wouldn't look up.

"Raheim? Did you hear what I said?"

I turned tha page. "Yeah, I heard."

"Well?"

"Well what?"

"You don't have anything to say?"

"Nah."

"You're not upset?"

"No, I ain't."

"You're not?"

"No."

"Then why won't you look at me?"

I did and then I went back ta readin, even tho' I wasn't.

"Raheim..."

"*What?*" I snapped.

"You're upset and you're trying to play it off like you aren't."

"I *ain't* upset."

"Yes, you are."

I got all up in his face. "*Don't* tell me how I feel! How tha *fuck* would you know?"

He jumped back. "Well, if you ain't upset, what are you?"

I threw tha blanket off me and jumped outa bed.

"Raheim, where are you going? Talk to me. How do you feel?"

"How do I *feel*? How tha *fuck* am I s'*pose* ta feel?"

"I don't know."

"You don't *know*?"

"I'm asking you, ain't I? I'm trying to find out. Just tell me what you think—"

"Tell you what I *think*? A'ight, a'ight, I tell you what I think: you a *fuckin* 'ho."

He turned away from me.

Ah, *shit;* I did it again. I climbed back on tha bed. I put my hand on his shoulder. "Baby, I...I ain't mean—"

He moved away from me. "—to say that? Well, if you didn't feel that way, why would you say that?"

I started pleadin my case ta his back. "That ain't it. It's just that...you just tell me, droppin a bomb and shit, and you expect me ta just say somethin...."

He turned ta me, cryin. "I didn't do it to hurt you...."

I wiped his tears. "I ain't know what ta say, Baby...."

"I didn't—I didn't think I would see you again; and...he, he was there for me, and..."

I took him in my arms. "But you just pushed me and pushed.... Don't cry, Baby, pleeze...don't cry."

He brushed his face against my chest. "I told you because I thought it was the right thing to do. I didn't want there to be any secrets between us."

"I know, Baby, I...I know."

"I'm sorry, Pooquie, if I hurt you."

"Nah, Baby, you ain't hurt me. I'm sorry...you was bein straight up wit' me...you did tha right thing."

Ha, I knew *that* was a lie. Why he tell me? I mean, I had a feelin somethin was up, but I ain't think that was it. Well, I sure as hell ain't wanna believe that *could* be it. I ain't stoopid—I saw tha body language between 'em. Little Bit was tryin ta avoid lookin at him, like he was guilty and shit. I saw it wit' my own eyes. But I had ta nix that cuz...ain't Babyface 'n' B.D. tagetha? Little Bit would break it down fuh me: how they both wanted ta kick it wit' other people befo' they "got married" (hunh?), and he was Babyface's choice.

Bottom line is they slept tagetha and, yeah, that shit irks tha *fuck* outa me. I hate tha idea of anybody else bein wit' Little Bit, even if they was wit' him when I wasn't around. That's why I came outa my face like that. Yeah, I was hurt cuz he told me and cuz he did it, and I wanted ta hurt him back. I know, I know, just me actin immature, not dealin wit' tha situation at hand. I almost had it under control. But I ain't wanna know, and I wish Little Bit ain't tell me. And I know it's *stoo*pid, but if Babyface was in fronta me when Little Bit said it, I woulda made sure he ain't look like a Babyface no mo' (of course, I mighta felt like it, but ain't no way I was gonna do it, cuz I would lose Little Bit).

It's not so much that they did it; I mean, it's done, and there ain't a thang I can do about it, right? No, my prob is that I wasn't around when Little Bit needed me. I fucked up—and I fucked *up* Little Bit— and somebody else had ta pick up tha pieces I left behind. If it wasn't Babyface, it coulda been somebody else. Shit, if it *was* somebody else, I woulda really been angry. Knowin tha kinda brotha he is, Babyface prob'ly told Little Bit not ta worry, that I'd be back. But any other mutha-fucka woulda told Little Bit ta just fuhget about me. All cuz I blew up and took off. Just runnin away from tha shit I create. I ain't never lettin that shit happen again.

Yeah, I was angry wit' *me,* and I took tha shit out on *him.*

Little Bit was right: how tha hell was he gonna know I was gonna come back? Was he s'pose ta wait fuh me? And I can't be goin off on him like that when I done slept wit' my boyz—and I did it when I was wit' Sunshine. Shit, I did it when me 'n' Little Bit was, too: that time he wouldn't gimme none, me 'n' David hit it. You know, it was just one of them thangz: I wanted it, and he wanted it. It was just that one time; it ain't mean a day-am thang ta me.

But Little Bit ain't gotta know about it. I'm just gonna keep my mouth shut so we ain't gotta go thru no mo' drama. I mean, Little Bit say he don't hate David, but I ain't gonna give him no reason ta be angry at *me.* Be straight up, hunh? Tellin tha truth and tha whole truth is tha right thing ta do, right? *Fuck* that. He ain't gotta know ev'rything. What he don't know won't hurt him.

Uh-huh, sometimes keepin a secret ain't such a bad thing.

REWIND '86

*I don't wanna hear it. I don't want to hear it, you hear me? I don't wanna hear one word you gotta say. You just sit, sit there and listen to me...*sit.

I just don't believe this. You know, I always was scared that this day was gonna come. It's the day that no mother wants to see. It's the day you pray real hard don't happen 'cause you know it happens all the time around here. Every single damn day I'm hearin about somebody else's son goin to jail. And every single damn day I say to myself, "Not mine. Ain't gonna happen to mine. Not mine."

What? *What you mean you wasn't in jail? You were handcuffed, right? You were put in a police car, right? You were driven to the station, right? You were booked and fingerprinted and photographed, right? You were put in a pen, right? Somebody had to come down there and get your ass out, right? Boy, you was in* jail.

Why didn't I come to the station? Why should *I have? You should be happy I sent the money to get your ass out. See, this is something that I just will* not *have. I promised myself that even if this happened, there was no way in hell I was goin down there.* No way. *Because I was not going to even give you the chance to get me used to it. I am* not *going to be like any of these other mothers around here. You go once, you go twice, you go three times, and before you know it, it's like a job, makin a daily or weekly or monthly trip to see their boys. Their* boys. *Ha, they still call 'em their* boys. *And that's the problem. You think you a man, you think you know what bein a man is about, goin out there and tryin to prove it to folks? Well then, don't come cryin to me when your ass gets caught, actin like a little boy who needs his mama. You make the bed, you lie in it, you hear me? I already been through this with your father, and I'm* not *going through it with you.*

Oh...I'm makin a big deal. You think so, hunh? Boy, you outa your damn *mind. Now, just what if Mad Dog hadn't stolen his aunt's car? And yes, he* stole *it, 'cause it don't belong to him and he didn't have permission to take it and he don't even have a driver's license to* drive *a car. All of y'all coulda been dead right now, or killed somebody else. And what if y'all wasn't lucky, runnin into that fence? What if it had been a tree or a pole or a building or a ditch? Do you understand how lucky you are to be sittin in that chair right now? You could be laid up in a hospital bed with tubes stickin all out of you. Or you coulda gotten roughed up by some cops who just can't wait to bash some niggers' heads in. Don't you know they just waitin...just* waitin? *Y'all lucky y'all wasn't bein chased by 'em. I'd be goin to the morgue right now, identifyin your body 'cause some trigger-happy cops ain't like their lunch hour bein disturbed. You wanna end up at Riker's like Mad Dog? That's* exactly *where he's goin. You can quote me on* that, *one of these days he'll be there, that'll be his second home.*

That's right, you and Derrick keep hangin 'round them raggedy-ass, rusty-butt niggers. They got your back, they got your back. They ain't *got your back, baby, let me tell ya. You keep puttin all your faith in them, you surely gonna find yourself by yourself. That Mad Dog, he ain't nothin but a secondhand hood: it only takes a second for him to get his hands on somethin that don't belong to him and for him to take it. And you just goin along for the ride. Ain't we talked about this?* Hunh? *I know I don't have to go over all that again, I* know I *don't. And I won't. I refuse to. I don't have to repeat myself. I only have to speak once, and that's it.*

Oh, so you know you hurt me. I'm glad you know that. But that don't make me feel any better. You *should be more concerned about hurting yourself, not me. I don't care what those niggers said, I don't care how much fun they said you would have, I don't care if they called you a punk if you didn't want to come.... If you don't stand for anything, you* fall *for anything, and you gonna be fallin flat on your face if you keep listenin to them. They ain't the ones who gotta answer for what you do wrong, and they ain't gonna be there when the chips are down,* believe *me. You better wise up. You ain't no fool, you ain't no dummy, 'cause I ain't raise no fool, I ain't raise no dummy. But I tell you this: you gonna feel like a fool, you gonna feel like a dummy, you gonna feel* real *stupid if you do some stupid shit like this again, 'cause I ain't comin. My mind is made up, and I ain't comin. You get yourself into it, you get yourself out.*

Now, get *out of my face. You ain't leavin this house anytime soon: You ain't goin* no-damn-where *for a whole month except school. Ah,* don't *say a word.* Don't. *The only thing I want you to do is* think. Think *about what you did and why it is best that you* never *do it again....*

THA WORLD ACCORDIN 2 GENE

"You don't like me, do ya?"

Me 'n' Gene was on B.D.'s balcony. B.D. and his dance company had made they debut and we—me, Little Bit, Gene, Babyface, and Carl—was at B.D.'s place fuh tha after *after* party. I don't know shit about ballet, but B.D. got tha moves down. And tha brotha knows how ta wear some tights. You just know Tha Kid had ta give him a big hug and squeeze that ass. He ain't seem ta mind. He just got one of them asses that yo' eyes can't help but follow wherever it go—you know, like the bouncing ball. It's a magnetic booty. When I think about Little Bit and Babyface havin a piece of that…it ain't fair they got ta have all tha fun. I mean, we all be even if I had some, right? If I even told Little Bit I was thinkin about it, he chew *my* ass out.

And speakin of Little Bit, he sang, and ya know he tore up. Some brotha gave him his card, sayin he a talent scout and could prob'ly get him some work doin background vocals. I told Little Bit ta just fuhget about him cuz all tha time this nigga was givin him his props he was busy clockin my Baby's ass.

Anyway, we came ta B.D.'s ta keep on celebratin. Little Bit, Babyface, and Carl was inside wit' B.D., who was gossipin about all tha drama that went on behind tha scenes. It was kinda cool outside, but I wanted ta see tha view. B.D. lives on tha twentieth flo' in this fly co-op; you can see tha whole fuckin city. Gene had already found his spot on what B.D. called "my linae" (what tha fuck is that, French?) when I stepped out there. We was talkin, but he was givin me so much static that I had ta ask him why—even tho' I already knew.

He sipped his drink and turned ta me. "My dear, what would ever give you *that* idea?"

"Don't *even* try it, G. Since me 'n' Little Bit got back tagetha, it's like you don't wanna be friends wit' me."

"Well, we weren't exactly bosom buddies *before* that time, now, were we?"

"Nah, we wasn't, but at least then you wasn't bein so frosty."

"All right, all right, Mr. Rivers. I guess I *have* been a little...distant. Since you've asked the question...yes, I *do* like you."

"You do?"

"Yes. Are you surprised?"

"Hell yeah. I mean, you don't act like it."

"Well, what do you want me to do...call you *Pooquie?*"

"Nah," I chuckled.

"I didn't think so. I happen to think, like Little Bit, that you are a very talented, intelligent young man. But there *are* several things about you that I do not like."

"Like?"

"For starters? You are belligerent, demanding, selfish, and egotistical."

"Yeah, I know, Little Bit already done told me all that. But I ain't tha only one out here who is."

I got him jood; he was gaggin. "Uh, are you trying to *come* for me, darling? Do not even *try* putting that 'ired' in *tired,* OK, for you would *not* want to raise *that* kind of an ire in me. I *know* you know better than that, and that you *are* better than that."

I laughed. "*Any*way..."

He sucked his teeth and rolled his eyes. "Uh-huh. *Any*way, you also hurt my best friend, so excuse me if I don't welcome you back into *my* life with open arms."

"But I told Little Bit—"

"Yeah, I know, I *know*...you never meant to do it, and you'll never do it again. Well, promises are empty, my dear. If I had to count on a promise every time my heart depended on it, I'd have to, in the immortal words of Mz. LaBelle, file love bankrupt."

Just then his face dropped. He looked like he was gonna have a seizure and shit. Uh-huh, he still got this hang-up about even *sayin* tha word "love." I don't see tha big deal, but then I can talk—I got it, I'm all in it. He still datin Carl, but they ain't in love as far as we know, cuz if they was, Gene be wit' somebody else now...or would he be? Carl done stuck by him; tha brotha took off a month from work ta help take care of him after he got gay-bashed and even went ta court ta make sure them mutha-fuckas got locked up (they did). So, tha way that word just slipped outa his mouth, it was like it *was* a natural thang, like he can say it cuz he got it, he all in it too. Wait till Little Bit hears *this*....

I let him play it off, like I ain't know why he was trippin, and started pleadin my case like he was a judge and shit. "I know I can just say it, but I ain't just sayin it. I *ain't* never gonna do it again. I know I was wrong. But I ain't a bad person."

"I never said you *were*. I don't think you are a bad person. You are a person who just happened to have done a very bad thing."

"So, you gonna hold that against me?"

"I do not believe I am holding *anything* against you."

"Seems like it ta me if you ain't gonna fuhgive me like Little Bit did. I mean, I ain't do nuthin ta you."

"My dear, let me correct you on a few things. One, it is not *for* me to forgive you; hell, you didn't do it *to* me and, as such, I ain't the one who has to sleep with you. Two, what you did *does* affect me, because when he feels pain, I do too. And three, just because *he* has forgiven you does not mean I have to."

He sipped his drink. I drank some beer.

I looked up at the sky. "You don't think Little Bit and me shoulda got back tagetha, hunh?"

"You really want to know?"

I ain't really wanna hear him say it, but I turned ta him and nodded yes anyway.

"No," he said, wit'out blinkin.

I had tha urge ta put my thumb in my mouth, but I caught myself. I put my arms over tha railin. "Why?"

"Look, maybe we shouldn't be talking about this—"

"No, I wanna talk about it. I mean, I really respect whatcha hafta say." And I did. Yeah, Gene can be a real smart-ass, but he is really a *smart*-ass mutha-fucka. I ain't stoopid, but I know he done seen a whole lot and been thru a whole lot. And if anybody knows Little Bit just as much as his family and could tell me tha best way ta handle all this, he could.

He sighed. I could tell he was tryin ta choose tha right words. "I don't think either of you are ready to handle what's ahead."

"Whatcha mean?"

He took a deep breath. "Now…I am happy for the both of you. I know Mitch does not believe me when I say that, but I am. And I do not doubt that you two feel the way you say you do about and for each other. Hell, all one has to do is *look* at you both and see it. But I don't know whether either of you can really be what the other needs…right now."

He musta figured out that *What tha fuck you talkin about?* look on my face cuz he grinned and went on.

"There is just a lot of growing that you both have to do. You both want to give a lot but you also *need* a lot, and sometimes it'll seem like *it* isn't enough. And because *it* won't be enough, one of you or both of you might think, at one time or another, that the other isn't giving enough, when you could *never* give enough."

I was understandin what he was sayin—but I really wasn't. He musta saw that, too. I swear, I saw tha lightbulb come on.

"You know that song by Luther, 'Never Too Much'?" he asked.

"Yeah."

" 'A million days in your arms, a thousand kisses from you'...many would like it to be like that, but it can't be. And I just hope neither one of you really thinks it's going to be like that and that *it* is going to solve your problems, 'cause it won't."

I thought about ev'rything he said fuh like a minute. He managed ta light up a cigarette wit'out puttin his drink down.

"So...you sayin I'm gonna hurt him again?" I asked.

He smiled. He took a puff, blowin a circle in tha air. "Yes, there is that possibility that you might, but it won't be through any fault of your own—" he stared at me, hard—"I *hope*. I mean, you wouldn't want to have to answer to me, now, would you?"

I tried ta smile but couldn't. That look on his face said he wasn't playin.

"But this particular pump, uh shoe, is not just on *your* foot. He can easily hurt you, too. And I don't want to see either one of you hurt, for any reason. You both have so much to prove to yourselves and to each other, and y'all got so much invested in this. And I know you're both expecting certain things because of *it*. So, with those emotions workin triple overtime, the last thing you want to be is disappointed or let down. And the chances of that happening are very high when you play the game of...you know."

I put my right hand in my pocket. "But I don't wanna play no game. I don't wanna play no game *on* Little Bit or *wit'* Little Bit. I want it ta be tha real thang, straight up, no mutha-fuckin chaser, ya know? I mean, I just wanna be—"

"Worthy of his, you know..." He winked.

"Yeah." I shrugged.

"Well then...I guess along the way you'll also show me that you are indeed worthy of *my* respect. And the fact that we are having this conversation tells me that that may happen...soon."

I sighed a smile. "A'ight."

"I don't mean to sound so skeptical. I just say what I mean and mean what I say. You both have good intentions. Unfortunately, we know where *that* can lead. But in spite of your faults and quirks, you two are committed to each other and working at it. And I guess that's the bottom line.

"But enough about what I think about you, and what I think about you and him. It's time for me to put *you* on the spot. Let's talk about what *you* think about *you.*"

Uh-huh, there goes my look again.

"Oh, please, Mr. Rivers, do not play dumb with me." He grinned. "I would expect that from B.D. I'm curious to know how you are dealing with coming out of the closet."

I looked around ta see if anybody heard, even tho' I knew there wasn't nobody out here but us. Day-am—not even Little Bit had asked me about *that* (at least not that way). So I did tha only thing I could do—*really* play dumb like B.D. "I ain't comin outa no closet, G," I said, laughin.

But he wasn't havin it. "Oh, no...no, you aren't. I'm sorry. You're trying to come out of a *walk-in* closet."

I choked on my beer.

He giggled. "Hey, I was giving you the benefit of the doubt. I could have said you were in the back of a hall closet in a hat box that ain't been opened in years, not to mention dusted off. But *no,* you just had to force me to take that trip, didn't you?"

"Uh-huh, yeah, well, be careful, cuz it's a one-way trip ta tha Bermuda Triangle, a'ight?"

He laughed. "Ah, trying to get vicious, aren't we? *That* was a good one."

He was still waitin fuh me ta answer his question; his eyebrows was raised, just anticipatin. I still wasn't gonna bite. "Fuh real, tho', G, I don't see myself comin outa no closet—"

"Well, correct me if I am wrong, but save Little Bit, the most important people in your life—your son, the mother of your son, and your mother—do not know. So, what do *you* call it?"

Now, why Little Bit had ta open his mouth?

"And *no,* Little Bit did not tell me...it was just an educated guess."

Day-am, he is too fuckin jood at this.

I went on tha defensive. "Yo, I don't know why it gotta be called *any-thing.* I mean, they don't know, but I do, and *I'm* tha one who gotta deal wit' it."

"Well, you don't just announce it to yourself and that's it," he argued. "It reveals itself to you every day in different ways. It's a part of you, and you just have to take it as it comes *out.*"

"You makin it all sound so fuckin simple, G."

"Well, I don't see why some of us make it so *hard.*"

"A'ight, then...when *you* come out?"

"My dear, I was never *in* the closet to begin with."

"You wasn't?"

"No, I wasn't. How *could* I be? Folks been lookin at me since I was two, chile, and sayin I was a faggot. Even my own father. So it wasn't like I could deny it when it was true." He puffed.

Think, mutha-fucka, think.... Got it. "A'ight, then check this out: if it comes ta ya in diff'rent ways ev'ry day of yo' life and ya don't just come out one time, then you *had* ta be in a closet ta keep comin outa one ev'ry day, *right?*"

I could tell by that grin I wasn't gonna win this one. "Your reasoning would be sound, my dear, if we were talking about the same thing. You see, there is a difference between coming out of the closet and coming *out*. I am in the latter category, for I have been in a place in my life for some time where I have accepted and come to understand just who I am. But every day I have to reaffirm who I am as a gay man living in a heterosexist world, and that means being *out* and challenging the homophobia in whoever and whatever I come across. Now, *you*, on the other hand, are just beginning to find *out* who you are and what your place is. And you can't affirm who you are if you don't know *what* you are affirming."

Day-am, he knows how ta lay that shit on; he got me again.

He knew it and went on wit' a smirk. "Now, I don't want you to take offense to this, but I do not understand why anyone would spend their entire lives trying to hide who they are. I mean, what's the point? *That* seems to be the only so-called choice we have—to be true to ourselves or to let someone or something dictate how we should live. And when you choose the latter you are, in essence, giving up power that belongs to *you*."

"Yeah, but—"

"And *here* we go again. I tell ya, we always doin da butt and no music has to be playin. Whatcha gonna say? That you would've been more open, that you might've come to acknowledge yourself sooner, *but*...you couldn't because you lived in a neighborhood, went to schools, grew up in a family, have friends that wouldn't accept it? Why decide what is best for you based on what others will or will not say, think, and do? I have *never* subscribed to that philosophy. My mother always said, 'Don't ever give nobody a stick to whip your ass with.' And she usually said this while I was actually *gettin* a branch for her to do just that!"

I ain't care—I was gonna go there. "Well, I shouldn't say it, *but*—" we grinned—"ev'rybody ain't like you, ya know? I mean, we ain't all come ta know...about this...tha same way, and we ain't gonna deal wit' it tha same."

He nodded. "Yeah, you're right. Nothing says that you have to walk around with a gold card that announces you are an avowed homosexual...like me."

We laughed.

"OK." He sucked in some nicotine. "So you don't see it as coming out of a closet. If that's what works for you, fine. You're still young. You have the time, the space, and the *energy* to explore it. And believe me, it *does* take a lot of energy. Some folks don't take that step until they are in their thirties or forties and, I'm sorry, but I do *not* believe in being a late bloomer. One should not be making this kind of declaration when their hair is falling out or all the kids have left the nest—or, worse, *because* those things are happening. You ain't on this earth to live *two* lives, just one."

"But how 'bout all tha pressure ta *be* somethin you ain't? It's ev'ry-fuckin-where...."

"So, is that what you've been doing: being something you're *not*?"

Ah, *shit*. This is why I ain't had this convo wit' Little Bit, cuz I knew somethin would come outa my mouth that I ain't want ta. I started trippin on my words. "Uh, nah, nah, uh...I mean...you—you know what I'm tryin ta say...."

He was enjoyin this shit. He struck his pose—right arm bent over tha rail, his fist under his chin—and he held his drink up over his head. Yeah, he was grinnin up a fuckin storm. "I never presuppose to know what another is *trying* to say. And *you* said it, not me."

Yeah, I said it, but I ain't wanna fess up ta it right then wit' him. "That ain't what I meant...I mean...I ain't talkin about me...let's drop it, a'ight?"

He shrugged. "Hey, you're the one who brought it up."

"*Yo*, I *said* I don't wanna talk about it, so just drop tha shit, *a'ight?*"

"OK, OK, it's dropped."

I ain't wanna look at him, cuz I knew I wouldn't like tha look on his face and would wanna knock tha shit outa him. I could just feel my temp rise, so I was glad when tha balcony do' opened and Little Bit came out carryin a tray wit' two bowls on it.

"Hey, how are you two doing out here?" he asked.

I tried ta smile. "We a'ight."

"Yes, we're getting to know each other...*and* ourselves," added Gene, takin a long puff. *Uh-huh.* He sees a flame but he don't put it out; he gets gasoline and just fires that shit up even mo'. Oh, yeah, just keep it up, mutha-fucka....

"Oh, well, I don't wanna disturb your conversation. I just wanted to bring out some of this pasta salad before Babyface and Carl eat it all up." He put tha tray down on a table sittin against tha brick wall. "Enjoy." He smiled, gave me a quick peck on my right cheek, and went back in.

Gene sashayed over ta tha table, sat, and looked at tha food. "My, my, my, this certainly looks...*jood.*"

He got me ta look at him and ta laugh, which he did too.

I sighed. "Uh, G...I'm sorry I, uh, snapped at ya, man."

"I know, I know," he said, pointin at tha empty chair across from him.

I joined him. "I guess it makes me...I don't know..."

He passed me a fork. "Testy?"

I shrugged.

"Well, it's supposed to make you testy, *and* it's supposed to test you." He took his last blow and put tha butt out in tha ashtray on tha table. "You don't have to supply me with any answers, 'cause no one can answer that and any other question you have about yourself but you. Just as long as those questions and answers bring you closer to not just living but living *life.*"

She-it, it was like I was back in school. "*Day-am,* G, you sound like fuckin Imhotep and shit. How you get ta be so fuckin phi-low-sah-phuh-cull?"

He smiled. "It's called wisdom, dear. And it comes with only one thing...*age.*"

We cracked up.

He raised his glass; I raised my beer can. "Here's to the trip *you* are taking," he toasted. "Let us hope that it is definitely one-way." We clinked.

Uh-huh, let's hope so.

THANKS 4 GIVING

I had walked back up in tha house at like nine, and there she was, in tha kitchen, stuffin tha turkey. I could smell tha ham, tha greens, and tha gravy as soon as I got ta our flo'. Little Bit can cook, but he can't cook like my moms. Tha Pilgrims and tha Indians ain't had nuthin like tha feast she turns out.

"Ma, you been up all nite?"

She grinned. "You ask me that question every year, and every year you know I say yeah."

"You want me ta help?"

"Uh-huh, and you ask *that* every year, and every year I tell you the same thing: no. You just can't cook, baby."

"I can cook."

"No, you can't. But you sure can *eat.*"

"C'mon, Ma, let me help."

She slapped my hand as I tried ta get me a taste. "You can help by stayin *out* of my way and *out* of my pots. Don't be dippin into nothin, you hear? You'll get to sample everything later."

"C'mon, Ma…"

"C'mon, nothin…and I done told you you too damn big to be sittin on my countertop." She slapped my leg. "I season meat and cut vegetables there."

"Yo, Ma, my butt is clean."

"Will you just get off!"

I hopped off. I bear-hugged her, nuzzlin her on her neck. She giggled. I stood against tha fridge.

"Is Li'l Brotha Man sleep in my bed?"

"You know he is. He just loves sleepin in his daddy's bed, knowin you gonna come in and join him."

"Did Sunshine say what time she was comin over?"

"I told her and Gloria to be here around four. Francie is gonna stop by with Laticia and Precious around six."

I nodded.

"Francie and I were talkin this mornin...."

Here it comes.

"It's...been some time, baby."

Yeah, I know.

"You...she just wants to tie everything up. And this is the last thing."

Yeah, I know.

She stopped cuttin onions and turned ta me. "Raheim?"

"Yeah, I hear you Ma, I hear you."

"It's time. You gotta face it. You can't ignore it anymore."

"I ain't ignorin it, Ma."

"What do you call it?"

I ain't know, so I ain't say nuthin.

"Francie thinks you should sell it. And I think you should too."

"Nah, nah, I ain't doin it."

"She's already got some offers. You won't have to do nothin. She's gonna hand the money over to you—"

"Ma, I don't want no money."

"Raheim, this is the best thing."

"No, it ain't!"

"Baby, I *saw* you. You couldn't drive it, you couldn't start it. It took forever for us to get you *in* it. Why are you torturing yourself over it?"

"I...I...I just can't, Ma. I can't."

She walked over. She gently held my face. "If you sell the Jeep, that doesn't mean you're erasing Derrick."

My eyes went down. I sighed.

"I know...it's painful to hold on to it, it's painful to let go of it. We all are just trying to make the best of a bad situation.... Let her sell it, baby. It's hard for her too. She feels the same way."

"Ah...yeah."

"You can buy yourself a car, something you've always wanted. You can put the money away for Junior. Or you can move the hell out of here."

I smiled. "You tryin ta get rid of me?"

"What do *you* think?"

We laughed.

She tapped my nose. "It's the best way to move on."

I shrugged.

She walked back over ta tha bird. "You two can talk about it."

I stared at tha ceilin. I knew I had ta say somethin, but then...

"Daddy!"

Leave it ta Li'l Brotha Man ta save tha day once again. There he came, zoomin inta tha kitchen, still in his pajamas. He had his arms out fuh me ta pick him up. Moms say he too old ta be pickin up, but I don't care.

"Yo, what's up, my man?"

He got his small arms around my neck. "You, Daddy."

"So, you still wanna go ta tha parade?"

He squeezed my neck. "You *know* I do, Daddy. Can I take my Happy Thanksgiving balloon with me?"

I chuckled. "Yeah, you can. You sleep a'ight?"

"Yes. I saved a place for you."

"You did?"

"Uh-huh."

"You pulled out that bed all by yo'self?"

"No. Grammy helped me."

"You musta had a lota space ta roll around in then. But I'm gonna be home tanite. You think there's gonna be room fuh me?"

"Yes."

"Jood."

Moms put her hands on her hips. "That's right, just *ignore* Grandma and talk about me like I'm not standin right here now that your father is home."

"Sorry, Grammy. Jood morning."

"Jood morning to you, too." She smiled. She pinched his right cheek. She frowned. "Young man, did you brush your teeth?"

He got that busted look. "No."

"Did you wash your face?"

He began ta shrink. It reminded me of me when I was his age. "No."

"What did I tell you about showin your face without washing up?"

"I'm gonna do it, Grammy."

"Uh-huh, and you will do it before I fix you somethin to eat."

"Ooh, ooh, can I have peanut butter and jelly?"

"For breakfast?"

"Yes."

"You sure you don't want some Wheaties?"

"No."

"Some pancakes?"

"No."

"*No?* You don't want some of Grandma's famous buttermilk pancakes with whipped cream and a strawberry?"

"No, I want peanut butter and jelly. It's been a long time since I had it."

"Junior, I made it for you last week."

"A week is a long time, Grammy. That's seven days."

"Yes, I know. All right, you can have it."

"Thank you."

"You're welcome." She looked at me. I had that *Me too* look. She knew it. "Uh, would *you* like a sandwich or two, too?"

I grinned. "Ya know it, Ma. Ain't nobody make 'em like you do, right, Li'l Brotha Man?"

He nodded. "Right!"

She laughed. "OK, OK. Now, *you*, go and wash up."

"OK. Daddy?"

"Yeah?"

"Will you help me pick out my clothes?"

I put him down. "You know I will. You can help me pick out somethin too. A'ight?"

"OK. Grammy?"

"Yes?"

"May I have chocolate milk with my sandwich?"

"Yes, you may. It will be ready for you when you come back."

"Thank you."

"You're welcome. Now go. You don't wanna miss seeing Kermit and Big Bird."

"OK." Off he went. We both looked at him and smiled.

Moms frowned. "He thought you were coming back last night."

"I was, but I got tied up."

"Well, the next time you get tied up, you can at least call this house and tell him that. He's big enough to understand, ya know?"

I ain't say nuthin.

"Oh, and you better check that high riser. It seems to get stuck."

"Whatcha mean?"

"I had a hard time pulling that other mattress out—even with Li'l Brotha Man's help."

"A'ight."

"It's probably time for you to get a new bed, anyway."

"Why?"

"*Why?* 'Cause you been sleepin on that one for more than half your life, that's why."

"So?"

"*So?* Well, you *are* 21 years old. You're not a kid, you're not a teenager. Don't you think it's time you got yourself a bed that ain't cut in half?"

"Yo, Ma, it's done tha job all this time. If it ain't broke—"

"Well, even if it ain't broke, all I'm sayin is that it may be time for you to go on to something else. To move on. *To let go.* You know what I'm saying?"

I sighed. "Yeah...yeah, I know.... You gonna buy it?"

"*Hell* no! Why should I? You got *three* jobs now. I'm scared of you. You should be buyin *me* a new bed."

"Don't worry...one day, I will, and a whole lot mo' ."

"Humph, well, that's somethin I sure do look forward to. In the meantime, will you please go and see about that child? He's probably still drownin his mouth in toothpaste. I keep tellin him that he don't have to pile it on the brush like he's putting icing on a cake."

I chuckled. "A'ight." I started ta leave.

"Raheim?"

"Yeah?"

"How many sandwiches you want?"

I shrugged. "Uh, I ain't greedy."

"Uh-huh. Will *four* be enough?"

I smiled. "Uh, yeah, that's cool."

"Fine."

"Ma?"

"Yeah?"

"I love you."

"I love you too, baby."

REWIND '87

"Pardon me..."

"Yes?"

"Uh, can I talk ta you fuh a minute?"

"What for?"

"Cuz I know you somethin ta talk ta."

"Oh, really?"

"Yeah."

"And why is that?"

"Cuz you one fly-lookin female."

"Well, my mother told me to never talk to a strange man."

"We can fix that."

"Oh? How so?'

"By just givin me tha opp ta get ta know ya. See, I'm a gentle-man, and I know if ya got ta know me, you gonna like me."

"Oh, you do?"

"Yeah. I been watchin you."

"You have?"

"Yeah."

"Why?"

"Cuz, Baby, you somethin ta watch."

"Hmmm, that sounds familiar. But I ain't give you permission to call me 'Baby.' "

"A'ight. You let me know when I can."

"Uh-huh, you might be waitin a long time."

"You said 'might'...so that means I got a chance. And yo, time is all we got, any-ol'-way."

"We? Uh, first off, there is no we...there is you, and there is me. And secondly, didn't your mother tell you it's not nice to follow and spy on people?"

"I ain't been spyin."

"Oh, no? What do you call it?"

"Just checkin you out."

"Uh-huh."

"So, can I walk ya home?"

"I think you're already doing that, aren't you?"

"Ha, yeah, I guess I am. And I guess ya don't mind, do ya?"

"No...I guess I don't. But you did say you were a gentle-man, right?"

"Yeah."

"Well, my mother says a gentle-man would introduce himself."

"Uh, sorry. Raheim."

"Crystal."

"Yeah, I know."

"You do?"

"Yeah. I told ya I been watchin ya."

"Uh-huh. And there is one more thing that a gentle-man would do—"

"And what's that?"

"Carry a young lady's books."

"A'ight, let me get 'em fuh ya."

"Thank you."

"You welcome. Uh, you go ta Science in tha Bronx, right?"

"Yes, yes I do. How do you...never mind, I know. You've been watching me, right?"

"You got it."

"Uh-huh. And I take it you go to Randolph?"

"Yeah. How ya know?"

"Well, either you do or you wearin somebody else's jacket."

"Ah, yeah."

"So, which is it?"

"It's mine."

"Oh. I thought it might be your girlfriend's."

"I ain't got no girlfriend."

"You don't?"

"Nah. You think I wanna talk ta you if I did?"

"Knowin how some of y'all can be? Yes."

"Some of y'all? Who is y'all?"

"Men."

"Well, I ain't no parta y'all. I'm me."

"So you don't have a girlfriend?"

"Nah."

"Well, would you talk to me if I had a boyfriend?"

"Nah. I don't hafta be messin wit' somebody else's female."

"What if I said I had a boyfriend?"

"You ain't got one."

"How you know?"

"Cuz one, like I said, I been watchin ya; and two, if you did, ain't no way he be lettin you walk home by yo'self from school ev'ry day wit' all these books."

"Hmmm…"

"See, I been doin my homework."

"Uh-huh. So, how old are you?"

"I'm fifteen."

"Fifteen? Are you sure?"

"Yeah, I'm sure. I mean, I should know my own age."

"Well, you look older."

"Well, you know, what can I say? How old are you?"

"Shouldn't you know?"

"How I'm gonna know that?"

"Cuz you been watchin me, remember?"

"Yo, I couldn't find out ev'rything. Ain't nobody perfect."

"No, they're not…but I can't tell you my age."

"Why not?"

"Because, you bein' a gentle-man, you should know better."

"Know what?"

"That no true lady ever tells her age."

"They don't?"

"No."

"Well, I guess us gentle-mans learn somethin new ev'ry day, hunh?"

"Yeah. But I guess I can tell. I'm the same age."

"Cool. There's somethin else we got in common."

"Oh, yeah? Well, what else do we have in common?"

"We both go ta high school, we live Uptown—"

"So you live around here?"

"Yeah, up on 130th and Fifth."

"Well, you sure are walkin a long way from where you live."

"Yo, I don't mind. I don't do nuthin I don't wanna do."

"So I guess I should feel special, hunh?"

"Baby, you—"

"Who?"

"Sorry."

"The way that word just falls out of your mouth, I bet you say it to all the girls."

"No, I don't. It only falls out when it fits."

"Oh, really?"

"Yeah."

"Well, I ain't been nobody's baby since I was two."

"But you special. And I only use that word wit' special people."

"Oh, really?"

"Yeah."

"So do you call your homeboys 'Baby' too?"

"Nah! You cray-zee!"

"Well, ain't they special?"

"I'm talkin 'bout tha ladies. You real funny."

"I know. Well, we do not know each other, so you can't call me that."

"I guess I hafta come up wit' another name, then."

"Why?"

"Cuz...Crystal is like...it's so ordinary."

"Oh, really? I'm sure my mother would disagree."

"I mean, it's a pretty name, but it ain't pretty enuff fuh you."

"Oh, really?"

"You really like ta say that word, don'tcha?"

"Don't even try it."

"I already did."

"Whatever..."

"Anyway, like I was tryin ta explain, you deserve a name that's you all over."

"OK. So what would you name me?"

"I don't know. Somethin that makes people take notice tha same way they do when they see ya. You got such a beautiful smile."

"Thank you."

"You welcome. And you bright on the outside and tha inside. You gotsta be smart ta go ta Science."

"Uh-huh."

"So I guess I'd hafta name ya Sunshine."

"Sunshine?"

"Yeah."

"Sunshine?"

"Yeah, Sunshine. Cuz you glow. And I can tell you warm and sweet."

"My...you certainly do know how to flatter a girl, don't you?"

"There's mo' where that came from...Sunshine."

"I don't know."

"What?"

"I don't know if I like the name. I'll have to sleep on it."

"A'ight, a'ight, that's cool."

"Well, this is me."

"You don't want me ta—"

"No, you don't have to walk me upstairs and to my door. I can handle it from here."

"A'ight. You sure you got all them books?"

"Yes, I got 'em."

"Uh, Sun—I mean, Crystal?"

"Yes?"

"Can I have yo' phone number?"

"No."

"No?"

"Yes, no."

"Why?"

" 'Cause it's a little too early to be askin me that."

"So, when should I ask?"

"I don't know...how about after you walk me home—tomorrow."

"Yo, I'm down wit' that."

"I'm not makin any promise...."

"A'ight, a'ight. But if I can't get it then, I'm gonna keep walkin ya home till I do."

"Oh, yeah?"

"Yeah."

"You mean you are going to keep doin this until I give it to you?"

"Yeah."

"And what if I decide not to—ever?"

"You will."

"I will?"

"Yeah."

"And why will I?"

"Cuz I'm a gentle-man."

"I see...."

"So, I guess I'll pick ya up at tha train station. Same time?"

"I'll be a little late. I have a meeting with my debate group."

"See, I knew you was smart. So, what time ya want me there?"

"Say, 4:40."

"A'ight. I'll be there."

"Well, thanks for walking me home."

"My pleasure."

"So, have a good night."

"You too."

"And Raheim?"

"Yeah?"

"Don't be late."

"Don't worry, I won't."

"YOU OUGHT TO BE IN PICTURES"

They don't call it Secaucus fuh nuthin.

All-American sent a white limo ta pick me up ta go ta tha photo shoot. When Tommy Boy told me where it was gonna be, I was like, *Where tha fuck is that?* Turned out it was in New Jersey, like a half hour away from Midtown. I was glad cuz I thought I was gonna hafta fly ta Cali or somethin. I ain't never been on no plane—and I don't wanna get on one. It ain't that I'm scared; it's just that you can't trust them airlines. Too many planes be crashin and shit, and ain't nobody I ever talked ta ever seen a brotha or sista at them controls. I just ain't willin ta put my life in tha hands of no white boy thirty thousand feet in tha air, ya know what I'm sayin?

Anyway, tha limo picked me up from Little Bit's Saturday mornin at like eleven (it was a half hour late). I wanted it ta get me from tha crib Uptown—you know, make 'em look and get 'em talkin—but then folks would be askin *too* many fuckin questions, tryin ta get all in yo' bizness and shit, and I wasn't feelin that. When we got ta Secaucus, it was obvious how it got its name: there wasn't nuthin but a sea of Caucasians walkin, runnin, ridin, talkin, workin, and playin ev'ry where I looked. Even tha folks sweepin streets and cuttin grass was white. What tha fuck is this, Forsythe County? I mean, I was just waitin ta see a Confederate flag and a NO NIGGERS ALLOWED sign. Folks don't think them kinda signs be posted, but they do. But they ain't gotta be up fuh us ta know we don't belong, and I wasn't feelin tha least bit jood about bein in Whitetown. No wonder they had me drivin in a limo wit' tha darkest fuckin windows I ever seen.

"Pooquie, will you relax, the KKK is not going to descend upon our limo," Little Bit chuckled. "You're just nervous. It'll be OK."

He *was* right; I was nervous as a mutha-fucka. I mean, this shit is really gonna happen. This is somethin that a lota folks dream about, that they leave home befo' finishin high school and head fuh tha Big Fuckin Apple ta do. I guess I shoulda been...happy? Excited? Well, chills was goin thru me, but they wasn't tha jood kind. I was ready ta tell A.J., tha white guy drivin, ta turn around and drive us back ta tha Fort. I ain't know what ta expect, and I was gettin cold feet.

I grabbed Little Bit's hand. He smiled and squeezed it. I ain't care if A.J. saw us.

I told Tommy Boy I was bringin my "associate" wit' me. I wanted ta say he was my "manager" or "agent," but Little Bit said they would view that as a problem; you know, some fuckin hot shot wearin sunglasses and carryin around a cell phone who would make things difficult, demandin shit like a big dressin room or arguin wit' tha photographer, tellin him how ta do his job. But I ain't care what he wanted ta call himself, just as long as he came wit' me. I ain't wanna be by myself.

When we pulled up in front of tha All-American buildin (ta my surprise, it wasn't red, white, and blue but green), Tommy Boy was waitin outside. And he gave me another surprise: he was wearin jeans. After he met Little Bit, I checked his label.

"What—you think I want to be fired!" He laughed.

"Just makin sure," I said. "I hope you got 'em in tha right size fuh me."

"Oh, yeah, we got your size. It's small."

"Man, I don't wear no small."

"I didn't say the size was small; I said it *is* small." He giggled.

Now, what tha fuck he mean by that?

When we got on tha elevator, he pressed "B." Uh-huh…basement. Me 'n' Little Bit looked at each other; we was thinkin tha same thing. How nice: doin bizness wit' tha Negro on tha down low.

As soon as we stepped off, *he* was waitin fuh us. *He* couldn't wait ta meet me. Tommy Boy did tha honors.

"Raheim Rivers, this is Sergio Guillermo. Sir Sergio, Raheim."

Tommy Boy told me this Sergio guy was famous fuh doin stuff fuh 'zines like *Esquire* and *GQ*, but that he been on tha All-American payroll since day one. Why? He jood and he cheap. He also from England. But wit' a name like that? Turns out he *really* from Madrid. I guess here, he be a white Hispanic: he got really pale skin, green eyes, and this shaggy light brown hair that he gotta keep pushin outa his face ev'ry two seconds. He looks young, maybe like in his late thirties, and is one *short* mutha-fucka: standin next ta Little Bit, he a munchkin.

"Sir Ra*heim*. The pleasure is in*deed…all mine,*" he announced, shakin my hand.

"Nice ta meet ya," I said.

"This—*this* is a face that *ought* to be in pictures!" he declared, holdin my chin wit' his left hand. He was still holdin my other hand.

Tommy Boy nodded. "I told you."

"You are even more *stunning* in person. I believe that this will be an experience we will never forget." He *still* ain't let go.

I tried ta smile. "I hope so."

Tommy Boy started pullin me away. "Well, we better get you ready."

Sir Sergio clapped his hands. "Yes, yes, *yes,* let us *not* waste any time, we are already behind schedule. Will see you in a bit."

"Day-am, I thought he was gonna try and keep my hand and shit," I said, shakin it.

Tommy Boy smiled. "I'm sure he'd like to keep *all* of you."

"Was he really knighted by the queen?" asked Little Bit.

Tommy Boy laughed. "Knighted by the queen? *Him?* He's never even *met* the queen. 'Sir' is just a nice way of making him feel impor-tant...and keeping him happy. The more we flatter him, the less likely he'll ask for more money."

"Well, that ain't gonna work wit' me," I boasted.

"Ha, we'll see." He winked. Ha, Tommy Boy wear jeans and he think he *is* Woody Allen.

He took us ta my dressin room. It was a box. I was hopin Little Bit *would* act like my agent any-ol'-way and say some shit like, "These accommodations are unacceptable," just ta see Tommy Boy gag. He musta read my mind again: we looked at each other and smiled.

There was somebody already in tha room, so I thought we was in tha wrong place. But he turned out ta be tha makeup man.

"My name is Giorgio," he said, gettin up from his chair. He was one of them *dark* Italians—you know, really thick eyebrows and lips, jet-black wavy hair in a ponytail (naturally), and olive-brown skin. He even had a nice little frame like Little Bit—includin tha ass (now, you *know* he must be a distant relative of Hannibal). Not bad...fuh a white boy.

"Raheim." We shook hands.

While Giorgio met Little Bit, Tommy Boy put his hand on my back. "When Giorgio is done with you, your outfit is in the closet. I'll be back in, say, twenty minutes to get you." He looked at Giorgio. "Take good care of him."

"Don't you worry, I will," he said.

Little Bit sat on a couch readin magazines as me and Giorgio talked about this bein my first time modelin and him not believin it ("You're kidding! With a face like that?"). After he set up his equipment, he called himself "analyzing" my head—graspin me here and rubbin me there, and sayin shit like "You have such a regal jawline," "Your skin is just *beautiful,*" "Your bone structure is intense"—then got ta work.

"First, we're going to make your skin a little richer," he said, applyin this stuff ta my face. Tha only place he ain't put it was in my eyes and on my lips. He even had me close my eyes so he could put a little on my eyelids. I looked in this mirror he had on tha table: yeah, it was still me.

"Now, we're just going to put a little powder and blush on."

A *little*? Man, I couldn't see fuh like a minute, wit' all that white puff flyin all over. All I could think was, *He tryin ta make me look like Michael Jackson.* And when he started puttin that stuff on my cheeks, I was like, *No matter how much you dab, my man, they ain't gonna turn red.* I checked tha glass again: same ol' me.

"Now I'm going to contour your eyebrows."

Hunh? What tha fuck is that? I found out. He outlined 'em, I guess ta make sure they even. And then he got out this little comb and started brushin my eyelashes. I was like, *I better not look like no Betty Boop.*

I didn't.

I ain't like none of this shit, but I was cool about it. I mean, it's just a part of tha program, right?

But when he got out that lipstick? Tha Kid was ready ta step.

"Mr. Rivers, I just want to make those lips more, uh, more luscious— you know, make them shine."

"Nah, nah, man, you ain't puttin that lipstick on me."

"It's not lipstick. It's just a little gloss."

"I don't care *what* ya call it. I ain't lookin like no female."

"Look, Mr. Rivers, I'm not going to make you look like a woman. If they wanted a woman for this shoot they would've hired one. My job is to make you look your best. And this is going to top everything off."

I looked at Little Bit; he mouthed "Go ahead."

"A'ight, a'ight...but don't be puttin a lot on."

"I won't."

He glossed me up. It tasted like...cherries? I inspected his work again: yeah, they looked even mo' juicy.

He grabbed me by tha chin, checkin out his creation from all sides and angles. Yeah, he was pleased. "I didn't think I could, but I've made you look even more handsome."

"Ha, thanks." I grinned. Little Bit rolled his eyes.

"I have the feeling you'll be doing this a while. You've got a special look. It was a pleasure meeting you." He grabbed his case. He stood up.

I did too. "You too." We shook hands.

He went fuh tha do'. "Good luck."

"Thanks."

"Oh, and 'bye, Mr. uh, Mr...."

"Crawford." Little Bit waved, frownin.

I closed tha do' behind him (yeah, I took a peek at that ass). I smiled at Little Bit. "He knows his stuff, don't he? I do look even jooda."

Little Bit wasn't impressed. "*You've* got a special look. Oh, puh-*leeze.*"

"Baby, what's up wit' you? He only speakin tha truth."

"Uh-huh. Well, it looks like he wants to speak some *more* truth to you."

"Hunh?"

"Look."

He handed me a card. It was Giorgio's.

"He left it on the table. I saw him take it out as soon as we walked in."

I looked on tha back. It had a phone number written on it and said, *Let's get together SOON.*

Little Bit sucked his teeth. "That ol' heifer."

"C'mon, Little Bit. Don't be jealous."

"I ain't jealous. It's just that he *knew* we were together."

"How he s'pose ta know that?"

"Please, Pooquie. They *all* do."

"Whatcha mean, 'They all do?' "

"Tommy Boy, Sir Sergio…how could they not?"

"You mean…they—"

"Yes, Pooquie, they are gay. In fact, everybody we meet today will be gay or might just swing that way if you look in their direction."

Funny, but that shit ain't even occur ta me till then. I mean, ain't tha fashion world s'pose ta be a breedin ground fuh faggots? Hmmm… that's prob'ly why Tommy Boy had raised his eyebrows when he met Little Bit.

Little Bit put his arms around my waist. "Giorgio had a *jood* time fondling your head, and I'm sure he would love to get his hands on the other one."

"Yeah, well…" I gushed.

"I think you're getting soft, Pooquie."

"*Hunh?*"

"I mean, you couldn't tell he wanted you? I guess you do only have eyes for me."

"You know it, Baby."

We kissed.

"Well, I think you better get that outfit on. Time is money, and Tommy Boy sure ain't payin you to be smoochin with me."

"Yeah."

I went inta tha closet, but there wasn't no jeans hangin up, only some bikini shorts in tha style of an American flag. So *this* is what Tommy Boy was talkin about. I put 'em on. A perfect fit.

"Pooquie, *you* are truly All-American." Little Bit grinned. "You think they'll let you keep it?"

"I don't see why not. Who they gonna give 'em to?"

We laughed.

"Are you ready?" he asked.

I shrugged. "Yeah...I guess so."

"Don't worry. You're gonna do fine. After all, you *are* fine."

I blushed.

Knock, knock.

"Yeah?" I said.

"May I come in?" It was Tommy Boy.

"Yeah, come on in, Boss."

He stood at tha do', takin in tha view. He grinned. "Wait till Sir Sergio sees you. He's not gonna believe his eyes."

He wasn't tha only one. When I came out inta tha studio, which was tha size of a gymnasium, I swear, you coulda heard a fuckin pin drop. It was like tha whole fuckin room just froze in time. Not only was ev'rybody still, but they mouths was on tha flo'. About tha only things movin were a few eyes, checkin me out from head ta toe, and a few tongues, makin contact wit' they chins.

And I was glad Little Bit came wit' me, cuz we was tha only Black folks up in tha place.

Somebody finally said somethin. "Sir Ra*heim*, you are...you are...*a Nubian king!*" declared Sir Sergio, his left hand over his heart, his right on his hip.

I blushed; Little Bit mumbled, "Oh, puh-leeze," under his breath.

Sir Sergio tried his best ta put his arm on my shoulder, leadin me ta this big, square marble block that he called my "little stage." After this queen sprayed me wit' H-2-O, rubbin it off my chest, my stomach, and my thighs and enjoyin it just a little too much, I climbed up on tha block and I started feelin them lights. We talkin high, neon-sign *boomin* lights. We ain't talkin 'bout no seventy-five-watt bulbs, ya know? You think we was makin a movie.

"Don't worry, Sir Raheim," said Sir Sergio, gettin behind tha camera. "It'll take a while for you to get used to the lights. Just relax, loosen up...uh, chill."

I tried ta relax, I tried ta get loose, I tried ta chill, but it was hard. *It* was hard, too, and it wasn't like I could hide it. Wit' all tha fuckin attention—folks still was just all tha fuck in it, even Tommy Boy—fuh tha first time in my life, I felt uncomf'table bein almost naked in front of people. I really felt like there was a price tag on me and ev'rybody was checkin out tha merchandise, just waitin ta put in they bid.

Now I knew how Kunta Kinte felt.

Tha whole thing took five hours. Can you image that shit—*five* fuckin hours. It prob'ly woulda took less time if it ain't take me so much time ta get useta tha lights and just bein there. Durin tha first hour, Sir Sergio ain't take no photos, cuz I was too fuckin tight. Once I got inta it, he started snappin. And he kept on snappin 'n' snappin 'n' snappin 'n' snappin.... I was like, *Day-am, how many fuckin photos he gonna take?* I also started thinkin about how much he was gettin paid. Do he get money fuh ev'ry snap? If he do, he gonna make ten times as much as I'm gettin. It seemed like he went thru a hundred rolls of film and shit. He used a dolly and even held tha camera, takin them far away and all up in my face.

That trainin B.D. put me thru ain't help. He call himself bein a coach, teachin me how ta sway, how ta turn, how ta walk a runway. I was like, *I ain't no fuckin RuPaul, and if they want me ta do that shit, I ain't.* All I did was stand there all that time. My hands did all tha fuckin work. Sir Sergio told me ta put 'em on my waist, put 'em on top my head, put 'em above my head, put 'em behind my head, put 'em behind my neck, put 'em behind my back, put 'em on my chest, put 'em on my nipples, put 'em on my dick, put 'em on my ass, put 'em on my thighs, put 'em on my knees, put 'em on my face, put 'em under my chin, put 'em on my underwear, put 'em *in* my underwear (just my thumbs), put 'em up ta tha sky, put 'em tagetha like I'm gonna pray, ball 'em up like I'm gonna fight, hug myself. And, each and ev'ry *fuckin* time I (or my hands) had ta change position, Sir Sergio always said tha same thing: "Smile." I just don't know how people can *do* this shit fuh a livin. Ta hafta smile on fuckin cue fuh hours? Yeah, tha money is tuff, but all that cheezin it up ain't fun. Add them lights, tha million fuckin poses and shit...we talkin about a Job wit' a capital *J*.

So you know I was too happy when Sir Sergio said, "All right, that's a wrap!" I hopped off that fuckin block and headed straight fuh tha dressin room. Of course, Tha Kid was mobbed on his way there.

"Congratulations!"

"Good job!"

"You looked marvelous up there!"

"You were great!"

"You were *fabulous!*"

You know I was lovin ev'ry word, but I was just *too* fuckin tired ta really enjoy it. How tired was I? As soon as my head hit that couch in tha dressin room, I was out. Those few little breaks I had, guzzlin down some o.j. and rappin wit' Little Bit, wasn't enuff. I ain't never work so hard in all my life. I was so tired, I ain't even wanna eat, so Tommy Boy and Sir Sergio postponed takin me out ta celebrate fuh another nite. I threw back on my clothes, and me 'n' Little Bit piled in tha limo and jetted. I slept on tha way home wit' my head in his lap.

Tha last thing I remember Little Bit sayin befo' I passed out in bed fuh tha rest of tha nite was: "Well, Mr. Rivers…welcome to show business."

ON THA ROAD, AGAIN

"So, whatcha think?"

"You really wanna know?"

"I'm askin, ain't I?"

"Well, I like the Camry. That color is really nice. I think the man said it was magenta or something like that."

"You don't like tha Jeep?"

"Yeah, I like it. But is it really necessary?"

"Whatcha mean?"

"Well, I thought you were gonna be practical."

"I'm bein practical."

"Are you? If the idea was to get a Jeep, you could have kept the old one."

"You know I couldn't do nuthin like that."

"Yes, I know. I'm just saying that you need something sensible."

"A Jeep ain't sensible?"

"No, it ain't."

"Why not?"

"Because, Pooquie, it's too sporty. You *cruise* in a Jeep; you *drive* a car. Besides, that color is awful."

"Yo, you tha one who said I look jood in bright colors."

"I said you look jood in bright-colored *clothes,* I ain't say nothin about a vehicle that's painted canary yellow."

"But I like it, Baby."

"I know." He smiled. "Ya know, you look so cute when you pout."

I blushed.

"You can still get the Jeep. I just don't think you should get it now. There's time. You need something that says you are a serious gentleman, a family man."

"A family man?"

"Yes, a family man."

I snickered. "And tha Camry says that?"

"Well, at least it doesn't stick out. It doesn't draw attention to itself the way the Jeep does. You said that you, D.C., and Angel were pulled over more times than you can count in it. May as well not give them a reason to do it again."

"Baby, they don't *need* no fuckin reason ta do it. It don't matter *what* kinda wheels you got. If you Black, you always gonna hear tha sound of da police."

He frowned. "You like the Camry too, right?"

"Yeah, I do."

"And you've had plenty of practice in it. You say you love drivin Angel's car 'cause it's a real smooth ride. And this is a 1994 make with a jood stereo system—"

"Yeah, that bass is bumpin."

"—and the price is right. Nine thousand dollars? They *givin* it away. That's what I call a holiday sale. Your down payment—not to mention the insurance, registration, and plates—won't be much. And I really like the color."

"I know, you told me."

"*And* I *love* the way you look in it."

"You do?"

"Yes, I do. Real sexy—sexier than you do in the Jeep."

"Yeah?"

He winked. "Yeah. And I think Junior seems to love the way *he* looks in it."

"Yeah, I guess he do. A'ight...we see what he say."

We walked back ta tha car. Li'l Brotha Man was in tha front seat, workin tha wheel, talkin wit' tha salesman, this skinny freckle-face white boy name Sal I knew was just waitin ta make a killin offa me. As soon as we walked in tha place, he led us straight ta tha Jeeps and almost had me sold. It's a jood thing Little Bit came wit' us. I knew Sal wasn't gonna be happy wit' our decision.

"So, whatcha think, my man?"

Li'l Brotha Man rocked in tha seat. "I like this one, Daddy. It's like Uncle Angel's. And I *love* the color!"

"You don't like tha Jeep?"

"Yes, I do. But I like this one better. There's more room for everybody."

"Ev'rybody?"

"Yes. You, me, and Mitch-hull." He said it like I was s'pose ta know. He smiled at us; we smiled back.

"A'ight, you da man." I looked at Sal. "We'll take it."

Sal tried lookin excited, but it wasn't workin. There goes that hefty commission. "Uh, great, great. You made a good choice."

"No, Sal, my daddy made a *jood* choice!"

Me 'n' Little Bit grinned.

Sal was lost and wanted ta know why. "Uh, *jood*?"

Li'l Brotha Man schooled him. "Yes, Sal, better than good!"

We all laughed.

Sal smiled. "You got yourself one smart little boy, Mr. Rivers."

I winked at Li'l Brotha Man. "Yeah, I know."

REWIND '87

> "Hi-ho, hi-ho
> It's off ta work she goes
> Da da da da da da da da da da
> Hi-ho, hi-ho
> Hi-ho
> Hi-ho, hi-ho
> Yo' mama is a 'ho
> Da da da da da da da da da da
> She is
> A 'ho."

"What tha fuck y'all 'hoin about?"

"Yo, what's up, money?"

"Man, we just chillin."

"Yeah, right. Who tha fuck y'all talkin 'bout?"

"Who else? Rockhead's moms. She ain't nuthin but a 'ho."

"Yeah, man, she just left ta get her paycheck on Forty-second!"

"What?"

"Yo, man, she walkin tha streets, workin them corners."

"How tha fuck y'all know that?"

"Cuz Mad Dog saw her last nite when he was breezin thru, doin his runs."

"Get tha fuck outa here!"

"Nah."

"Yeah. Now we know why that mutha-fucka can't get no pussy."

"Why?"

"Cuz he done seen his moms give it up so much, nigga prob'ly turned gay and shit!"

"Yo, man, that shit ain't funny. Ain't none of this shit funny."

"Man, whatcha mean it ain't funny? It is too."

"You niggaz wouldn't want nobody talkin 'bout y'all's moms like that, so y'all just need ta chill tha fuck out."

"Man, what tha fuck is up wit' you?"

"If his moms is a fuckin prostitute, that shit ain't funny."

"Man, kill that noize. I think tha brotha is gettin soft."

"Smooth, we ain't talkin 'bout yo' dick, a'ight?"

"You tryin ta break on me and shit? Nigga, I fuck you up!"

"Nigga, you ain't fuckin nobody up!"

"Man, who tha fuck you s'pose ta be?"

"Mutha-fucka, you don't get tha fuck outa my face, you gonna find out."

"Will y'all niggaz quit this shit?"

"Get tha fuck outa tha way, D.C. I'm gonna fuck yo' boy up."

"Nigga, pleeze, don't be wastin my fuckin time. You ain't worth spittin on. I'm outa here."

"That's right, that's right, punk! Just get tha fuck outa here!"

"Yo, Brotha, hold up!"

"Man, D.C., let that nigga walk. He always runnin off and shit. Ol' punk."

"Yo, Brotha!"

"Brotha Man, get off me!"

"Raheim, chill, Brotha, chill. What's up wit' you and shit?"

"Man, what's up wit' you? Y'all standin in front of that nigga's house, talkin that shit. That shit is cold as mutha-fuckin ice."

"Man, since when you care 'bout how that nigga feel?"

"This ain't got nuthin ta do wit' how he feel. How 'bout if somebody was talkin that shit about yo' moms in fronta yo' house? Y'all niggaz can't find nuthin else ta do? That shit shows just how much class y'all got."

"Man, how you gonna dis me like that, yo' Brotha Man?"

"Cuz sometimes, man, it's like you ain't even thinkin. You just listenin ta them okie-doke mutha-fuckas like they know shit, when they don't."

"Man, all we doin is havin fun. You fuckin trippin. See, that's what happens when you pussy-whipped."

"What?"

"Pussy-whipped. Little ol' Mary mutha-fuckin Sunshine got you just wrapped all tha fuck up, ain't she? Man, I knew this shit was gonna happen.…"

"Man, I ain't no fuckin pussy-whipped. Yo' problem is you ain't gettin no pussy like Smooth and all them other knucklehead mutha-fuckas you hangin 'round."

"Man, fuck you."

"Fuck you, nigga."

"Man, Smooth is right. You ain't nuthin but a punk."

"I'm a punk? Nigga, you suck my dick, I don't suck yours, so who is tha real punk? Just get tha fuck out my face and stay tha fuck away from me!"

"Fuck you, nigga!"

MERRY XMAS, BABY

"You don't like it?"

"What do you think?"

I rubbed my chin. "You don't like it."

"It's not that I don't like *it*. I don't like it for *him*."

"Sunshine, it ain't nuthin but a fuckin toy."

"Didn't we have this conversation before?"

"Yeah, we did."

"And?"

"And nuthin. If I wanna buy my son somethin, I'm gonna get it fuh him."

"You know how I feel about this, Raheim."

"So."

"So?"

"Yeah, you heard. I'm tired of you always tellin me what I can and can't do fuh him. Why don't you let tha boy be, let him be a boy?"

"And what is *that* supposed to mean?"

I couldn't resist this one. "Uh, what part of that statement *ain't* you understand? How he s'pose ta know what bein a man is all about?"

"Uh-huh. And what exactly *is* bein a man supposed to be about?"

"All you want him ta do is play wit' blocks, watch *Sesame Street,* and keep his head in a fuckin colorin book."

"And what's wrong with that?"

"What's wrong is that that ain't all there is ta life, and he gotta know that."

"So you saying that this is gonna make him see what being a man is all about?"

"Sunshine, he see tha shit on TV all tha time. And we ain't livin in no suburb."

"I know, Raheim, and that's exactly why I don't want him to have it. I don't want him to think that it is something he should like, that there's nothing wrong with having one."

"He five fuckin years old and shit. I had one, and I ain't strapped."

"No, you ain't, but some of your homies are. Where you think they get the idea it's OK?"

"Tha streets. But all Li'l Brotha Man doin is havin fun—"

"And that's my point. The streets are out there telling him one thing, so I don't want to send him the same message. I don't want him thinking that it is fun to have one. And I think giving it to him says that."

"It don't."

"Yes, it does."

"It do not."

"OK, OK. What about D.C.?"

"What about Brotha Man?"

"Junior knows that a gun took away his godfather. What are we saying to him if we let him keep it?"

"You act like we givin him a Nine and shit. He know tha diff'rence."

"To me, there *is* no difference."

"Look, I want him ta have it."

"I *don't*."

"A'ight, a'ight. I know. Let's let him decide."

"Let *him* decide?"

"Yeah. He ain't no dummy. He smart. He know all about what's goin on in tha streets. Let him be his own judge. I bought it fuh him."

"He's not old enough."

"He is too."

"No, he isn't."

"Look, I ain't takin it back. We doin it like this."

I opened her bedroom do', clearin tha way fuh her ta go out first. She sighed real heavy, mumbled "Fine," and went inta tha livin room, where Li'l Brotha Man was still openin his presents. She sat on tha right side of tha couch, where their Christmas tree was. It was one of them fakes—you know, tha kind ya put tagetha in like ten minutes. I should know: I did it wit' Li'l Brotha Man. Ever since he was a baby, he just loved puttin on them bulbs, tha tinsel, tha candy canes, all that shit. And ev'ry year, he put tha star on top. I do it wit' him cuz he like me ta and it makes me, Sunshine, and him seem tagetha, like we a family. I ain't really have that, so I wanna make sure he do.

"Oh, wow! Look, Mommy! Look, Daddy! Look what Mitch-hull gave me!" It was one of them jigsaw puzzles. And, big fuckin surprise, it was of Dr. King. Just about ev'rything Little Bit give him gotta teach him somethin. But I don't think Li'l Brotha Man even care. Little Bit could wrap up a fuckin lollipop, put a ribbon on it, and Li'l Brotha Man would love it.

"Ooh, that's really nice," said Sunshine, takin it from him. "You have to make sure you thank him for your gifts, OK?"

"Yes, I will."

I grabbed tha gun; it was a silver pistol. It was part of a cowboy ensemble (he was wearin tha hat and holster). I knelt down in fronta him.

"Li'l Brotha Man?"

"Yes, Daddy?"

"C'm'ere."

He did. I wrapped him up in my left arm.

"We wanna talk ta ya about somethin."

He looked at Sunshine. He looked at me. "What?"

I held up tha gun wit' my right hand. "We wanna know how you feel about this."

"How I feel?"

"Yeah."

"What do you mean, Daddy?"

"Do you like guns?"

He shrugged. "I don't know. I never had one before."

"Well, you think kids should play wit' 'em?"

"Not if they real."

I looked at Sunshine. I smiled. "Do you like this present?"

He nodded. "Yes, I do."

"Do you wanna keep it?"

He looked at Sunshine; he knew how she felt.

"It's OK if you want it, Junior," she said.

He smiled. "Yes."

I squeezed him. "A'ight, then. You can keep it."

"I can?"

We both looked at Sunshine, grinnin. She couldn't help but bust out laughin. "Yes, you can."

He jumped up, clappin. "Jood!" He took tha gun from me and started playin wit' it.

I rose up off my knee. That's my son.

"Junior, come here for a second," said Sunshine.

"OK."

She took him by his shoulders. She smiled. "I am so proud of you." She kissed him on his nose.

"Can I wake Grammy now?"

"Yes, you can. Ask her to run your water for you."

"OK." And off he went, tha gun in his hand.

She got up and went inta tha kitchen. I followed her.

"So?" I asked.

"So, what?"

"I told ya he could handle it."

She sighed. "Yeah."

"What's wrong?"

"Nothing."

"If there ain't nuthin wrong, why you look all sad?"

"I'm not sad."

"Then you must be angry."

"Why would I be angry?"

"Cuz he said he wanted it, and you know you ain't want him ta."

"I might feel that way, but that's not what I'm feeling right now."

"So…what's up?"

"I just realized something, that's all."

"What?"

She stopped gettin stuff out tha fridge and came up ta me. "That my baby is no longer a baby."

I knew this was my cue. I hugged her. She held me tight.

"Nah, he ain't no baby no mo', but he always gonna be our—"

"—Li'l Brotha Man," she finished wit' me. We laughed. I let her go, but she still held on.

She frowned. "I don't want him to play with it outside."

"Why?"

"Because somebody might mistake it for a real one."

"It don't look real."

"Uh-huh, that's what all those cops say after they shoot some kid they thought had a real gun."

She had a jood point. "A'ight. You compromise, I compromise."

"Ya know something?"

"What?"

"I'm proud of *you,* too."

"Oh, yeah?"

"Yeah."

"Why?"

"'Cause you are his daddy…and you are so jood at it."

I chuckled. She got me on my lips.

"Merry Christmas, Raheim."

"Merry Christmas, Sunshine."

"Yo, yo, yo, Happy Ha-lee-day, Bay-bee!"

I wish I had a camera ta save that look on Little Bit's face when I fell up in his place dressed ta tha Red. That's right—cap, jacket, and pants. Only tha boots was black, courtesy of my man, Karl Kani. Tha rest of tha set I got at this costume place Uptown a few years back. I useta put it on fuh Li'l Brotha Man, ta let him know that Santa Claus ain't no white man, he a Black man, his daddy. This another thing Sunshine ain't like, but I was like, *Fuck that*. I wasn't havin my son dreamin of no white Christmas, thinkin he gotta be jood tha other three hundred and sixty-plus days of tha year so some fat, pasty-face mutha-fucka can come down a chimney and give him shit his moms and pops can't. Besides, kids are hip these days—they don't seem ta believe in all that shit we did when we was they age.

Anyway, I ain't wear tha suit this year cuz Li'l Brotha Man wasn't hyped about it. But I'm glad I ain't throw it away. And Little Bit's reaction told me he was glad too.

"Pooquie, where did you get that?"

"That's Santa ta you, young man." I scooped him up and carried him inta tha livin room, where Be Be and Ce Ce Winans was jammin on "Jingle Bells." I wanted ta get one of them giant trees fuh tha house so we could fix it up tagetha, but Little Bit got one of them teeny-weeny table trees that had a big red bow. It was sittin on tha coffee table. Little Bit ain't wanna put no lights on it, so he let me string some along tha bedroom window that spelled MERRY XMAS.

He giggled. "OK, uh, Santa. But aren't you like twenty-four hours late?"

"I had ta make a lota stops. Anyway, ain't you heard that phrase, 'Better late than never'?"

"Yeah, I guess I have. But you're still not off the hook. How are you going to make it up to me?"

I put him down on tha carpet. "How 'bout this?"

Our tongues did a serious dance. Uh-huh, just gimme that Holiday Love...Cuz U a Holiday 2 Me.

"Uh, Santa?" he moaned.

"Yeah?" I groaned.

"Aren't you supposed to be deliverin presents?"

"Whatcha think I'm doin?"

"How do you know this was on my list?"

"Ha, I got yo' fuckin list, Baby, *trust*."

"Well, shouldn't we be doing this under the mistletoe?"

"We don't *need* no mistletoe."

We giggled.

He played wit' tha white ball on tha tassel of tha cap. "So, did you actually walk through the streets of Harlem in this?"

"You *cray*-zee? I put it on when I was leavin tha house."

"So Junior didn't see you in it?"

"Nah. He way past that, Baby. He call you?"

"Yes, he did. He said he loved his gifts."

"Sunshine did too."

"I know. She told me."

"She did?"

"Yes. She thanked me, too. She said Junior looked so good in the outfit I gave him. But he corrected her, saying, 'No, Mommy, I look *jood*!' "

We cracked up.

He grinned. "And *you* look jood too."

I grinned too. "I know." I started lockin him in tha position. "So, you want yo' other presents now?"

"No, wait. Before you *really* start giving me my gifts, I have some presents for *you*, Santa."

"Oh, yeah?"

He eased up from under me and grabbed a shoppin bag next ta tha coffee table. He handed it ta me. "Here."

I peeked in it and saw two boxes and a small, square, thin package. I hit tha mutha-fuckin jackpot. "So, what are they?"

"I don't know. I didn't give them to you."

"Nah?"

"No."

"If you ain't give 'em ta me, who did?"

He sat down on tha carpet and crossed his legs. "Well, there's only one way to find out, right?"

That was true, so I went ta work. I went fuh tha big ones first cuz Tha Kid knows that tha best presents come in small packages (uh-huh, like Little Bit). There wasn't no card. I just tore tha wrap off like Li'l Brotha Man do. I was just feelin too jood.

I opened tha box, and there was no doubt who bought me this present. It was a really thick red, black, and green scarf wit' a matchin hat. Tha card inside said, *Happy Kwanzaa, Your Brother in the Struggle, Babyface.*

"That's really nice," said Little Bit, as he checked tha set out. I was busy openin tha other box. It turned out ta be a gray sweatshirt. It had POOQUIE & LITTLE BIT in a heart on tha front and HERE'S 2 LOVE on tha back. Its note said, *To Pooquie...Merry Xmas. If this don't keep you warm this winter, I don't know what will. (Yeah, right!) All My Lust, B.D.*

I smiled. "This is tuff."

"I told him you were gonna like it. He gave me one too."

"He did?"

"Yeah."

"So, what, we s'pose ta walk around like twins and shit?"

He rolled his eyes. "No, we don't."

I knew by tha shape of tha last present it was some kinda CD, and I was right: *The Best of Rap, Part I.* It had all tha jams from back in tha day, like "The Message," "The Breaks," "My Adidas," "Roxanne, Roxanne," and, of course, "Rapper's Delight." Day-am, I ain't heard none of them cuts in years. But I was really in shell shock when I saw tha note: *Mr. Rivers: Betcha Didn't Expect This, Hunh? My Dahling, I Am Full of Surprises. Happy Holly & All That Jazz, Gene.* I mean, I was surprised ta get somethin from all of 'em, but ta think that Gene spent money on me? That threw me fuh a fuckin loop.

"This is a *jood* hits package," said Little Bit, lookin at tha CD. He smiled. "You cleaned up."

I shrugged. "Yeah. But I ain't get them nuthin."

"So? This is a time for *giving*, Pooquie. They certainly didn't do it because they were expecting something in return."

"But why they do it?"

He got on his knees between my legs and took ahold of my head. "I don't know. Maybe because they know how much you mean to me. Maybe because they like you. Maybe they want to welcome you into our little family. Maybe all of the above." He kissed my nose. "And speakin of family, my mother, Anderson, Adam, Aunt Ruth, and Alvin wish you a merry Christmas."

"Yeah? So, how they doin?"

"They're all fine. My mother sent you two big plates of food—"

"A'ight!"

"—and Aunt Ruth made you a pie."

"Cool. What kind is it?"

"Your favorite."

"Nah! Lemon meringue?"

"Yup."

"*Get* tha fuck outa here!"

"I can't. Then I wouldn't be able to see you open up *my* presents."

He got up, reached behind tha couch, and came up wit' three packages. Hmmm...I had been lookin there ev'ry day fuh tha past two weeks ta see if that's where he was hidin my gifts. I took tha one that was so thin it seemed like nuthin could be in it. It was a pair of black leather gloves.

"Yo, Baby! Just what I needed!"

"I know. You've been saying that the past two months. I can take a hint."

I had 'em on, admirin them. I grinned. "Thanks, Baby."

"You're welcome."

I pulled them off, and I shook and opened tha slim, rectangular box next. It was a *Jeopardy!* board game.

My eyes popped. "Yo, Baby, I been wantin this a *long* time!"

"I know. Now we can play anytime."

I slapped him on his ass. "Ha, I think we do that already."

He gushed. "Just open the other one, silly."

It was a light blue terry cloth robe wit' my initials on it.

"Baby, I *love* this."

"I'm glad. Now you can give Adam *his* robe back."

"Yeah." I laughed. "Thanks, Baby."

"You're welcome."

I grabbed him. Our tongues did battle again.

I grinned. "Now, we saved tha best fuh last."

I went inta my little red bag of treats. He knelt on tha flo', just anticipatin. I guess he could tell tha first one was a CD too. But when he saw who it was, his face almost broke in two.

"Oh, my *God*, Pooquie," he said, not believin his eyes. "*Where* did you get this?"

"I got my sources." I grinned. My "source" was Arthur at Simply Dope Records, who got it fuh me when he went ta Germany.

Little Bit kept starin at it. "I didn't know they released this in the United States."

"They ain't. You prob'ly tha only person who got it."

It was *The Very Best of Randy Crawford, Volumes I & II.*

But that wasn't it. He was so shocked he ain't even bother ta turn tha two CD set over and see what was taped on tha back. When he finally did, he found two tickets ta see...you know who.

"*Oh, no! Randy Crawford in concert?*" he squealed like Li'l Brotha Man.

"Uh-huh. Two front row seats, Baby."

He jumped inta my arms, kissin my face all over. "*Oh, Pooquie! Thank you, thank you, thank you! You know I've never seen her before! Oh, I can't wait! Oh, I love you, I love you, I love you so much!*"

I giggled. "Yo, yo, yo, *chill*, Baby. You got two other presents comin. You ain't gonna have no energy ta handle 'em."

I reached back in tha bag and took out a small, thin, long box. He opened it. His eyes bulged, and he drew back a breath. His mouth opened, but nuthin came out. It was like he couldn't speak. His tears did tha talkin.

I grinned. "What's wrong, Baby…cat gotcha tongue?"

"Oh, Pooquie…it's…it's *so* beautiful."

"I know. Here, let me put it on ya."

He turned around so I could. He played wit' tha charm. Yeah, it said LITTLE BIT.

I wrapped my arms around his waist. "You like it?"

"No, I don't like it…I *love* it."

"Uh-huh, and I love *you*."

He turned around ta face me and gave me one of them deep-throat jammies.

I laughed. "Baby, why you still cryin?"

He giggled. "Because, Pooquie. I'm just so happy."

I wiped his tears. "I got somethin else ta make you happy. You got another present comin."

"You've already given me so much."

"Baby, you ain't gonna wanna turn this down."

I stepped back. I took off my boots and socks. I unbuttoned and slid off tha jacket. I took off my T. I unsnapped my suspenders and let my pants drop off. I just stood there in my red briefs. I folded my arms against my chest and grinned.

He did too. "Uh, Santa?"

"Yeah?"

He eased up ta me. "I've been really naughty this year."

"Jood."

He started circlin me. "Jood?"

"Yeah."

"Well, ain't I supposed to be nice to get what I want?"

"You mo' than nice, Baby. And you mo' than naughty." I wrapped him up. "And that's why you can have it *both* ways."

"Hmmm." He held me by my ass. "I think I'm gonna enjoy goin up *your* chimney, Santa."

I blushed.

He smiled. "Uh, will you keep the hat on?"

"Yo, I'm still on duty."

We cracked up.

"Merry Christmas, Pooquie."

"Merry Christmas, Baby."

STICKS & STONES

I was takin Li'l Brotha Man ta Little Bit's place ta spend tha weekend wit' us when…

"Daddy?"

"Yeah, my man?"

"What's a faggot?"

Day-am, where tha fuck *that* come from?

Li'l Brotha Man is just too fuckin much. He smarter than I was when I was his age. But since he started school, he be askin even mo' questions. He say his teacher tells him not ta be afraid of askin, and I don't think he should be. But sometimes, them questions just be wild.…

"Daddy, what are the clouds made of?"

"Daddy, how does the sun know when to come out?"

"Daddy, how does the moon know when to come out?"

"Daddy, if the world is round, how come when it turn we don't fall off?"

"Daddy, if there is a God, how come we can't see him?"

"Daddy, how do we know God is a *him?*"

"Daddy, how do they get the Rice Krispies to talk to me?"

But this question was straight-up *wack.*

Well, I guess it ain't that tha question was wack but that he was askin it. I mean, he only five. So, I just had ta know…

"Where you hear that word?" I asked, tryin ta look at him and drive at tha same time.

"Terrence."

"Terrence? Who he?"

"Remember, Daddy, he's my friend at school."

"Oh, yeah."

"He has a twin sister. Her name is Theresa."

"Uh-huh…did he call you that word?"

"No. He said that's what his daddy called Michael Jackson."

"Michael Jackson?"

"Yes. I asked him what it mean, but he didn't know. He said that his daddy said it because he didn't want him to watch Michael on TV because of what he did to those boys."

"Did his daddy say what Michael did?"

"That Michael touched them, and that he slept in the same bed with them."

Me 'n' Sunshine had already talked ta him about lettin people "touch" him, so I know I ain't had ta go over that again. Li'l Brotha Man, he real sharp. But this? I had ta take a real deep breath.

"Li'l Brotha Man, listen ta me real close, a'ight?"

He folded his hands in his lap, his eyes wide, and looked at me. "Yes."

"We don't know if Michael did anything ta them boys...they just allegations. Can you say that word? A-lee-gay-shuns."

"A-lee-gay-shuns." He just loved soundin words out.

"Right."

"What does that word mean, Daddy?"

"A allegation is somethin that ain't been proved yet. You know, it's just one person's word against another. So we don't know if what them boys say is true or not."

"You mean...they could be tellin a fib?"

"Yeah, they could be tellin a fib."

"Why would they do that?"

"I don't know...maybe cuz they parents know they can get some money from Michael.... Anyway, we don't know if anything happened, so it ain't right ta prejudge somebody. You know what that word mean, prejudge?"

"Pre-judge? I think so. Is that when you think something about someone without knowing anything about them?"

"Yeah. How you know that?"

"We talked about that in class. Misses Scott says it's not nice to prejudge."

"That's right. And you wouldn't want nobody saying things about you that ain't true, or prejudgin you by what somebody else say, right?"

He shook his head. "No."

"So, I don't want you goin 'round sayin things you don't know ain't true or not."

"OK, Daddy."

He smiled. He seemed a'ight wit' what I said. I was glad, cuz explainin shit ta him is hard. But then....

"Daddy?"

"Yeah?"

"You didn't answer my question."

Day-am...I almost got away.

I tried playin it off. "What question?"

But he wasn't havin it. "What is a faggot?"

Shit. What tha fuck do I say? This is one of them times when bein a parent ain't tha least bit cute. You gotta explain things that are hard ta explain, 'specially when they so young.

I took another deep breath. "Li'l Brotha Man, it's a bad word...some people use it when...well, they say it ta boys who...boys who don't act like boys."

"Boys who don't act like boys...? What do you mean, Daddy?"

"Uh..." Day-am, where's Little Bit when I need him? This is somethin he be jood at. "Some boys don't wanna be boys...they wanna be girls...see, there are boy things and girl things...like, jumpin rope is a girl thing, and if you see a boy doin that, jumpin rope wit' girls, people will say that he tryin ta be a girl, that he is...that word."

Tha tip of his left thumb went inta his mouth. He was thinkin. It reminded me of...me. "So Terrence's daddy said that because Michael jumps rope with girls?"

I chuckled. "No, Li'l Brotha Man. I guess Terrence's daddy called Michael that cuz...some people think that Michael don't act like a man...cuz he wear makeup, and he got a high-pitch voice...but you callin somebody outa they name when you do that, and it ain't right."

"So it's not a nice word?"

"No, it ain't, and I don't want ya usin it or callin somebody it. You don't like it when somebody calls you a bad word, right?"

He nodded. "No, I don't."

"So, don't do it ta nobody. It's like you prejudgin somebody cuz of tha way they look, or act, or talk, or sound."

He understood; I could tell by tha look on his face. We was quiet fuh a bit, and I was able ta breathe a *big* mutha-fuckin sigh of relief.

I smiled. "You like Michael?"

"Yes, I do. But Terrence says I shouldn't."

"Well, if you like him, you like him. Don't be listenin ta what Terrence say. People always comin down on Michael. I mean, I don't really like him, but it prob'ly ain't easy fuh him, bein tha richest Black man in tha world."

He looked at me like I was buggin. "Michael Jackson is *Black*, Daddy?"

"Yeah, he Black. Whatcha think he is?"

"He looks white!"

"I know he do, Li'l Brotha Man, but he Black."

I laughed.

REWIND '88

"So, when were you gonna tell me?"

"I...I don't know."

"Well, you picked one fine time, two weeks before she due."

"I—I ain't know how ta tell you."

"So, that explains it all."

"What?"

"Why you been walkin 'round this house lookin all lost for the last seven months. I knew somethin was up. I don't know why you do that to yourself...just like your father."

"I ain't like him."

"You gonna tell me? I know both of y'all better than y'all know y'allselves."

"I ain't even gonna be like him. I ain't runnin off. I'm a man, and I'm gonna take care of my son."

"A son? Y'all know it's a boy?"

"Nah...I just know it is."

"Uh-huh. And I told you 'bout talkin bad about him, right?"

"Ma, why you always stickin up fuh that nigga—"

"Boy, you better watch your language in this house! You ain't talkin to one of your little homeboys out there, you hear me? Do you hear me?"

"Yeah."

"So...you a man, hunh? You gonna be able to take care of...your son?"

"Yeah."

"Uh-huh...and just how do you propose to do this?"

"Whatcha mean?"

"I don't think I'm speakin a foreign language: how you gonna take care of him when you can't even take care of yourself?"

"I'm gonna get a job."

"A job. What kind of job?"

"I...I don't know, somethin..."

" 'I don't know'? 'Somethin'? You better know, and it better be somethin. How come you don't already have this job?"

"I been lookin."

"Lookin where?"

"Uh, all over."

"And what kind *of job you lookin for?"*

"Somethin that pays real money."

"Real money? What *is real money?"*

"At least ten an hour."

"Boy, what kind of job you think you gonna get that pays ten dollars an hour? You fifteen years old…you be lucky to get a job that pays three-fifty an hour."

"I'm gonna find me one, Ma…."

"Uh-huh. And while you are searching for this job that pays real money, your son needs diapers, food, clothes—"

"Ma—"

"Boy, don't Ma me, OK? You ain't gonna find that *job, so I suggest you go down to that McDonald's around the corner and fill out an application."*

"Mac-Donald's?"

"Yes, Mac-Donald's."

"Ma, ain't no way I'm workin there—"

"Why not?"

"Cuz they ain't payin no money."

"Forty billion burgers sold? They must be payin somethin."

"Ma, it ain't enuff."

"Excuse me? 'It ain't enough'? It's gonna be more than what you makin now: nothin."

"I can't be workin there."

"Why not?"

"Cuz, Ma, it ain't no real job."

"A real *job? Boy, you gotta start someplace, and* there *is a better place than nowhere."*

"But Ma, all my boyz come up in there."

"So? You'll just have to do to them what you'll have to do to everybody else: serve 'em with a smile."

"Aw, Ma."

"Don't, OK? Don't. *You can't afford to be frownin up your nose at no job and thinkin 'bout what your so-called* boyz *are gonna think. You suppose to be thinkin 'bout your* son."

"But Ma—"

"I don't wanna hear it. You don't know what you doin, you don't know what you gettin into. You a man? You a man? *Then* act *like it. I expect you to have not one, but* two *jobs by the end of this week."*

"Two jobs?"

"You hear very well. That's right, two jobs."

"I don't need—"

"Boy, how you gonna tell me what you need? I know. See, you ain't thinkin, you ain't think this through. You gonna take care of your son? Well, you have to do more than that: you gotta raise him. And for you, it ain't gonna happen with just a job. You right: you need a job payin real money, but you ain't gonna find one, 'cause you don't even have a high school diploma yet. That means you gonna have to try twice as hard and work twice as hard."

"But Ma, how about—"

"—your summer vacation? You may as well kiss that and every other summer vacation good-bye, at least for the next eighteen years. I ain't had no summer vacation since you been around. Believe me, you get used to it."

"That ain't fair...."

"Fair? Fair? I tell you what ain't fair: you mouthin off about how you gonna lose out on runnin the streets with them no-good hoods when your son should be all you thinkin about. You livin for him now, not for yourself. You done stuck it in and now he's comin out, so I suggest you get it together. I ain't takin care of him, I ain't raisin him, and you ain't havin my grandchild on no welfare because you lazy. And you better not even think about makin this a habit. You ain't bringin no more children into this world, at least while you livin under this roof. How many other taskets you been puttin your tisket in?"

"Huh?"

"You heard. You better not be toilin no other girl's soil out there. And how come you ain't use no protection?"

"I did."

"You did, hunh? Well, you obviously didn't put it on right, now, did you?"

"Ma—"

"Please, don't—just don't. I don't care if you packin groceries, sweepin the streets, or makin french fries, you got a lot of catchin up to do. And I think you better start right now."

"Huh?"

"You heard. I advise you to take a walk and see if anybody around here is hirin."

"It's gettin dark, Ma."

"And? So what? Take off that sweat suit, put on a pair of pants and a shirt, and hit the pavement. And don't be lookin at me like that. I ain't make this bed, you did. Go on and change. And give me Crystal's number again."

"Why?"

"Boy, if I gotta tell you why, then you shouldn't be the father of nobody's baby."

"You don't need ta talk ta her, Ma. I got it all under control."

"You got it under control? If you did have things under control, you *wouldn't be a father at fifteen, now, would you? You can't even control your own erection, Junior. Puh-leeze."*

"Don't call me that."

"Don't call you that? See, your idea of bein a man is talkin a good game like these no-count Negroes out here. 'I'll take care of it.' 'I'm in control.' Bull shit. *You gonna do right by this child and its mother, and there ain't gonna be no half steppin. So leave the* damn *number before you go.... Do Crystal's mother know?"*

"Yeah, she know."

"Well, how nice of you two to tell her and not me."

"Ma, I ain't—"

"Yeah, I know, I know, we already been over that. Just go on and do what I say. Pick up your feet. And don't take forever.... Crystal don't need to be raisin two babies, and I was through changin your diapers a long time ago, so you better change your attitude and quick, you hear?"

SCHOOLIN HIM OUT

I take Sunshine out ev'ry year fuh her birthday, January 22 (and, whatcha know, this year she turnin twenty-two). She loves plays, so I got us tickets ta see *A Raisin in the Sun* at the National Black Theatre. Esther Rolle was playin tha moms; I ain't seen her since *Good Times,* and she ain't changed. She was just too tuff. We caught tha matinee and then went ta Sylvia's ta eat. It was packed; there was a line comin outa tha place—it was tha church crowd, little ol' ladies named Hazel and Gussie wit' blue hair and hats you just know they blew their whole SSI check on—but Sunshine wanted ta wait (it was only twenty minutes). Tha Kid got tha usual: a slab of ribs. Sunshine claim she was on a diet just havin a veggie plate, but she woofed down like five slices of cornbread.

I was pattin my very full stomach and tha waitress had just taken away our dishes when she put a pamphlet in fronta me.

I frowned. "What's this?"

"Remember that school I mentioned? This will tell you a little bit about it."

I looked at it; there was five white kids, one Black, one Asian, and one Puerto Rican, and they was all showin their teeth. "Why you want him ta go there?"

"Because it's a damn jood school, that's why." She smiled.

I didn't. "Who say?"

"What?"

"Who say it is?"

"It's known throughout the city, Raheim."

"Yeah, right."

"In fact, it was graded one of the best elementary academies in the country."

I sat back. "See, there's tha prob."

"What?"

"We *s'pose* ta be sendin him ta tha first grade, not no academy."

"That's what we'd be doing."

"C'mon, Sunshine. Academies is where stuck-up white folks send their kids."

"*Black* kids go to them too, and there are Black kids at Alexander."

"Yeah? How many?"

"According to the director, Miss Dewhurst, the Black student population is 10 percent."

"That don't tell us nuthin. How much you wanna bet there's only one or two of us?"

"Raheim, there are five hundred students at the school, which means there are at least fifty of us. He's not gonna be the only one."

"And I take it them digits ain't gonna be risin no time soon, huh?"

"Meaning?"

"Meanin one in ten ain't enuff."

"There are other groups, Raheim."

"Uh-huh, and I bet none of 'em come close ta tha white folks, right?"

"So what if whites make up the majority of the students? The school is integrated."

"That ain't no integration, Sunshine. White folks got a majority of tha pie and we just thrown a few crumbs and shit?"

"There's nothin wrong with him going to a school where he's in the minority. God knows it's gonna be that way for him the rest of his life, anyway."

"Well, you can just fuh*get* that. I don't want my son bein *nobody's* experiment."

"He won't be."

"He will too. And I bet they ain't got no Black teachers, neither."

"I asked, they do, and it's more than one or two."

"Uh-huh, and I betcha they don't teach no *real* subject like math or science."

"Raheim—"

"What about MLK?"

"King Elementary?"

"Yeah."

"MLK isn't jood enough."

"*Why?* It was jood enuff fuh me."

"Raheim, you were in elementary school over a decade ago. A whole lot has changed since then."

"Like?"

"Like, for one, the size of the school. MLK has almost twice as many students as Alexander, and it shouldn't. There isn't enough classroom space. You want him learning his times tables in a bathroom?"

"Funny, real funny." I chuckled.

She didn't. "You hear me laughin? I've heard the stories from folks. How is he gonna get the attention he deserves if he's one in forty or fifty in a class? How is he gonna learn in a building that's falling apart?"

"I don't want him goin ta no school where they ain't gonna be teachin him who he is."

"Meaning?"

"What tha fuck I just say? I don't want him endin up thinkin he white."

"Number one, don't curse at me, and number two, that's ridiculous."

"No, it ain't."

"Why would he think that?"

"If ev'rything he see, if ev'rything he read, if ev'rything he around is white, whatcha think is gonna happen?"

"I went to a lily-white high school and college. I turned out all right. And it's not who goes to the school that's important but how the school is run. Is it such a bad thing that I want something better for our son?"

"Better. Better as in *white*?"

"Will you get off this white kick, already—"

"Nah, cuz you know that's what it comes down ta. Ain't nuthin wrong wit' a Black school."

"I never said there was."

"That's what he gonna think."

"He goes to a Black school right now, so he knows they exist. He knows they're OK."

"Why can't he go ta a Africentric school?"

"I don't have a problem with that. But it may be too late."

"Whatcha mean, 'too late'?"

"The few I looked into all have waiting lists, and folks put their kids on them as soon as they are born. Everybody I've talked to said we should consider Alexander. At least its admissions process isn't complicated. It's run like a private school but it's really a public school, so there's no waiting list. There's just an application and an interview."

"An interview?"

"Yes."

"Why they wanna interview him? It ain't like he applyin fuh a job or goin ta college."

"They want to interview *us*."

"Us?"

"Yes, *us.*"

"Why?"

"'Cause they want to check us out."

"Uh-huh, don't ya mean *cancel* us out?"

"No. This gives them the chance to find out more about Junior, what his needs are, and what we need as his parents. And we get to check them out. And they mean business. They had already called us by the time I was told about them."

"Huh?"

"Well, they don't just wait for the best people to come to them. They compile a list of the brightest students in the city to recruit. And Junior was at the top of the list that his school submitted to them."

Uh-huh, that's my son. But… "I don't want him bein bused far away ta no white neighborhood."

"He ain't gonna be bused far away to a white neighborhood, 'cause he wouldn't be *leavin* the neighborhood. The school is next door, less than a mile away, in Morningside Heights."

I sucked my teeth. "Morningside Heights? That's Harlem, Sunshine. White folks just can't say they live in Harlem, so they call it somethin else."

"Look, I don't want him endin up at MLK or any other school in the neighborhood that can't do the job. The least you can do is go with me and visit Alexander before you say no."

I picked up and flipped thru tha pamphlet. "A'ight, a'ight, I'll go wit' you. But I ain't sayin yes unless I like what I see and hear."

"Fine. And if you think there's another school he can go to, we'll check that out, too. But I think we should make sure we look into every opportunity."

Just then, our waiter came up ta our table singin "Happy Birthday." I was glad when tha other waiters and waitresses joined him, cuz tha brotha couldn't carry no tune. He put a chocolate brownie down in front of Sunshine. It had a single candle on it. Sunshine blew it out. Folks clapped.

She smiled. "Thanks, Raheim."

I grinned. "You welcome."

She pushed tha brownie in fronta me.

"You don't want it?"

"No. I'll enjoy watching you eat it."

I dug in.

She sipped her coffee. "Don't worry."

"Hunh?"

"Don't worry about him."

I shrugged. I chomped.

"He can handle himself. You know that better than anybody."

I nodded.

"He knows who he is. How could he not, with a daddy like you?"

I blushed.

She smiled. "He's not gonna come home sayin he's in love with a little white girl named Daisy Lou or Mary Sue."

I almost choked. She laughed.

"HERE COMES THE...?"

I never thought I would be at a weddin and there ain't no bride.

When Little Bit first told me that B.D. 'n' Babyface was gettin married, I laughed. I mean, I just knew he was jokin. I ain't never heard of no men gettin married. Well, I had read stories about two men and two women *wantin* ta do it, but none about 'em doin it. But then I knew it wasn't no joke when...

"Hello? Raheim?"

"Yeah...who this?"

"Well, how soon they forget.... It's B.D."

"Oh. What's up?"

"So much is up that I wouldn't want to bore you with it all, darling."

"Little Bit ain't here. You want me ta—"

"I didn't call to speak to him. I called to speak to you."

"Me?"

"Yes, you. I was wondering if you would be free on Valentine's Day."

I laughed. "Yo, what's up, G, you tryin ta step ta me?"

"As *lovely* as that idea sounds, no. I want you to be an usher at our wedding."

"Yo' *weddin*? Who you marryin?"

"Silly, who do you think? Babyface."

When he said it, it just hit me like a brick.

"Hello? Hello?" He tapped tha phone. "Is this thing on? Raheim?"

"Yeah, yeah, I'm here."

"So, can I count on you to bless us with your magnificent presence? I'm sure the Children will *love* having you greeting them and escorting them to their seats."

"Uh, uh...I don't know."

"Well, what's wrong? Oh, I'm sorry. Do you have plans that evening?"

I didn't, but he gave me an easy out. "Uh...uh...yeah...yeah, I do. Me 'n' my Li'l Brotha Man. We got somethin really, uh, special planned...a surprise fuh Little Bit."

"Oh, how nice. A *family* outing.... OK, Raheim, tell me why you don't want to come to my wedding."

Uh-oh.

"You can tell me. Don't worry. I may be a little bit fragile, but I won't break. You won't hurt my feelings."

"Uh..." *Get it tagetha, mutha-fucka.* "B.D., it's just that I...I don't think I would be comf'table, that's all."

"May I ask why? I mean, it's not like I'm asking *you* to marry *me*—even though, if the truth be known, I would if Little Bit and Babyface weren't in the picture."

I blushed.

"Uh-huh, go on ahead and blush."

Day-am, how he know?

I was drownin, so I tried ta save myself. "B.D., it's all just...new ta me. I mean, I ain't never gone ta no weddin where...you know...."

"Believe me, darling, the only difference will be that *this* bride will not wear a veil or train—and that's because my soon-to-be husband won't allow me to—and almost all of the guests will be fine Black men on the arms of *other* fine Black men. So you will be *very* comfortable. You will be amongst your peers. You'll be in, to borrow a phrase, *jood* company."

"I...I don't know."

"Listen, I don't want to push you to do anything, and I don't want you to do anything you don't want to. But I would love for you to come. And I'm sure Little Bit would too."

Yeah...I know he would.

"Will you at least think about it?"

"Uh...uh, a'ight...I don't know if I'll change my mind, but I'll think about it."

Well, I thought about it, and I still ain't wanna go. Tha whole thing was just rubbin me tha wrong way. I mean, I don't really believe in no God; you know, all that Adam and Eve not Adam and Steve shit. But tha whole thing felt...I don't know...funny. Just what tha fuck is gonna happen? How they gonna do it? B.D. said he was the "bride," which means Babyface must be the "groom," right? Is B.D. gonna walk down tha aisle on his daddy's arm? Is he gonna throw a bouquet? Are they gonna have a best man and a bridesmaid and all that other traditional shit? Are they gonna say some kinda vows? And *who* is gonna perform tha ceremony? I ain't never heard of no preacher joinin two men tagetha in holy matrimony. I ain't wanna ask B.D. or Babyface about it cuz I ain't wanna seem dumb. I also ain't wanna seem curious. I mean, we know what that shit did ta tha fuckin cat, ya know?

Yeah, I just knew I couldn't go. I also knew Little Bit would want me ta. But thinkin it's all about me and believin that he'd do anything fuh his Pooquie, I did a real *stoo*pid thing: I asked him not ta go.

"Pooquie, you should know better than to even ask me that."

"Why? I'm yo' man."

"*And?* What does that have to do with anything?"

"I don't feel right wit' it, so I don't want ya ta go."

"Uh-huh."

"I mean, *we* should be spendin that day tagetha, Baby. Just us. It's gonna be our first Heart Day."

"Uh-huh, we *can* spend it together…at the wedding."

"C'mon, Baby—"

"C'mon, *nothin.* Not wanting to be an usher is one thing, but asking me not to go just because you think you won't be comfortable is another."

"Yo, ain't I important ta you?"

"Yes, you are, Pooquie. But two of my very best friends plan to embark on a new life together, and I plan to be there when they do it— with or without you."

"You mean…you go wit'out me?"

He ain't miss a beat. "Yes, I would."

"Why?"

"*Why?* Why *not?* I'll be damned if I'm going to miss one of the happiest days of their lives just because *you* don't want to go."

"Whatcha sayin? You love them mo' than me?"

"Raheim, don't even try that. This has nothing to do with my love for *them;* this has to do with your love for *me.*"

"Fuh *you?*"

"That's right, for *me.* Did it ever occur to you that I might want you to go with me because this will be one of the happiest days of *my* life?"

"What tha fuck you talkin about?"

"I'm *talkin* about sharing a very special experience, a very important moment with you, the man I love. This whole day, this whole event is about love. But all you can talk about is you, you, you."

I ain't know what ta say, cuz he was tellin tha truth.

He sighed. "I should've known this was coming."

"Pardon me?"

"First, we had to take down your drawing of me and put away the photo of us in the Village because of Junior. Then it was the movie poster in the bedroom. Then you decide to sleep on the floor in the living room with him sometimes, for appearance's sake. Then you refuse to go with me to any Brotherhood meetings. Now, this. I'm sorry: I will work with you on being, as you say, more comfortable about yourself, about us, but that doesn't mean I'm gonna live in *your* shadow."

"My shadow?"

"Yes. I know you want to be careful because you are not ready to tell Junior, your mother, or Crystal—even though they already know...."

"Yeah, we already been over that, a'ight?"

"Yeah, I know. Junior is too young to think that, and your mother and Crystal would never think a man like *you* could be *that* way, right? Well, fine. I can handle that because that is where you are right now. But as you trip over stuff like that, you also have to be careful of how you treat my love, how you treat us. You can't let your fear come between us."

"I ain't."

"Yes, you are. What if it were us, Raheim?"

"Hunh?"

"What if *we* were getting married? Would you leave me at the altar because the whole thing makes you uncomfortable? Or would we never even get to that point?"

Jood questions. I ain't really know.

He gave me his bottom line. "If you don't want to go, fine. But if you don't, you'll be spending Heart Day alone."

I still ain't wanna go but did any-ol'-way cuz if I didn't, he was gonna go wit'out me. In a way, he was forcin me, cuz he knew I wanted ta spend tha day wit' him. I musta gave him that impression, cuz he said straight up, "Don't go because I want you to or because you feel you have to." But I ain't want him fallin up in there by himself. All them folks knew we was tagetha, and they would just know that somethin was up if I ain't show. Gene would get so much mutha-fuckin satisfaction out of me not bein there, mo' proof fuh him that we ain't s'pose ta be tagetha. I know it's fucked up and that once again it comes down ta me, but I was goin ta show that I could stand by Little Bit.

Uh-huh, I was standin by my man.

I don't know what I expected ta find when I got there, but one thing was fuh sure—I wasn't uncomf'table. There was like fifty people there. Just about ev'rybody was in a suit and tie, but most of 'em looked like brothas from around tha way. And they all had it *seriously* goin on. B.D. wasn't lyin. There was brothas who were little like Little Bit, and tall, dark, and lovely like Tha Kid. If I wasn't wit' Little Bit, I woulda been clockin me a few numbers—or at least tryin ta. Just about ev'rybody was wit' someone. Tha wild thing is, some of 'em had already gotten hitched like Babyface 'n' B.D. was gonna do, and they had been tagetha fuh like years. After tha ceremony, Babyface 'n' B.D. had three couples take a bow cuz they all had tied tha knot on Heart Day too. One couple, Jameson 'n' Devon (he was gettin everything on video-tape), been tagetha fuh fifteen years. *Day-am!* I can't even imagine bein wit' anybody, even Little Bit, that long. Now, you *know* there's gotta be a whole lota love there....

Anyway, tha ceremony was really cool. Ta my surprise, it was held in a church called Unity Fellowship, not far from Little Bit's crib. Tha program said Unity was "a place of worship for same gender loving people of African descent, but its doors are opened to people of all colors, persuasions, and orientations." (Hmmm... "same gender loving?" I'm gonna leave *that* alone.) B.D. ain't walk down no aisle, and ain't nobody give him away. Both "bride" and "groom" was sittin in tha front row, Babyface wit' us, B.D. wit' his moms (who came all tha way from down South) in tha row across. They was both dressed in matchin black tuxedos. B.D. had on a long red silk scarf, and Babyface, a green one. Tha music started, and they grabbed hands, got up, and stood in front of one of tha few sistas there, who turned out ta be tha preacher. She said a few words about love bein love, no matter what form it comes in (there wasn't no "Dearly beloved..."). Then Babyface 'n' B.D. said they vows—I guess that's whatcha call 'em—tellin each other how they felt and why they was takin this pledge, makin it official by ex-changin rings. Babyface even got on one knee when he said his. Little Bit, B.D., B.D.'s moms, and a few other folks started pullin out Kleenex and shit. Yeah, it was touchin.

Tha best part, tho', was when Little Bit sang. He ain't even tell me he was gonna be singin. I woulda been so fuckin angry if I had stayed home and then found out I missed him. I had heard him a few times hummin and singin "You & I" by Stevie Wonder in tha house but ain't think nuthin about it. I'd tell him, "That sounds jood, Baby," and he'd thank me. But when he rose outa his seat and took his place by tha piano, tha cat was outa tha bag. I was shocked but so fuckin proud. When he sat back down, I grabbed his hand and gave him a kiss, knowin folks was lookin. Yeah, he was surprised by it. And then it hit me: I just kissed him in front of ev'rybody *in a church!* Yeah, I started ta shrink in my seat....

Tha preacher went on about commitment, blessed them, had us all pray, and then two sistas came up ta tha front carryin a broom. I was like, *What tha fuck they gonna do wit' that?* And then it clicked: like they did in *Roots*, they was gonna jump tha broom. And whatcha know, I was right: after tha preacher pronounced them "soul mates," they took that leap. Then B.D. leaped inta Babyface's arms, and they kissed. Little Bit, who was snappin shots of tha whole thing, really started lettin them tears flow. I ain't never seen him so worked up about somethin befo'. It was then that I understood....

Ev'rybody congratulated them, and tha festivities continued a block away at this brotha's house named Godfrey. (I stayed outa his way—turned out we had gotten busy a coupla years back. Uh-huh, he was another one I couldn't remember, but fuh a jood reason: tha sex was *wrecked*.) On one flo' they had small black tables wit' red tablecloths on 'em and green chairs (nobody but Babyface) and one big table wit' a weddin cake (no, it wasn't white; it was chocolate) that was three stories and—I ain't lyin—had two little Black men holdin and kissin each other instead of a man and a woman on tha top. Its base said, BABYFACE & B.D.—LOVE IS FOREVER—FEBRUARY 14, 1994.

They thanked ev'rybody fuh comin; B.D. looked straight at me when he said, "And thanks to those for not *depriving* us of their esteemed company" (yeah, I blushed), and introduced his moms, who was *still* cryin. She said she was "so, so, *so* happy" ta see her son "settle down," and that she "couldn't have asked for a better son-in-law." Babyface ain't had nobody on his side of tha family givin testimony; Little Bit told me his parents ain't wanna have nuthin ta do wit' it. His only brother, Tracey, was there, but he ain't say a word. He left when they started cuttin tha cake.

After they fed each other cake (they was really eatin it off and out of each other's mouth) and opened their gifts (they cleaned up—a weddin album; bottles of bubbly; gift certificates galore, dumb dollars, and *stoo*pid checks; a trip ta Jamaica from B.D.'s moms; lingerie fuh B.D. and silk pajamas fuh Babyface; and, of course, HIS & HIS matchin towel sets and robes from me 'n' Little Bit)—they had us go upstairs. It was time fuh their first dance, and "Always & Forever" was their song (I think that must still be *the* slow jam folks play at a weddin). When L.V.'s "Here & Now" came on (prob'ly number two on that playlist), Babyface stepped aside fuh B.D.'s moms, and other folks started dancin. Little Bit looked at me.

"Come on, Pooquie."

"Baby, I don't wanna dance."

"Since when *you* don't wanna dance?"

"I ain't up ta it."

"Well, would you mind if I danced with somebody else?"

I wanted ta say "Yeah," but I decided ta play it cool. "Nah, Baby, I don't mind."

Yeah, he was gaggin. "You...you don't?"

"Nah. Why should I? I mean, just be-cuz I don't wanna dance don't mean you don't hafta."

He just looked at me; I know he thought he was dreamin. "Uh...are you sure, Pooquie?"

"Yeah. Go on ahead. Have fun, Baby."

"OK." He smiled. He gave me a kiss on my cheek. "I'll be back in a bit."

It looked like he was gonna ask Jameson ta dance when Babyface swept him up. I know you ain't gonna believe me, but I wasn't jealous. I knew that Little Bit was dancin wit' somebody who had a special place in his heart, but it wasn't like what he felt fuh me. And wasn't nobody in tha room—not Babyface, not Gene, not B.D.—and there ain't nobody in tha world could love Little Bit tha way I do. He mine, so what I gotta worry about?

So I stood there by myself, against tha wall, just watchin them dance when...

"Excuse me?"

I turned ta my right ta see these two queens, Mutt 'n' Jeff, who had been scopin me out. They was just waitin fuh Little Bit ta leave my side, schemin. I just knew they was prob'ly tha only two brothas up in tha place that wasn't wit' somebody. I mean, who would want 'em? They looked and acted so fuckin desperate. When I smiled at them, they was just too thru. Yo, if I had just nodded in *that* direction, both of 'em woulda been on they knees befo' I could say, "Wanna taste?"

"Yeah?" I asked.

"Uh, I'm Eric," said tha tall one, "and this is Julius." Julius nodded at me—or, should I say, my piece. His eyes ain't move from below my waist.

"Raheim," I said. I wasn't about ta hold out my hand, since my hand wasn't tha thing they wanted ta shake. Besides, Eric was busy talkin wit' his hands and Julius was afraid ta show his—he was hidin them behind his back.

Eric giggled. "Uh, this is going to sound crazy, but...could you be that guy in the All-American ad?"

Befo' I had tha chance ta answer, Julius gave me what he was hidin: a copy of *YSB*. Yup, that was me. I had seen tha photos they had decided ta use but only mock-ups of tha ads. This was the Real mutha-fuckin McCoy. There I was, wit' nuthin but tha American flag wrapped around my waist, lookin straight at tha camera wit' that devilish smirk, my arms folded across my waist, my body just arched a little ta tha left. Tha background was white, and tha tag line read, THE RED, THE WHITE, THE BLUE, & THE BEAUTIFUL: ALL-AMERICAN 4 ALL TIMES. THE JEANZ 'N' THANGZ COMPANY (I came up wit' that last line, and it got me an extra thou). Tommy Boy said I wouldn't be seein myself till March, but I guess they was able ta squeeze inta this issue.

I was kinda miffed—not only cuz it was tha first time I was seein it. I wanted Little Bit ta be tha second person ta see it.

"Yeah, that's me," I said, tryin ta smile about it.

"*I told you, I told you, I told you it was him!*" screamed Julius, who pushed a pen in my face. "Would you please, please, *please* sign it? 'To Julius, Love, Raheim.' "

"Sure…" And I did. And then Julius went around ta almost ev'rybody at tha party ta tell 'em we had "a star in the house" (yo, those was his words, not mine, a'ight?). You think I was Denzel Washington and shit.

Now, I said he went up ta *almost* ev'rybody. Tha one person he ain't show 'n' tell was Little Bit, who, even tho' he was happy tha ad was out and that it looked jood, was not happy I signed Julius's magazine wit' "love."

"Baby, it's what he wanted me ta say," I argued as we came inta tha house. "What tha fuck was I s'pose ta do, say no?"

He locked up and turned ta me. "Yes."

I followed him inta tha bedroom. "Now, how that sound? We talkin about my fans. I gotta keep 'em smilin."

"Uh-huh, and what else were you plannin on doin to keep that tired child smilin?"

"Whatcha talkin about?" I said, takin off my clothes.

"You know what I'm talkin about, Pooquie," he said, doin tha same. "All you had to do was drop your pants right there, and he would've swallowed you whole. And what fans do you have to keep smiling? We're talking about *one* person."

"Yo, ev'rybody wanted ta talk ta me about it."

"Maybe so, but they all weren't askin you for your autograph. Anyway, that is not the point. I don't think it is necessary to sign your name with 'love.' I mean, it may give some of these children the wrong idea. And I hope you're not going to let this go to your head."

I grinned. "Which one?"

"Funny, very funny."

"Baby, don't be so serious."

"Well, you *have* to take it seriously, Pooquie. You are a spokesperson for a corporation now; you represent them. So every time you are in public, you have to be mindful of that. And people can be funny. You write 'love' on their picture, and they think that means you *do* love them."

"But I wrote '*Peace* and love,' so why would he think that way? That's cray-zee, Baby."

"I know, but it happens. Ask all those stars who are stalked by fans who mistake their being gracious and friendly for something else. I just want you to be careful, that's all."

He kept takin off his clothes wit' that low face.

"Little Bit?"

He sighed. "Yeah?"

"You ain't gotta worry about nuthin, Baby. You ain't gonna lose me."

"What are you talkin about, Pooquie? Why would I think that?"

I took him in my arms. "Cuz just like me, you just saw this whole thing as being fun. But now that it's out there fuh ev'rybody ta see...I ain't gonna change, Baby. I ain't goin nowhere."

He looked at me; he sighed. "I guess...it's a little scary."

"But it's a'ight ta be. And it's a'ight fuh you ta be jealous."

He pushed me away. "*Jealous?* Now, why would I be jealous?"

"Cuz of tha attention I get. Like tanite. I mean, it's only natural."

"Uh-huh. And I guess that would be the way you feel about B.D., Babyface, and Gene, hunh?"

"Huh?"

"Admit it. You are jealous of what I have with them."

"Baby, you cray-zee. Why would I be jealous of them?"

"Because, Pooquie, it is a part of my life that exists apart from you. And even though you know you can be a part of that, it's hard for you to because it's all new."

Day-am...he just read me like a book.

His clothes all off, he got in bed, pullin tha blanket back and settlin under them on his right side. "Am I right?"

I eased in too, restin on my left side. "Yeah...I guess."

"It's OK.... You know, I'm sorry if I sounded so demanding about you going. But I really wanted us to share this day together. I knew you would have a jood time...didn't you?"

I shrugged. "Yeah, I did. I mean, it did feel a little weird. But I'm really happy fuh Babyface 'n' B.D. And I *did* enjoy bein crowned a star."

He sucked his teeth. "Uh-huh, by that no-class queen."

I chuckled. "Ha, yeah..." I held his hand.

"Pooquie?"

"Yeah?"

"I'm proud of you."

"Yeah?"

"Yeah. I know how much it took for you to go tonight. And Gene, Babyface, and B.D. were really happy about you coming."

"I know. They told me. But I'm surprised Gene ain't faint or somethin."

"What do you mean?"

"I mean, as many times they said tha word *love*?"

He laughed. "Well, I guess Carl has something to do with that. They look jood together."

"Uh-huh. And you *sounded* jood, Baby."

"Thank you, Pooquie. I was singin it for them, but I was really singin it to you."

"I know. That's why I kissed ya."

And I kissed him again.

"Baby, I'm sorry."

"Sorry? About what?"

"About bein so...so..."

"Pig-headed? Domineering? Overcautious and overprotective? *No.*"

He giggled. He pecked me on my nose.

I frowned. "I couldn't give ya ev'rything ya wanted."

"What do you mean?"

"You know...not dancin wit' ya tanite."

He rubbed my head. "You gave me what I wanted, Pooquie. I loved my card. And the candy. And the flowers. And the BE MY VALENTINE balloon. *And* Pooquie Jr.!" He smiled at tha small black teddy bear I gave him; it was sittin on tha windowsill wit' tha other Pooquie. "And I *love* the way your gift looks on you." He gave me five pairs of bikini briefs in diff'rent colors. They all had red hearts on 'em. I wore tha blue ones tanite.

"Ya want me ta put 'em back on?" I asked.

He pulled me on top of him. "No. I'll only want you to take them back off anyway." He frowned. "But—you wanna know something?"

"What?"

"*I* wanted to get your first autograph."

"Don't worry about it, Baby. Julius mighta got tha first autograph, but you can always get somethin better."

"Hmmm. Now, *that* sounds better than an autograph." He squeezed my ass. "It *feels* better than one, too. And I *know* it's gonna taste better than one. With a giant chocolate kiss like you, *every day* is Heart Day."

I blushed.

"So, can I have some now?"

I licked them honeysuckle lips. "Baby, you ain't even gotta ask."

REWIND '89

"*You* what?"

"*I need more money.*"

"*What tha fuck you mean, you need mo' money? I just gave you two bills on Friday.*"

"*Yeah, well, what you gave me ain't cover half the bills that been pilin up. I told you on Friday it wasn't gonna be enough.*"

"*Yo, I gave you all I got, a'ight? That was all I had. What else you want from me and shit?*"

"*What I want from you is to see that you can't just say to your son, 'That's all I have.' *"

"*I ain't sayin that ta him, I'm sayin that ta* you.*"

"*Well,* he *needs this, I don't. When are you going to stop seeing this as a* you versus me *thing?*"

"*I* don't *see it that way.*"

"*You do too, Raheim.*"

"*So what, now you gonna fuckin tell me how I* see *shit?*"

"*We go through this all the time.*"

"*We go thru* what *all tha time?*"

"*You gettin angry with me. For what, I don't know.*"

"*I ain't angry wit' you, a'ight?*"

"*Then what is it?*"

"*I'm angry wit'* me, *a'ight?*"

"*Why?*"

"*Whatcha mean,* why? *How you think you feel if you couldn't give yo' kid ev'rything he need?*"

"*Raheim—*"

"*I mean, I'm kickin my ass, workin three jobs and shit, tryin ta save all tha fuckin funds I can, and it* still *ain't enuff.*"

"*Raheim, will you—*"

"*I ain't angry at you, I ain't angry wit' you, I ain't angry at Li'l Brotha*

Man, and I ain't angry wit' him, a'ight? So don't *fuckin* tell me how I feel
when you don't know."

"Raheim, will you please *stop cursing at me?*"

"And don't tell me how ta fuckin *talk,* a'ight?"

"Look, Raheim, I know, I know you're doin the best you can, so don't think
that your best isn't good enough."

"*It* ain't."

"*It* is."

"Sunshine, if it was, we wouldn't be talkin 'bout this right now."

"Raheim, don't beat yourself up because we are struggling. We knew it was
gonna be like this. And we promised each other we wouldn't turn on *each other*
when things like this happened."

"I don't wanna let my man down."

"You're not."

"I am, Sunshine."

"You *are* not, Raheim."

"I don't wanna do ta him what he did ta me."

"What?"

"I don't wanna do ta Li'l Brotha Man what my pops did ta me."

"What do you mean?"

"I'm talkin 'bout not bein there fuh him, Sunshine."

"You *are* there for him, Raheim."

"No, I ain't."

"Yes, you are. You can only do what you can do. And you are not *your*
father. Why would you even think that?"

"Cuz, Baby...that's all I can think about...I don't wanna fall out."

"Raheim, don't torture yourself. And don't fight me. I am not against you, I
am on your side."

"But I ain't got nuthin else."

"Well, can't you ask your—"

"Nah, nah, I ain't askin my moms."

"Why not? I ask mine."

"Cuz."

" 'Cause what?"

"Cuz it's diff'rent fuh you."

"Why?"

"Cuz you ain't no man, Sunshine."

"Raheim, do not even hand me that."

"See, you don't understand—"

"Oh, yeah, I understand. You a man, and you supposed to be able to take
care of yours, and that means you can't be askin anybody for help—especially
your mother, right?"

"Sunshine—"

"Don't 'Sunshine' me, OK? I'm workin two jobs too, and *goin to school. But I know I can't do it all. I'm not ashamed to ask for help because I know if I don't get it, Junior suffers. So the least* you *can do is be practical and not proud when it comes to your son."*

"So, what, I'm s'pose ta look like a chump?"

"A chump? Is that what you think you're gonna look like making a decision to put food in your son's mouth? It ain't gonna make you less of a man to borrow thirty or forty dollars from your mother. And if you really think it will, then you ain't got nobody to blame but yourself if you believe you followin in your father's footsteps. I have to go to work. I'll talk to you later."

Click.

WORD GAMES PEOPLE PLAY

"Why you use that word?"

"Why?"

"Yeah, why?"

"Because, Pooquie, that is what I am."

"Who says so?"

"Who says so? I do."

"Just cuz they call themselves that don't mean you hafta."

"*They?* Who is *they?*"

"*You* know. Them white boys."

"They're not the only ones who use it—"

"Yeah, but they tha ones who came up wit' it. I don't be followin no white boy's lead."

"I'm not followin *any*body's lead."

"You is, too."

"Well, I don't really know *who* came up with it or *where* it comes from...."

"Then why you usin it?"

"Uh...jood question. I...I don't know."

"Then you shouldn't be usin it."

"Uh...yeah. Yeah, you're right: you shouldn't call yourself something if you don't know what it is or where it comes from. I guess I'll have to do a little research and find out. But it's hard *not* to call yourself it, though."

"Whatcha mean?"

"Well, when you're around folks, and that's the language they use, you use it too."

"Just cuz they use it, don't mean you hafta."

"I know, Raheim."

"You obviously don't."

"I do. It is just very convenient. I think most people use it because it is shorter and less politically charged."

"Hunh?"

"You know. *Homosexual* is such a loaded term. You say it and people stop whatever they are doing, look, and gag. Now, *gay*? They do it with *gay*, too, but it's not as direct. It kinda like softens the blow. I guess it's a nicer way of saying it, cuter...."

"*Cute*? Baby, ain't nuthin cute about tha word. And I don't know why it could be called that, seein how folk ain't tha least bit gay about bein it."

"Well, it's hard to be gay about being gay when you're constantly told you're not supposed to be gay about being gay."

"*Hunh?*"

"*You* know what I mean."

"Yeah, yeah, I know."

"I would guess that they—whoever *they* are—chose that word because they *wanted* people to feel gay about being gay. Besides, I'd rather be gay than queer. Better to adopt the title created by a white *gay* man than a white *straight* man."

"You ain't gotta adopt nuthin nobody say, 'specially somebody white."

"I know. And speaking of *straight:* I wonder if heterosexuals came up with that in response to *gay...*?"

"Prob'ly."

"It's funny that they would call themselves that, if they did choose it. I mean, if they are straight, does that mean gay people are crooked?"

We laughed.

"Nah, cuz *ev'rybody's* straight-up crooked, Baby."

"Uh-huh, *especially* straight folks.... Uh, Pooquie?"

"Yeah?"

"You don't like being labeled gay, right?"

"Nope. It ain't got no meanin ta me."

"So...would you say you are bisexual?"

"Nah."

"No?"

"Yeah."

"Well, you've slept with men and women, right?"

"Yeah."

"Do you find men and women attractive?"

"Yeah, some of 'em."

"So why wouldn't you say you're bi?"

"Cuz, just cuz I think somebody looks attractive don't mean I'm attracted *to* 'em. You can think somebody look jood wit'out you wantin ta get wit' 'em."

"Well…you can't be straight…are you?"

"No."

"Then what label would you choose to describe yourself?"

"I ain't gotta choose no kinda label. I'm just me, and that's all I gotta be."

"Yeah, you're just you, but exactly what are you?"

"I ain't a *what*, I'm a *who*."

"I know, Pooquie, but you have to identify as something."

"I do? Who say?"

"Well, nobody says you have to, but—"

"Uh-huh, and if somebody said I did, I ain't doin it."

"Well, I'm not saying you *have* to…but I *want* you to."

"Why?"

"Because it is important for me to know exactly who the man I love and I am in love with is."

"Baby, you know who I am—"

"No, I don't. That's why I'm asking."

"So you wanna try and tag me?"

"Tag you?"

"Yeah, try ta sum me up and shit."

"That's not what this is about. This is about how you view yourself in relation to me. You love me, right?"

"Yeah."

"And you're in love with me, right?"

"Yeah."

"So, what does one call a man like yourself who is in love with and loves another man?"

"Whatcha just said."

"Hunh?"

"I call him a man that's in love wit' and loves another man."

"But what is your name for it?"

"Baby, it ain't gotta have no name."

"It's got to have *some*thing."

"No, it *don't*. Ain't no label gonna say who I am."

"You don't think so?"

"Nah. How one word gonna tell ev'rything there is ta know about somebody?"

"Well, it won't tell you everything, but it will give you some idea of the type of person they are."

"That's only if people see it tha same way."

"What do you mean?"

"Just cuz somebody calls themself somethin don't mean it means tha same thing ta ev'rybody else. It can mean so many diff'rent things that it ends up meanin nuthin."

"I see...so what about being Black?"

"What about it?"

"Well, if a label doesn't say who one is and it can mean so many different things, then why use Black as a label?"

"Black ain't a label, Baby, it's a fuckin legacy."

"A legacy?"

"Yeah. Just look at me, look at you. Tha color says it all."

"So...are you saying that color, which we can see, is a legacy, but sexual orientation, which we can't see, is a label?"

"Nah. It's mo' than color, Baby. White folks think that's all it is, like goin ta tha beach gonna give them some melanin. It's all about a culture, a spirit. It's a *science*."

"Gay people have a culture...."

"They ain't got no culture, Baby. Whatcha call 'culture,' gay bars and shit?"

"Pooquie, there's more to gay life than bars and clubs."

"There is?"

"Yes, there is, and bars and clubs are not a cultural thing, they're a social thing."

"Baby, a culture is when folks have tha same beliefs and traits in common and shit. All people who call themself gay got in common is sex."

"It's not the sex that we have in common, Raheim, it's who we love. Just like heterosexuals. *That* is a cultural marker."

"Well, wit' bein Black or bein gay, ain't no contest."

"I didn't say it *was* a contest."

"You tha one tryin ta compare 'em."

"I'm not. All I'm saying is that both are identities that people who are both should embrace."

"I agree."

"You do?"

"Yeah."

"How is that possible, if you don't believe in labels?"

"That's right, I don't believe in 'em. But you should be who you are wit'out somebody tryin ta box yo' ass up."

"So...are you saying that the label is not so much for the person it's supposed to describe but for society's benefit?"

"You got it. It's like wit' African-American. Some of us don't wanna be called that. Some wanna be Black. Some still trapped in that seventies mode and shit, goin 'round callin themself Afro-Americans. That shit is *wack*. Yo, I ain't no Afro, ya know what I'm sayin?"

"Ha, yeah, I do."

"And some folks still usin Negro and colored, like my moms. That's what she like. And some mutha-fuckas think they can be as dark as me and just be American. *Yeah*-mutha-fuckin-right. I can't go fuh that. But that's me. You gotta be comf'table wit' you, and if that means you down wit' this label and not that one, it's yo' thang, do whatcha wanna do. And if you ain't down wit' no labels, you ain't down wit' 'em. But don't call yo'self somethin just cuz society say so."

"OK, so correct me if I'm wrong. You are a Black man—"

"Uh-huh, wit' a c-a-p-i-t-a-l *B*, Baby."

"—thank you, who is in love with and loves another Black man with a c-a-p-i-t-a-l *B*. Right?"

"Yeah. Ain't no way one word gonna describe that, Baby."

"Hmmm...ya know somethin?"

"What?"

"I think I can hang with that."

SKELETONS

"Will you *please* pull up your pants?"

Me 'n' Moms was doin some prespring cleanin. Since Little Bit was in Jersey visitin his moms, I was also "at home for the weekend—for a change," as Moms put it. So, not knowin if there'd be another time when I'd be up in tha house fuh mo' than a day, she put me ta work. Just my luck: I had ta clean out tha hall closets. I mean, I don't mind doin tha bathroom or washin tha windows. They ain't nuthin but surface things, all laid out in fronta you. All you gotta do is roll up yo' sleeves and scrub. But this job requires a whole lota courage, cuz you don't know whatcha gonna find hidin up in that closet (don't *even* go there, a'ight?). Shit that been packed up fuh years, just waitin ta jump out and take you places you ain't been and may not even wanna go. But some of them discoveries I made brought back a lota jood memories: there was my set of *Encyclopaedia Britannica*s (that's where I got all tha knowledge) and a treasure chest of toys: a glow-in-tha-dark yo-yo that don't glow; a slinky that still did its thang; a box of Legos; an electronic train set minus tha train; a baseball bat and glove (but no ball); a water gun; two Army men; a Mr. T doll (don't ask, a'ight?); and games like Operation, Connect Four, Lite Brite, Twister (it got me 'n' Brotha Man "started"—ya know what I mean?), and, of course, Monopoly.

I was checkin out my Tonka truck—its yellow fadin but still rock solid—when Moms had ta say somethin about my low-ridin pants.

"What's up, Ma?"

"Once again, it's not what's up, it's what's down. I just don't understand why you insist on walkin through life without a belt on."

"Ma, you always ask me that—"

"Yes, I know, and I'm gonna *keep* asking you about it until you give me a reason I can believe."

I spun Tonka's wheels. "Check it out, Ma. It's still in jood condition."

"Humph, it better be. Those trucks came with a lifetime guarantee. They don't make stuff like that anymore. Junior would probably love it."

"Hunh? *I* love it. I had *mad* diesel fun wit' this. This mine."

She took it from me. "And what exactly are you going to do with this? You're not five years old."

"This just ain't somethin you pass on down. This somethin you keep in a vault fuh safe keepin, like a artifact."

She grinned. She handed it back. "Well, so long as you keep it in your *own* closet. I want this one cleared out." She headed fuh tha kitchen.

I put ol' Tonka down. I kept on searchin ta see if I was gonna find any other treasures when...

"*Ma!*"

She came runnin. "What? What is it?"

"Look."

She smiled. "Ahhh...you would blow your allowance on these comic books every week."

I smiled. "Yeah." I started flippin thru 'em. "Hold up...I don't see no Spider-Man or Incredible Hulk."

"You had too many of those books for them all to fit in one box. And you never threw any of them away. So they must be in there somewhere."

So I charted that territory like York did fuh Lewis 'n' Clark, and I found that box. Day-am...I useta lay on my bed fuh hours, just studyin 'em. That's right, studyin 'em. I almost never read tha stories; I ain't care what Jughead or Richie Rich was up ta. I was like eight or nine, just analyzin tha way tha people, places, 'n' things was drawn, and I would copy 'em. Man, I had a jood eye fuh detail, outlinin shit ta tha bone.

I was checkin out my sketches of the Jackson 5 and Fat Albert and the Cosby Kids (I did these lookin at TV and studyin record albums) when Moms joined me.

She sighed. "God, you were so talented."

"*Were?* Whatcha mean, 'were'? I still got it."

"I haven't seen you draw something like that in years."

"Yo, how 'bout all that stuff I do fuh Simply Dope?"

"First, do not address your mother with the word 'yo.' And secondly, all I've seen you do for them is fancy stuff with letters and symbols."

"That ain't been all I've done. And how 'bout tha stuff I did of you, and Li'l Brotha Man, and Sunshine?"

"Yeah, you've done some jood stuff of us, but it's all been sporadic. You go months at a time, a year, without doin somethin like this. Back then, you were tackin somethin up on that refrigerator every single day."

"Yeah, I was." I frowned at her. "But I still got it."

"OK, OK, OK. You still got it. But you better start usin it more, and in other places, or you're gonna lose it."

"I ain't gonna lose it."

"OK. I just don't want you wakin up one day and that dream done passed you by."

"How you know that's my dream?"

She squeezed tha back of my neck. "Because you are my son. And I know that your dream sure as hell wasn't to be a model."

"I thought you liked me bein a model...?"

"Well, I do. You make me look real jood down at the office. Those women at the job are just *too* through with me. But I'm not the one who has to like it, 'cause I'm not the one who is doin it. One thing is for sure, though: it ain't somethin you're gonna be able to do for the rest of you life."

"Who say? You got one fine son, Ma."

"Uh-huh, but everything gets old, my dear"—she grabbed my chin—"and that includes this face. Everybody's gotta have *som*thin to fall back on."

"Ma, I know whatcha gonna say—"

"All right, then...I won't have to say it. Anyway, I'm goin to the store to get some Comet and ammonia. I'll be back...oh, excuse me: I'll be *Black* in ten minutes." She winked.

I grinned. She pecked me on my cheek. She was about ta walk by but stepped back, grabbin a belt loop on my pants. "Pull 'em up, pull 'em up, pull 'em up. I saw that as much as I wanted to when you were a baby, OK?"

I laughed. I knelt back down, goin thru tha other comics. A few minutes passed when...

"Yo, what's up?"

Now, I knew *that* wasn't Moms.

I turned. I looked up. It was Angel. He had a basketball.

"How you get in here?" I snapped.

"Yo, be cool, brotha. I ain't break in. Yo' moms was comin out. She told me you was in, that tha do' wasn't locked. I knocked, but you ain't hear me."

I nodded. I returned ta my work.

"So, what's up?" he asked, again.

"Nuthin."

"You wanna play some ball?"

"Nah."

"Nah?"

"Nah."

"*You* don't wanna play no ball?"

"You heard."

"Ha, since when?"

"Since now."

"Man, you gonna pass up a chance ta razz me? You know I ain't got nuthin on you."

"Ha, you right about that," I huffed.

"But I been workin on my skillz, man. Wit' this new brotha. Well, he ain't really a brotha."

He waited fuh me ta bite. I didn't.

"His name is Charles. Folks call 'em Chuckie. His pops own that Korean grocery up tha block. He can play some mean ball. He down at tha court now. I'm tellin ya, he got some moves. I told him about ya. We can go down and shoot some hoops now and—"

"Can't ya see I'm busy?"

"Yeah. Yeah, I see. I see you busy. You been so busy, you...you can't even call me back."

I picked up tha box. I dusted pass him. He followed me inta my room.

He huffed, "Man, what's up wit' you?"

I dropped tha box on my bed. "Ain't nuthin up, a'ight?"

"*Some*thin's up. How come you don't wanna hang or nuthin no mo'?"

"Hang?"

"Yeah. We was real tight, and—"

"We was *never* tight."

"Huh?"

"Man, what tha fuck is wrong wit' you? How come I gotta keep repeatin myself and shit? What part of that statement *ain't* you understand?"

He stood there, lookin hurt. Then his whole face changed; it was one of them *Nigga, I fuck you up* looks. But even he knew he couldn't do that, and that's prob'ly why he turned ta leave. But then he turned back around.

He sighed. "It ain't my fault."

I stopped goin thru tha box. I looked up. *"What?"*

"It ain't my fault."

I put my hand on my hips. "It ain't yo' *fault?* Nigga, what tha *fuck* you talkin about?"

"It ain't my fault he dead!" he yelled. He held tha ball ta his stomach, cradlin it like it was a baby. "You—you blame me, don't ya?"

"Blame you?"

"Yeah."

My hands went up. "Why would I do that?"

He put tha ball on his left hip. "Cuz...cuz *I* wanted ta go ta tha party."

I put my hands in my pockets. I looked away.

He sighed. "I wanted ta go...y'all didn't...if we ain't go—"

"Man, I don't blame you fuh nuthin. That's *stoo*pid."

"Yeah?"

"*Hell*-fuckin-yeah. How you even gonna *think* some *stoo*pid shit like that?"

"Man, what tha *fuck* am I *s'pose* ta think? It's like you don't wanna have nuthin ta do wit' me. I call you here, I call you at Mitch's crib. You don't wanna play no ball. You don't wanna watch tha playoffs, you don't wanna hang out, you don't wanna do nuthin. You even dissed me at tha courthouse."

I did. But it wasn't like I was doin it ta be mean. I just...I just ain't feel...right. Seein that mutha-fucka who killed Brotha Man, wantin ta pound his ass. Havin ta get up in fronta all them people and tell tha judge that, no matter what nobody say, this wasn't no drug killin, that my Brotha Man was clean, that he left that shit behind a long time ago, that he was just mindin his own bizness when this *punk*-ass mutha-fucka started shit, and that he deserves tha max—fifteen years. I mean, it was bad enuff they let him plead guilty ta manslaughter, not murder (wit' some twenty witnesses, he woulda been *stoo*pid ta go ta trial, anyway). But that judge looked dead at me, dead at Brotha Man's moms, dead at Angel, and gave him eight years. *Eight* fuckin years. Can ya *believe* that shit? That nigga could be out in two. His ass be doin *eighty* years if he had killed somebody white. Our lives don't mean shit ta white folks. Seein him only get eight...that shit hurt. It just ain't fair. It just ain't fair....

I turned my back on him. "That ain't it, " I mumbled.

"Then what's goin on, man?"

"I...I don't know."

He sighed. "I...I don't know, either, man." Snifflin like he was cryin, he said somethin else befo' he left—somethin I already knew but never gave him tha chance ta say...

"Just remember, brotha: you ain't tha only one who miss him."

REWIND '90

"Yo, Brotha, check it ouuut."

"Yeah, yeah, you got bank."

"Man, you can get paid, too."

"I already told you, nigga, I ain't inta that shit."

"Man, I ain't inta it, neither, I'm just gettin mine."

"Yeah, and tha way you doin it is straight-up wack."

"Why you gonna be like that, Brotha? How you gonna pull it out? It ain't gonna happen.…"

"I ain't doin no shit like that, man, and if yo' moms find out, she gonna have yo' ass."

"She ain't gonna find out. Any-ol'-way, I'm doin what I gotta do ta take care of mine."

"Brotha Man, don't even hand me that shit. You ain't gotta do no shit like that."

"Brotha, it ain't nuthin but a thang. It's just da life."

"Just da life? Man, you criminal minded. You been blinded. Keep on clockin wit' them simple mutha-fuckas and you ain't gonna have no fuckin life."

"Man, why you buggin?"

"I ain't buggin, you buggin. We seen what that shit do. You ain't doin nuthin but fuckin us all up."

"Man, whatcha talkin 'bout?"

"You know what tha fuck I'm talkin 'bout. That shit bringin us all down, man."

"Man, don't even come at me wit' that. I ain't hurtin no-fuckin-body. I'm payin tha bills."

"And? Nigga, you ain't tha only one payin tha bills."

"But look at ya, Brotha. You ain't gotta sweat it out fuh no white man. Haulin his fuckin boxes, bein a fuckin toy cop on tha lookout, followin us around his store and shit—"

"I'm earnin my keep, mutha-fucka."

"Yeah, right, nigga. What you earn in a week I make in a fuckin hour."

"That's right. I know when I get my paycheck, it ain't cuz somebody shootin up or gettin shot."

"Man, only them stoopid-ass niggaz be gettin caught out there like that."

"Uh-huh, and how about when yo' ass get caught out there by them 5-0s?"

"Man, them fuckin cops be up on it too. They know what time it is. They ain't comin after nobody as long as they get a cut too. Why you think they be standin by watchin tha shit go down all tha fuckin time?"

"Ha, that ain't what you gonna be sayin when them DTs 'n' DEAs swoop down on yo' ass and you doin twenty ta life in a federal pen."

"Man, you know how many niggaz been up on it and still standin? It's E-Z, man, E-Z. Yo, I'm just collectin them coins fuh that rainy day. I'll be makin my exit soon. And I'm gonna get me some wheels."

"Nigga, yo' sorry ass can't even drive."

"No prob, man, no prob, I get it taken care of. I'm gonna have a dope Jeep, man, be livin high 'n' fly. Man, you cray-zee not wantin a piece of this. Yo, Mad Dog 'n' Smooth hook you up. You get L.B.M. ev'rythang he need and then some, and then mutha-fuckin some. C'mon, Brotha, we be partners again. We don't be hangin no mo'. Why you bailin out on me?"

"I ain't bailin out on you, nigga. You bailin out on yo'self."

"A'ight, a'ight...be like that. I'm outa here."

"And do somethin fuh me, a'ight? Don't come tha fuck back up here talkin that shit and wavin yo' green up in my face. I don't want no parta that shit, a'ight?"

"Cool, Brotha, cool. But tha off is still there, man. It's still there...."

"INTRODUCING...OUR ALL-AMERICAN"

"Good afternoon...welcome to All-American's spring launch. I am Thomas Grayson, vice president of image and media relations for the company. Today, all of you will witness history in the making. You will get to see, for the first time, the promotion that will make the entire apparel industry take notice—*and* take notes. I could stand here forever and praise its worth, celebrate its value, but seeing is believing—and we know that after you see it, you won't believe it."

And wit' that, tha curtain was pulled and there was a giant replica of tha ad, as big as a movie screen. This mighta been tha first time tha white folks in tha room was seein it, but it wasn't fuh me 'n' Little Bit. And Tommy Boy was right: tha folks just couldn't believe what they was seein. When they stopped oohin 'n' aahin, gaspin 'n' geekin, and givin tha ad a standin ovation, Tommy Boy said it's gonna have its premiere in *Rolling Stone*. Hmmm...maybe Little Bit would have a story in that issue, too. But hold up: if this is tha premiere, what about *YSB*? I guess tha Black press don't count, hunh?

Tommy Boy continued. "*This* is the new face of All-American, a face that we believe represents all that *is* American. And now, ladies and gentlemen, I am pleased to introduce to you—*that* face. Our one and only All-American...Mr. Raheim Rivers."

Folks clapped—some of 'em even whistled and screamed—as I went up ta tha podium. This time I *was* wearin a blue pair of All-Americans, wit' their red T-shirt and white cap. I really looked—and felt like—tha flag. "Don't worry, you're gonna do fine," whispered Tommy Boy as he went back ta his seat.

I wasn't worried; Little Bit prepped me. Since this was gonna be my first interview, Little Bit had me tape it, so years from now he could say, "I knew you when."

As soon as I nodded and smiled, them bulbs started flashin, cameras started clickin, and they just started throwin questions at me....

"*Mr. Rivers, how does it feel to be a model?*"

"I never modeled befo', so it's all new ta me."

"Is this something you've always wanted to do?"

"No."

"Is modeling like you thought it would be?"

"It's...in-ter-es-ting." They laughed.

"Well, how interesting? What do you like about it and what don't you like?"

"I don't like them lights; they can be so hot. And ya gotta stand in one position so long. And all that smilin." I really cheezed it up; they laughed. "And it can take hours ta get that *one* photo. But tha thing I do like? Tha finished product." I looked up at myself. I smiled. "It was worth it."

"How did All-American find you?"

"Uh, Thomas just walked up ta me in Washington Square Park one day and asked me if I'd like ta do it. And here I am."

"In the bio it says you are a bike messenger and a graphics artist at Simply Dope Records. Any plans to quit your day jobs?"

"I don't know. If I can make a comf'table livin just modelin, yeah. But it's too soon ta tell."

"What type of education do you have?"

"I went ta A. Philip Randolph High Uptown."

"Uptown?"

"Yeah, Harlem."

"Do you still live in Harlem?"

"Yeah."

"Do you have plans to move?"

"Nah. Why should I? It's my home."

"Did you go to college?"

"No."

"It also says in the bio that you have a five-year-old son. Is he just as handsome as his father?" They laughed.

"If I can be modest? Yeah." They laughed again.

"How does he feel about his father being a model?"

"He's excited. He loves showin tha ad ta people and sayin, 'That's my Daddy.' "

"How does the rest of your family feel?"

"They cool wit' it."

"Would you let your son model?"

"I don't know. If he wanted ta do it, I guess."

"Are you married?"

"No."

"Have you ever been married?"

"No."

"Are you single?"

"Nah. I'm seein somebody right now."

"How do you think the black community will react to the ad?"

"I think tha brothas 'n' sistas will like it. It shows that we just as beautiful as white folks—and that we are All-American, too."

"Is that the message you hope people get when they see the ad?"

"Yeah."

"Do you think it's going to sell a lot of jeans?"

"If I'm gonna keep this job, it better." They laughed.

"The ad's purpose is, I assume, to sell jeans, but you're not wearing jeans. So what is it really selling?"

"It's sellin jeans, but it's also sellin an attitude."

"What kind of attitude?"

"An attitude that says you all that, that you got it goin on, and there ain't nobody like you. That you can claim yo' own space and yo' own place."

"And wearing All-American jeans will help the person who wears them achieve that?"

"I guess so. I mean, we in America, right?" They chuckled.

"In the last few years, we've seen more minorities, particularly black men, in ads for mainstream companies. Why do you think that is?"

"Cuz they prob'ly figured out that so-called minorities got money ta spend just like white people."

"Could the same be said for All-American?"

"I guess so. Hey, better late than never, right?" They laughed.

"You are wearing briefs in the ad, and you almost never see black men in ads like this, whether they are actually selling underwear or not. The last mainstream company to have a black man do it, I believe, is Michael Jordan, for B.V.D. Why do you think it has been that way?"

"Folks got a lota hang-ups about us. They don't feel Black men can be sexy like white men, and they threatened by our sexuality."

"When you say 'folks' and 'they,' do you mean white people?"

"Not just white people. Some Black folks can't handle it neither."

"To that end, do you think the ad in any way challenges negative stereotypes of Black men being, say, criminals and absent fathers?"

"Uh, not really. Ain't no way one image gonna challenge all that. But it does present us in a way people almost never see us."

"And what way is that?"

"As human."

"Well, then, how does it feel to be a spokesperson for the black community, presenting a different image?"

"I ain't a spokesperson fuh tha Black community, cuz it don't *need* a spokesperson. I can only speak fuh me."

"You have a very rugged street look. Given that All-American's core audience for the past two decades has been rural and Middle America, do you think that market is ready for an image like that?"

"I don't see why not. Besides, I may look rugged, but I ain't dangerous."

"Speaking of that image, the mainstream first got a taste of this with Marky Mark modeling Calvin Klein underwear. Do you think that exposure has made it easier for you to come along?"

"No. We two totally diff'rent people. Anyway, he was perpetratin. He couldn't open no do' fuh me, cuz he was tryin ta be somethin he ain't."

"Can we assume, then, that you think Calvin Klein should have used a black rap artist for those ads?"

"Let's just say he obviously ain't want tha real thing." They grumbled.

"Some might say the ad is an example of reverse sexism—that you, a man, are being exploited for the pleasure of women. Do you see yourself as being a sex object?"

"Nah, I don't. I mean, ain't nuthin wrong wit' admirin tha body. It's a natural thing."

"Then would you have a problem being viewed as a sex symbol?"

"Nah. Ain't that many brothas who get ta be that, so if I do, that be cool."

"Are you a professional bodybuilder?"

"No."

"Do you work out regularly?"

"Yeah, ev'ry mornin. But I do it cuz I like ta, not cuz I want people ta look at me. I do it fuh me."

"Do you work out at any particular gym in the city? I'm sure there are a lot of people who may want to join it." They laughed.

"Nah, nah, I do it at home."

"Are you athletic? Do you play any sports?"

"I shoot hoops a lot."

"What are some of your hobbies?"

"Uh, I like ta read. I watch *Jeopardy!* on TV. And I love hangin wit' my son."

"What do you like to read?"

"Just about anything. Magazines, books..."

"Do you have any favorite authors?"

"Zora Neale Hurston, James Baldwin, Richard Wright, Gloria Naylor."

"When you play Jeopardy! *do you usually win?"* They chuckled.

"Yeah, I do." They gasped.

"Would you like to be a contestant one day?"

"Yeah, I would."

"Do you like rap music?"

"Yeah, I love it."

"What rap artists do you like?"

"Public Enemy, KRS-One, Ice Cube, Dr. Dre, 2Pac, Naughty by Nature, L.L., Arrested Development, Wu-Tang Clan, Snoop."

"Do you think some rap artists, particularly in the gangsta genre, have gone too far?"

" 'Gone too far'?"

"Well, some of their lyrics are racist and sexist and anti-Semitic, and they endorse violence.... "

"I ain't a music critic."

"Somewhat on the same subject, some have used their rap credentials as a way to break into acting. Models have done it too. Do you have any desire to do that?"

"Nah, I ain't really think about that."

"What if you were approached about doing a movie or being on a TV show— would you consider it?"

"Yeah."

"Are there any goals you would like to accomplish, outside of modeling?"

"Uh, just ta be able ta raise my son tha best way I can. He my heart."

"Do you have any influences or role models who have shaped your life?"

"My moms. She raised me, and believe me, I was a lot ta raise." They laughed.

I felt a hand against my back; it was Tommy Boy. "Our All-American will answer any other questions you have personally after the marketing presentation. Let's give him a chance to catch his breath." He smiled at me and started clappin. I was kinda happy ta relax a little, but I was just gettin started. I was on a fuckin roll. I could get useta givin interviews, ya know what I'm sayin?

Tommy Boy's talk went on fuh like a half hour, and then I got ta mingle wit' tha crowd. Six people gave me cards, sayin they was agents and was int'rested in representin Tha Kid. But none of 'em had *my* int'rest, since they was all white. I mean, it's bad enuff I was gonna be makin All-American a lota Black money; I ain't wanna line tha pockets of yet *another* white boy. A few folks wanted me ta sign their press books. Can ya believe that shit? And just about ev'rybody wanted ta pose wit' me, includin tha All-American Good Ol' White Boys and Girl (yeah, there's just one female on tha board). All them flashes was makin me see spots.

When it was all over, Sir Sergio and Tommy Boy finally got tha chance ta take me out. We went ta some Italian restaurant where no drink was less than ten dollars and no plate was under thirty. They drank a lot; me 'n' Little Bit ate a lot. And we had two other guests fuh dinner: Sir Sergio's "companion," Humberto, a too-tall Dominican half Sir Sergio's age, and Ralph, Tommy Boy's "friend" from J.R.'s stompin ground, Dallas, who was darker than me, but it was obvious Black wasn't no state he was useta bein in. He was tryin so hard ta be down—callin himself talkin about hip-hop and tha hood wit' me and Humberto, who grew up in El Barrio. Tommy Boy wasn't happy about him frontin, neither: he called him away from tha table, and when they came back, "Ralphie Boy" (Tommy Boy's nickname fuh him) ain't had shit ta say fuh tha rest of tha nite—unless Tommy Boy "said so" (wit' his eyes, that is). Little Bit said Tommy Boy is prob'ly puttin Ralphie Boy thru law school and Ralphie Boy is givin up most booty (which he do got) as a trade-off. He just s'pose ta be seen and not heard; all that was missin was his leash. Day-am, talk about sellin out....

But Ralphie Boy ain't spoil me 'n' Little Bit's fun. We kept on cele-bratin when we got home. We was comin down from our high when Little Bit dropped another bomb on me.

"I'm surprised about what you said today."

"What I say?"

"You said you're seein somebody right now."

"*And?* I am."

"Well, I know you are, but I didn't think you would tell the world the way you did. I mean, you practically said you were seeing a man."

"*Hunh?*"

"Pooquie, you didn't say you were involved with a woman. You didn't say there was a special lady in your life. And because you didn't, you said it indirectly."

He knew that *Oh, shit* look on my face by now. He rubbed my head.

"Don't worry about it, though. I mean, most of the people there prob-ably didn't pick up on it. Journalists in the mainstream are not that sharp; they just assumed you were straight because in their eyes, you look it. Gay journalists probably picked up on it but assumed you are gay; they know most men in the business are in the life, be they behind or in front of the camera. And those people who read what you say and can read between the lines will discuss it with their friends, and your sexual iden-tity will become gossip for the rumor mill, just like it has for those other celebs, male and female, who are suspected of being one of the Children. And *the* Children will claim you—but only silently."

"How they gonna claim me when they don't know?"

"Well, it's better that they don't."

"Whatcha mean?"

"Well, let's say you were heterosexual and they found out. Knowing that would be a *major* blow, a major loss. So not knowing gives them the hope that you could be. And as far as they know, you playin it safe, droppin them a clue that only they can pick up on. The way it came out, that's what I thought, too."

"Ah, a'ight. But whatcha mean, *you* thought I was playin it safe?"

"I guess I just thought you would say you were dating someone who is female."

"Like who?"

"I don't know. Crystal, I guess."

"How that sound, Baby? It ain't nobody's bizness who I'm gettin busy wit'. "

"Well, it's true that it isn't anybody's business, but now you're a public figure. And whether you like it or not, people are gonna make it their business."

"Y'all journalists is some *no*sy mutha-fuckas."

"Thank you. I'll take that as a compliment."

"But I ain't inventin no girlfriend, Baby. I ain't gotta prove nuthin ta nobody. What's tha point? And I'm kinda hurt."

"Hurt? Why?"

"Cuz you think I was tryin ta play it safe. Like I was gonna stand up and say I'm in love wit' some female and you sittin right there in fronta me? I ain't gonna dis you like that."

"I'm sorry, Pooquie. I didn't mean to hurt you. I only thought that because that's the way most folks in the public eye deal with it. I guess you've found a middle ground you are comfortable with."

"It ain't no middle ground, Baby. It's just where I'm at. I can't be callin mutha-fuckas out about perpetratin a fraud and doin it myself."

"Hmmm…I wish most of us had that kind of integrity. I'm so proud of you."

Lip lock time.

He smiled. "And I'm so proud of the way you handled yourself today. You had them eating out of your hands, especially when you were puttin them in their place."

"Ha, yeah."

"You really made such a jood impression. I can't wait to see what they write."

"Me too."

"And if you could've seen your face when they said 'Michael Jordan.' "

"Whatcha mean?"

"Don't try it, Pooquie. Your eyes were dancing. It must've been some sensation, being told you followin in his footsteps."

I gushed. "Yeah, I guess so."

"You *know* so. Ain't that many Black men who get the chance to show what they got to the American people in a pair of briefs. But ya know somethin?"

"What?"

"He ain't got nothin on you."

2 OF A KIND BROTHAS

"Sur-prise!"

Little Bit was so surprised that he started cryin right on tha spot. Tha Kid pulled it off: I wanted ta give him a birthday party, and the Three Musketeers—B.D., Babyface, and Gene—was all too happy ta help. Gene kept Little Bit out all day, goin ta a movie and shoppin, while B.D. cooked and Babyface helped me clean up and decorate.

It was just tha regular crew. Carl brought tha cake. Adam came wit' a fly little honey named Lynette. Me 'n' Angel talked, and I let him come wit' his boy, Chuckie (yeah, they make a cute mix: red beans 'n' rice). Chuckie got what most Asians don't: height and muscle. He also think he a boy from da hood, wearin brotha gear. But at least he ain't come outa his face wit' no "ghetto speak" (you know, that language mutha-fuckas who ain't Black talk when we around, droppin their *g*'s and throwin out *ain't*, thinkin that makes them down). Little Bit's cousin, Alvin, came wit' some big Hulk Hogan brotha named Monte that Little Bit swears he saw in some fuck movie (and yeah, he was gettin busy wit' a brotha). Alvin's twin, Calvin, ain't come; Alvin say he just can't handle Tha Kid. And I invited Little Bit's friends from his old job, Michelle and Denise. When they showed wit' no dates I asked why.

Denise broke it down. "Be*cause*, Mr. Rivers, no heterosexual man could be in a room full of gay men and not feel that everyone wants him."

"Besides," added Michelle, "no heterosexual man would be able to handle all of the masculinity in this room, not to mention the beauty. I mean, look at that face, those eyes…those *thighs.*"

I blushed as she squeezed 'em.

As soon as Little Bit stopped cryin, caught his breath, and gave ev'rybody a hug, it was time ta eat. B.D. whipped up some mean hot wings, vegetables in brown rice, and cornbread. Little Bit, who says he wishes *he* could cook like B.D., gave tha brotha his props.

"B.D., everything is just fab, especially the salad."

"Thank you, darling, but I can't take credit for that. Pooquie did it."

"Pooquie? Pooquie who?"

"Who you think?"

"*My* Pooquie? *My* man?"

I hugged him from behind. "Yeah, *yo'* man."

He looked up at me like he ain't believe it. "*You* made the salad?"

"Yeah, *I* made it."

"Since when do *you* make salad?"

"Since today," answered B.D. "I wasn't about to have him sittin up on that counter lookin cute, entertainin himself by watchin *me* do all the work. It don't take that much skill to break a head of lettuce and cut up some tomatoes."

Little Bit smiled at me. "Well, it *is* jood. I guess you're just not jood at *tossin* a salad, hunh?"

"Uh-huh, there *is* a rumor goin 'round about that," said B.D.

Little Bit frowned. "And just *who* started *that* rumor?"

B.D. smiled at me. "Guess."

I grinned.

"But he shouldn't be braggin about what he can do, 'cause *some*body might want to see if there is *truth* in advertising." He wiggled that big salad bowl of a booty. We all laughed.

When tha feast was done, ev'rybody settled in tha livin room. Adam and Babyface rapped about tha criminal *in*justice system. Carl tried ta weasel that recipe fuh tha hot-wing sauce outa B.D. Gene and Alvin giggled over knowin tha *real* T about Calvin. While Angel just listened, Chuckie and Monte asked me about becomin a model. And Little Bit filled Lynette, Denise, and Michelle in on his lawsuit against *Your World*. Tha askin price on tha table is a cool three mil, but he don't really want tha money—he wants 'em ta admit they fucked him over cuz he Black. Michelle and Denise both agreed that he stood a better chance of collectin tha funds than an admission of guilt, but said they would still testify fuh him in court. There ain't gonna be no conflict of int'rest cuz they left tha magazine two months after Little Bit did. Denise is workin at *Cosmopolitan* now, and Michelle went back ta school ta be a dentist. Michelle was a secretary at *Your World,* so ain't much she can say, but Denise was there when *all* that shit went down—and they know, and I know, and *you* know, ain't no way a jury of white folks gonna discount tha testimony of one of their own.

Anyway, B.D. asked about Little Bit meetin L.V., and that got ev'rybody's attention. That booty-clockin talent scout came thru—he got

Little Bit gigs doin background vocals fuh Roberta Flack (she still killin 'em softly), Chanté Moore (she Minnie Riperton reincarnated), and a coupla new artists: Brandy (she was on that TV show, *Thea*) and Cindy Mizelle, a sista who can blow like Whitney and scream like Patti. Cindy loved him so much, she brought him ta L.V.'s session. And L.V. loved him so much, he asked *my* Baby ta sing on his remake of that old school jam, "Going in Circles." When ev'rybody started buzzin about tha photos of Little Bit and L.V. ("Oh, *no,* Luther, you lost the weight *again?*"), I realized Adam was missin in action. I found him outside, sittin on tha stoop, puffin away.

I slapped him on tha back and sat down. "Yo, man, I ain't know you smoked."

"Yeah."

"Little Bit know?"

"Nah, he don't. I mean, I quit a couple of years ago.... He wanted me to, but...what can I say, I got the bug again. I know I shouldn't do it. But, as crazy as it sounds, it relaxes me."

"You tense about somethin, man?"

"Uh...yeah, I guess you could say that."

"Well, what's up?"

He inhaled. He exhaled. He grinned. "You know."

"I do?"

"Yeah. 'Cause you goin through it too."

"Hunh? Man, whatcha talkin about?"

He inhaled. He exhaled. He sighed. "It's Lynette."

"Yeah...?"

"I'm in love with her, man. And I *hate* it."

"You hate it?"

"Well, it ain't that I really hate it. It's just that...man, I been tryin to avoid this shit."

"Yo, I know whatcha mean, Brotha."

"Somebody gets your heart, and it's over for you. I tell you, man, she got me trippin."

"I know."

"I hate not bein in control. All she gotta do is look at me, man, just *look* at me."

I laughed. "Oh yeah, I know how *that* is."

"The more I fight it, tryin to keep it in check, the more it fights me back. It's a tough bitch."

"Yeah, you got that right."

"I was dodgin it real...uh, how ya say it?"

"Jood."

He slapped my thigh. "Man, you a fuckin genius. That word describes it to a *G*. Mitch always said it was gonna sneak up on me and knock my ass down. But I always said, not me, not The Kid."

I grinned. "You too, hunh?"

"Ya know it. He said he couldn't wait for that day to come, to see *that* look on my face."

"Uh, is that why you been avoidin him?"

"Yeah. But he gonna figure it out, especially since I ain't never bring a lady to one of his parties. And he and Lynette are just hittin it off. You think they was the best of friends."

We stared at tha stars.

I sighed. "Man, I tell ya...love might be a natural thing, but it *ain't* a rational thing."

Did *I* just say that?

He agreed wit' me. "That shit is so fuckin true, man. It's so true." He inhaled. He exhaled.

"Brotha, tha shit ain't easy ta deal wit'. But ya just gotta take yo' time, go wit' tha flow. And don't be suckin up no fumes. That ain't gonna help."

"Yeah, yeah...you right." He put it out. "Ya know somethin?"

"Yeah?"

"I'm glad y'all workin things out."

"You are?"

"Yeah."

"Ya know, I...I'm really sorry about what happened."

"Sorry? Man, you ain't gotta apologize to me."

"I, I just want ya ta know...you can trust me. I ain't gonna hurt him."

"Hey, in spite of what went down, my brother has faith in you. And he loves you. And I trust him. And if he's all right with it, I am too."

I nodded.

"I gotta admit that I wanted to fuck you up."

"Yeah?"

"Yeah. But even if I saw you in the street, I wouldn'ta done nuthin. I ain't the violent type. People think I am just because of my size. And we ain't even gotta talk about the fact that I'm the wrong color."

I could testify ta that. "Brotha, we is *def*initely on tha same page."

"See, you don't hear me, tho'. I useta wear that T-shirt: NO, WHITE LADY, I DON'T WANT YOUR PURSE. There it was, in big, bold, black letters...and they *still* afraid of your ass."

"I know how it is, Brotha."

"One night me and Lynette was out and I had it on, and this white lady turned her nose up at us. Lynette turned to her and said, 'Uh-huh, and he don't want your pussy, either!' "

We cracked up.

"I tell ya, she had me goin. I tell her she should be a comedienne. She got such a sharp tongue."

"So…what else ya love about her?"

"Well…you can see she one fine female."

"You got that right. Yo, if I was still walkin on *that* side of tha street, you be in trouble."

He rubbed my head. "Ha, yeah, right. Anyway, she so fuckin sweet. And I just love her smile. It's like I can *feel* it, ya know? And she so fuckin brilliant. She got a Ph.D. in physics."

"Physics?"

"Yeah, man, physics. Ain't that many sisters with doctorates in science, so you know she got it *seriously* goin on up here. But she might have a lot of book smarts but she got a whole lot of street smart in her, too. She was born and raised in the South Bronx. She a little older than me, but it don't seem to matter."

"How old is she?"

"She 35."

"Yeah? *Day-am*, Brotha. She look *jood* fuh her age."

He grinned. "I know."

"But, yo, what is this, man? First yo' moms, then Little Bit, now you. This younger man thing seems ta run in yo' family, hunh?"

He chuckled. "Yeah, I guess so."

"So, when y'all settin that date?"

"Yo, don't even try it, man. I should be askin *you* that."

"Me?"

"Yeah, *you*. Look like y'all the ones who done set up house and shit." I shrugged. "Yeah, I guess."

"We ain't talkin about stuff like that—"

"Yet."

He smiled. "Hmmm, maybe we'll have a double wedding."

We looked at each other.

"Hell no!" we both laughed wit' a brotha slap.

He noogied my head. "Man, I tell you…you a real cool Brotha."

"Yo, it takes one ta know one, ya know?"

"Yeah, I guess it does…but there's one thing you gotta do, and then we be set."

"Yeah? What?"

"You gotta pay up."

"Pay up?"

"Yeah. Don't you remember the little bet you made with me about the Bulls winnin the championship?"

Did I? I did. But… "Man, we made that bet when Jordan was king."

"Well, King Jordan or no King Jordan, you gotta pay up."

"A'ight, a'ight." I went in my pocket and pulled out eight dimes. I dropped 'em in his open palm. "I'll give ya tha other twenty cents when we get upstairs."

"Thank you. I always like a man who sticks by his word." He rattled tha change.

"Yo, I don't make no promise I can't keep."

"Yeah? Well, I'm gonna hold you to that."

We both nodded.

He sighed. "Well, I guess we better get back upstairs. It's about time to cut the cake and open the presents."

"Yeah. I just can't *wait* ta see Little Bit's face when he opens up his present."

"Uh, Raheim?"

"Yeah?"

"Thanks."

"Fuh what?"

"You know…for listenin."

"Yo, anytime, Brotha, anytime."

We shook hands, tha brotha way. We embraced. We got up and went upstairs, arm ta arm.

REWIND '91

"We have to talk."

"About what?"

"About Junior."

"Yeah?"

"He said some words that I never wanna hear come out of his mouth again."

"Words like..."

"Words like fuck—"

"Nah!"

"—and nigger—"

"Hunh?"

"—and shit."

"He said all that?"

"Yes, and I don't think it's funny, and I don't know why you're so surprised. Who do you think he learned them from?"

"Oh, so this my fault?"

"What do you think?"

"How you know he got it from me?"

"Because your mouth is the only mouth I hear those words come out of on a regular basis."

"Yeah-fuckin-right. Like you don't curse?"

"Yes, I do curse, but I do not do it around my son."

"A'ight, a'ight, just hold it. Number one, he ain't just yo' son. And number two, how you know he ain't pick it up from TV or from somebody else?"

"Somebody else like who?"

"I heard yo' moms say them words."

"That's right. You've heard her say them, and chances are, she was sayin them to you. But she knows better than to say those types of things in front of him."

"Whatcha tryin ta say?"

"What I am sayin is that we have had this conversation before, have we not?"

"Yo, don't be talkin ta me like I'm fuckin stoopid."

"*I'm not.*"

"*You is too. How you fuckin sound—*"

"*And please,* don't *curse at or to me.*"

"*And don't be* fuckin *tellin me how ta talk.*"

"*Look, Raheim, getting angry at me is not going to help things.*"

"*And now you gonna tell me I ain't got no right ta be angry, hunh?*"

"*Look:* our *son has said those words, and I don't want him to hear them come out of* either *of our mouths again.*"

"*Who* you *s'pose ta be? My moms and shit?*"

"*Raheim—*"

"*I ain't even tryin ta hear that, a'ight? He sayin shit you don't like, we just tell him not ta say it.* End *of discussion.*"

"*No, that's* not *the end of the discussion, because we can't tell him* not *to say these things and then five seconds later, they're comin out of* your *mouth.*"

"*Uh-huh, just keep it up, a'ight?*"

"*Excuse me?*"

"*You heard. Just keep it tha* fuck *up. You just askin fuh it.*"

"*I'm* askin *for it? Exactly what am I askin for, Raheim?... Hello, I'm listening...I'm waiting.... OK, since you won't say it, I will: I'm* askin *to be slapped, right? I...I just can't believe you, Raheim. Here I am, discussing something very important, and you...you don't like what I'm saying so you threaten me.*"

"Threaten you? Bitch—"

"*That's it. There's another word I don't want him picking up. How could you call me that, Raheim?* How? *I wanted to have this conversation with you face-to-face, but I'm glad I didn't.*"

"Why?"

"*Because you can't take criticism and you act like you know everything, and I was afraid it might come to this, that we would have to go down that road again.*"

"*What tha* fuck *you talkin 'bout?*"

"*You know* damn *well what I'm talkin 'bout.*"

"*Uh-huh,* you *can curse but* I *can't, right?*"

"*This is not about that, Raheim, and you know it. This is about you not being able to control your temper and not being able to control* me. *I'm sorry, but you're gonna have to get it together....*"

"*Get it* tagetha*?*"

"*Yes. I don't want* our *son growing up around that. I...I just can't believe you...look, when you want to come over, make sure I'm at work or school, all right?*"

"*Hunh?*"

"*I don't want to see you for a while, OK? I just don't.*"

"What's up wit' you? You can't take a joke?"

"Don't, Raheim. Please don't try to push it off. Ignorin it ain't gonna make it go away, and it ain't gonna change things."

"Yo, Sunshine, I—"

"And don't *call me that*. I don't have anything else to say. Good-night."

"Nah, nah, don't—"

Click.

BLASTS FROM OUR PASTS

It was Little Bit's idea fuh us ta watch movies on video ev'ry Friday nite. He thought this would be tha best way fuh us ta spend "quality time" tagetha, ta really get ta know each other. He felt that tha type of movies we wanted ta watch would tell it all.

Now, we could agree on some of 'em: *She's Gotta Have It* (uh-huh, just like me 'n' my Baby); *Beverly Hills Cop* (Eddie ain't never gonna top it, so why he even tryin?); *Shaft* (uh-huh, he was a *bad* mutha-fucka—and not bad-lookin, either); *To Sleep With Anger* (it's tha deepest mutha-fuckin movie I ever saw, and ev'ry time I see it, I see somethin new); *A Soldier's Story* (tha best military flick ever made); *Sparkle* (tha original *Dreamgirls*); and *Let's Do It Again* (tha funniest movie Bill 'n' Sid made tagetha). And neither one of us wanted ta see any "great white hope" movies—you know, where tha all-knowin, all-seein, all-*that* ofay shows us niggers (or spics or injuns) da way.

But we couldn't see eye ta eye on nuthin else. I wanted ta watch shoot-'em-up-bang-'em-up-knock-'em-out flicks—you know, anything wit' Bruce Lee, Chuck Norris, Steven Seagal, Da Arnold, Sly, or my fave, Jean-Claude Van Damme. Not only is J-C movies hyped, but he got a hyped body, too. I mean, I ain't one ta be scopin out no white boys (I don't play in no snow, ya know what I'm sayin?), but he got Ass—that's right, wit' a c-a-p-i-t-a-l *A*—and I would gladly do a dance up in that jammy.

Little Bit is tha melodrama type—you know, shit like *Mahogany* (I can't *stand* Miss Loss, and Billy Dee don't do shit fuh me); *The Color Purple* (as jood as Whoopi, Oprah, Danny, Margaret, and Adolph was, Mr. Close Encounters of the *Worst* Kind Spielberg *fucked* Alice's book up); and *Mommie Dearest* (that "No wire hangers…*ever*!" thing was wack; I mean, Christina ain't bring tha mutha-fuckas up in tha house, and she wasn't even big enuff ta reach tha fuckin closet rack, so why Mommie go ballistic on her?). He tried ta force some scary movies on me, too, but I wasn't havin that. Yeah, I admit it (even tho' I won't ta him): I'm a fraidy cat, a'ight? But he tricked me wit' *The Silence of the Lambs.* "It's a psychological thriller, Pooquie. There ain't no Jason slicin and dicin people at a camp left and right." No, but there was Hannibal "the Cannibal" Lecter, and he wasn't no joke. He fucked wit' Jodie's mind—and mine too. That mutha-fucka have you doubtin yo' own name and shit. I couldn't shake his face or his voice fuh like a week, and ev'ry time Little Bit would nibble on me, I almost jumped outa my fuckin skin. Uh-huh, I found out what "psychological thriller" meant.

Anyway, sometimes when we be watchin Little Bit's movies of tha week, I would doze off (yo' eyes don't hafta be closed ta do that, ya know?). But some of 'em, ta my surprise, were on tha one, like *Prizzi's Honor.* Wit' all that schemin 'n' lyin 'n' stealin 'n' killin goin on, there was as much action as a J-C flick. And it was funny, but in a wack way— sorta like *The Godfather* meets *The Munsters.* (My only prob: it was called a "black" comedy when it shoulda been called a "white" one since there wasn't no Black folks up in it except some maid they called "the girl.") And there was a few that I ain't wanna see but I was glad I did, like *Dangerous Liaisons.* When Little Bit told me it was about eigh- teenth-century aristocrats, I was like, *You have gotsta be cray-zee!* But I gave it a chance. It wasn't easy. I kept crackin up durin tha first ten min- utes cuz of them costumes; I just couldn't stop thinkin about Carol Burnett and that curtain rod, ya know? But all that dirty talk got me 'n' Little Bit so fuckin worked up, we ended up gettin busy right there on tha couch. Yeah, tha movie ended up watchin us.

But we couldn't just *watch* tha movies Little Bit wanted ta see: he always had ta turn ev'ry fuckin viewin inta a Q&A session. Like when we was barely ten minutes inta *Kramer vs. Kramer* (which I was fallin asleep on), he stopped tha tape, turned ta me, and asked, "What if Crystal were to just up and leave you tomorrow, Pooquie, just drop off the face of the earth: could you take care of Junior by yourself?" Of course, I said *hell yeah;* I mean, I'm his daddy, and can't nobody take care of him better than me. But then, after seein ev'rything that Dustin Hoffman went thru, I realized I take a lota shit fuh granted—like Sunshine, my moms, and even Little Bit bein there fuh Li'l Brotha Man and me. I mean, ain't nuthin wrong wit' him knowin he got other folks in his life who are there fuh him, but if I couldn't count on all that help, where would I be? Yeah, tha shit got me thinkin....

Then there was tha time we watched *Big.* That title was enuff ta get me int'rested. But then I found out what it was about. Yeah, it was funny and yeah, Tom Hanks was cool. But...it ain't tha kinda flick that's gonna be in my collection, ya know what I'm sayin? But then

Little Bit Q'ed me wit' "If you could have one wish, Pooquie, what would it be?" When he asked it, I was like, *Who you s'pose ta be, tha genie in tha fuckin lamp?* But it made Tha Kid do some serious thinkin. How serious? I ain't answer him till tha next day: "I wanna be at peace." He smiled; I ain't hafta explain.

Tanite we checked out *Ghost.* Whoopi, who was tha movie, was just too funny. Little Bit was a little too quiet thru it and when it was over. I was hopin he wasn't thinkin of somethin ta ask me. I mean, I liked ta talk ta him about tha movies — shit, I really loved bein all cuddled up in tha dark, sharin a big bowl of popcorn and a soda—but I always felt like I was in school takin a quiz. I knew I was home free when we was in bed on our way ta sleep. But then...

"Pooquie?"

"Ah...yeah?" I was almost out.

"Do you believe in ghosts?"

"Nah."

"No?"

"Nah, Baby." I moved in closer ta him. "Ain't no ghosts."

"Why do you think that?"

"Cuz when you dead you dead, there just ain't no comin back, Baby."

"Well, I believe."

I chuckled. "C'mon, Baby, you soundin like Whoopi."

"I'm serious, Raheim.... After seeing the movie...I just know that it *did* happen."

"What happened?"

"My uncle...my Uncle Russ, I told you about him."

"Yeah, you told me. He's tha one who died of AIDS, right?"

"Yes. He was here."

"Hunh?"

"He came here. He visited me."

"He ain't visit you, Little Bit."

"Yes, he did, Pooquie."

"Baby, it was a dream."

"No, it wasn't."

"It had ta be."

"I always thought it was, but...after tonight..."

"A'ight, Baby, a'ight. Tell me about it."

We sat up, and I held him.

"I was wide awake, sitting in that very chair." He pointed ta it. "I was workin on a story about AIDS, and it was hard to write."

"So, what, he helped ya write it?" I joked.

He ain't find it funny. "Yes, in fact, he *did* help me write it. I still had not come to grips with his dying of it. He came to me...he told me that I didn't have to be afraid of it...that I was wrong to feel that I was doing the story too late because he was gone. And I *did* feel guilty. I guess in the back of my mind I always felt that I was somehow responsible for his dying."

"Why would ya think that?"

"I know it sounds crazy, but...I was the last family member to see him alive. I mean, why didn't I see it? Why couldn't I tell? Why couldn't *he* tell *me*?"

"That ain't yo' fault, Baby."

"I know that now, but that's how I felt. When he visited me he said I had to write the story because people needed to know. He said that it would save someone's life."

By this time he was cryin. I kissed away his tears.

"So I do believe in ghosts. I did think it was a dream, but after seeing the movie...I don't think I would have been able to finally grieve for him if I didn't experience that. And he knew that. That's why he came back. He was here. It was him. And I know it was real. I know it was."

What he said stayed on my mind all nite. I couldn't sleep. I got him up early so we could take a trip ta Long Island. I ain't tell him where we was goin; he figured it out when we pulled inta tha driveway. First, we went in a flower shop across tha street and bought some roses, and then he walked wit' me, hand in hand, ta tha grave.

It was tha first time I was seein him this way. I never told Little Bit that I ain't get out tha limo that day we buried him. But I had been here befo': me 'n' Brotha Man came so he could visit his pops, who got inta a fight over a card game and was stabbed. He was only twenty-two. *Day-am.* They was tha same age when they died. And Brotha Man told me, standin over his pops' grave, that he knew he was gonna die young just like him....

I wiped off tha dirt coverin up his plot wit' a handkerchief. *Carter, Derrick "D.C.," Jr., 1971–1993.* I rubbed his initials. I put tha roses in tha vase and called myself tryin ta arrange 'em in a nice way. I stared so hard at tha ground; I guess I wanted him ta just come on up and talk ta me. Little Bit held one of my hands; tha other hand he had on my right shoulder.

"Do you want me to leave?" he asked.

I nodded no.

"Do you want to say anything?"

I nodded no again.

I sighed. I squeezed his hand tight. He rubbed my shoulder.

"Are you sure you don't want to say anything?"

I nodded yeah. He held me from behind. We just stood there like an hour. I poured some beer in tha ground.

I ain't say a word when we was drivin back, and I ain't say hardly nuthin tha rest of tha day. Shit, I ain't even wanna eat, so ya know Little Bit was worried.

"Pooquie, you don't want to talk?" he asked, closin tha bedroom window.

I was in bed, naked, flat on my back, my hands behind my head. "Nah." I really didn't, cuz I ain't know what ta say.

He made his way around tha bed and got in on his side. "Well, I know I sound like a broken record, but are you sure? I've never seen you like this."

I rose up and grabbed his hand. "Don't worry, Baby. Ain't nuthin you can do."

"Well, I'm here for you."

"I know, Baby."

"Good night."

"G'nite."

We kissed, and he turned off tha light.

"Yo, Brotha, wake up!"

My eyes popped open.

"Wake up!"

My head raised up, real slow. I couldn't believe my eyes.

"Yeah, man, it's me. Betcha ain't expect ta see me again, hunh?"

He was sittin on tha edge of our bed. *Nah, no way, man, this just couldn't be happenin....*

I sat up and swung my legs off tha bed. I checked him out from head ta toe. He was wearin tha same clothes he had on tha nite he....

He held out his hand. I just looked at it. He laughed. "It's a'ight, Brotha. I ain't gonna bite ya...unless ya want me ta."

I reached out wit' my left hand. He grabbed it. I jumped. My heart started ta race. It felt so real. It felt like...*him.* He tried ta let go, but I wouldn't let him.

He laughed again. It sounded just like him. "It's a'ight. I ain't goin nowhere just yet."

Seein him, there was so much I wanted ta say, so much stuff was fillin my mind. "I...I...I..."

He giggled. "What's up, Brotha, cat gotcha tongue? Ha, I'm gone fuh like nine months and you ain't got nuthin ta say?"

"I...I..." I was goin there again. "I...I...I love you, Brotha Man."

"Yo, Brotha, I know. You ain't know I did, you ain't think I did, but I did."

I was gonna say somethin else—what, I don't know—when he put his right thumb ta my lips. "Shhh...you ain't gotta say nuthin, man. And you ain't got nuthin ta be guilty about. You did all you could. You looked out fuh me, like you always did. And I love you too, Brotha."

He got up and stood in fronta me. He grabbed both my hands and pulled me up. I felt so light. He wrapped his arms around me and squeezed me tight. Oh, he felt so *jood*. I cried on his shoulder fuh...I don't know how long it was.

Then he sat me back down. He bent down on his right knee. He wiped away my tears and kissed me on tha lips. He held my face wit' both hands. "You gonna be a'ight, Brotha. You got so much right here—" he looked over at Little Bit, still asleep, and smiled—"and you got so much here—" he pointed ta my heart. "Don't be scared of it. Go fuh yours, boy, fuh you *and* me. And don't fuhget...I'm always here wit' ya."

He got up but held on ta my hands. "And thanks fuh keepin yo' promise. That beverage was *jood.*" He smiled. I did too.

He winked. He turned, facin tha window. I ain't want him ta leave. I tried reachin out fuh him, but I couldn't move. I tried ta call out fuh him, but nuthin would come out.

Next thing I knew, Little Bit was shakin me.

"Pooquie, it's me, wake up, wake up!"

I opened my eyes. I was in tha exact same position I fell asleep in. "What—what's goin on?"

He stroked my head. "You were calling out for D.C."

"I was?"

"Uh-huh. Did you dream about him?"

"Yeah, yeah, I did."

He sat up. "What happened?"

"Uh...he said...he said he loved me."

"He did?"

"Yeah, Baby. I told him I loved him. And I held him. He kissed me. It was so real."

He hugged me. He kissed my cheek. "I'm glad, Pooquie, I'm so glad. Do you feel better?"

"Yeah, yeah, I do. Thanks, Baby."

"For what?"

"Fuh just bein you."

"I'm here for you."

"I know. I love you."

"I love you too, Pooquie."

We kissed.

He smiled. "Let's go back to sleep, OK?"

"A'ight."

I was about ta cradle him in my arms when...

"Pooquie?"

"Yeah?"

"Did you open the window?"

"Nah."

"Are you sure? I know I closed it before we went to sleep."

"You want me ta close it?"

"Please. It's kind of chilly."

I got up ta do it.

"I just don't understand how it got open." He shrugged. "Hmm, must have been a ghost."

I closed it. "Yeah...musta been."

HIGH SCHOOL DAZE

"Hey, Supermodel!"

I was makin my weekly appearance at Simply Dope. Since me 'n' Little Bit work at home, tha only times I really come ta tha office is ta drop off or pick up my assignments. It ain't like they got space fuh me, any-ol'-way: folks got these little cubby holes they like ta call offices, and I don't see how they get any work done cuz things are so cramped and tight. You need advertisin? That brotha can be found just a few feet in fronta tha sista who *is* tha finance department. But I can see where tha brotha who runs tha place, Z.Z. Middleton, is comin from: keep them costs low and those returns are gonna be high. They ain't Def Jam or Death Row, but Simply Dope can hang: ev'ry month, they got a record goin gold or platinum. So I prob'ly don't hear folks complainin about movin ta a bigger office cuz Z.Z. be lookin out where it *really* counts.

And I had come ta get *my* piece of that action: it was payday, and I don't trust no mailman. I showed up when ev'rybody was buzzin about this group called HigHopes that looked and sounded *too* much like En Vogue (don't they all?). They're tha first Simply Dope act ta have a top ten hit on tha white charts (some call it "pop," but I call it what it is). Tha song ain't new: a remake of "Best of My Love." They shoulda left it alone, cuz they ain't no Emotions. Tha only reason it's a hit is cuz they pumped it up wit' a hip-hop beat. Even tha video is better than tha song—and I ain't sayin that cuz I'm in it. Maxine, one of them HigHopes, spotted me in tha office one day and asked me ta play her boyfriend (yeah, she wanted me ta *keep* on playin it, but I'm taken). This was my video debut, but it wasn't *nuthin* compared ta my second shoot. Some castin agent saw me in *YSB*, got in touch wit' Tommy Boy, and tha very next day I was filmin SWV's "Anything." And when I walked inta that studio, I just *knew* I was back at Heaven: there was nuthin but brothas wit' boom*bah*stic bootiez and bodiez, walkin around half-naked in G-strings and towels. I couldn't concentrate on any directions from tha director, cuz I kept gettin fondled and flashed (one brotha's towel always seemed ta be comin undone when I was standin behind him). Yeah, I'd be lyin if I said I didn't enjoy it (who wouldn't?), that I didn't do some fondlin 'n' flashin of my own (gettin a "hug" or givin a "brotha pat" don't fall in them categories, do they?), and that I didn't think twice about goin out fuh a drink or meetin at so-'n'-so's hotel room fuh a *any-thang ya wanna do* party. But I knew who I had waitin home fuh me. I clocked a few numbers (yo, I ain't ask, a'ight, they just gave 'em up), but I ain't keep 'em. I wasn't about ta have Little Bit goin thru my pockets and findin some nigga's digits.

Anyway, I got my check and was waitin fuh tha elevator, registerin Warren G on my radio (he mad cute and, whatcha know, he look just like my Baby), when somebody called me. My boss, Arthur, gave me that new title. He would just love ta see me wit' nuthin but some briefs on, but he knows that copy of tha All-American ad he ripped out of a magazine is tha only way that dream is gonna come true. Ya know he was too thru when I signed it. It's on his desk in a frame.

So I knew it was gonna be him when I turned around. But it was Gene, wavin a card.

I took off my headphones. "What's up, G?"

"Nothin much. I'm glad you're here. Would you please give this to your hubby?" He handed it ta me.

I took it. "What is it?"

"If you must know, it is an invite to his high school reunion."

"His high school reunion?"

"Yes. If turnin twenty-eight doesn't make him realize that the years are flyin, this will."

"How you get it?"

"Angela Martin gave it to me. She and Mitch graduated together. They expect him to say a few words. They've been trying to find him for months. Tell him to call the school for more info." He raised his eyebrows. "I trust you will see to it that he re*ceives* this in *jood* condition...?"

"Yeah. I mean, I do that kinda thing fuh a livin, ya know."

He grinned. "Jood."

It hit me when I was on my way home why Gene was gettin wise on me: Little Bit was prob'ly gonna see his coach at this reunion. *Day*-am. That means I gotta go. I read tha card:

To our esteemed alumni

You & a guest are invited to attend
the 10th anniversary reunion of the
Class of 1984
on Friday • June 3, 1994
8:00–11:00 P.M.
Edward R. Murrow High School
RSVP by May 8 • Ida Gray • 718-655-8934
Bring your memories!

Ain't I doin somethin that nite? I am: Li'l Brotha Man 'n' me gonna celebrate cuz he graduatin tha very next day. Uh-huh, my son, he movin on up. I gotta get shit done fuh his graduation/birthday party, and that's happenin on Saturday, too. Is that a lucky break or what? I gotta admit that I would wanna roll on that fuckin coach, takin my Baby's virginity and his heart. He fucked over Little Bit, *big*-fuckin-time. But this is somethin totally diff'rent from B.D. 'n' Babyface gettin hitched. I mean, am I ready ta go ta somethin like this? What would I be—his "man," his "boyfriend," his "friend"? How about if somebody recognizes me: do I play it off and say I ain't *him*? Wit' us bein tagetha, I knew shit like this was gonna come up. But I was kinda glad Li'l Brotha Man gave me a easy out. Ain't no way I can break my date wit' him.

I knew Little Bit wasn't gonna be happy about me not goin, but he ain't seem that happy about goin himself. He was tryin ta play it off, tellin me 'n' Gene (who called ta get tha scoop) he couldn't wait ta go and see what happened ta his class, if ev'rybody did what they said they wanted ta do. I knew he was holdin back on me.

It finally came out when we was in bed playin *Jeopardy!*

"OK, Pooquie. You need one more answer and you've won."

"So, what else is new?"

"Don't be cocky about it, OK? Your category is famous dates. The answer is, 'The Titanic sank on this day, claiming over 1,500 lives.' "

"Aw, c'mon, Baby, can't you do better than that?"

"What's the question, smarty pants?"

"What's April fifteenth, 1912?"

"Now, how do you know that?"

"Cuz I'm a smart mutha-fucka. And in case you fuhgot, my Baby was born on that day."

I smiled. He frowned.

A'ight...I'll try again. "I mean, I knew I was wit' somebody who was up there, but *day-am*! That means you eighty-two, not twenty-eight, Baby!"

He pushed me, but his expression ain't change. "Ha, ha, ha. Corny but cute. So, you wanna play again?"

"Do I wanna play again?"

"Yes, do you wanna play again. That's what I asked."

"Hold up, Baby, hold up…I just whipped yo' ass—*three* times—and you wanna play again?"

"Yes. Why?"

"Cuz three is yo' limit, remember? Three strikes and you out. What's goin on?"

"What do you mean?"

"I mean, what's goin on?"

"Nothing's goin on, OK? You wanna play again?"

"Nah, I don't."

He sighed. He shrugged. "OK." He started packin it up.

I just stared at him. He got tha hint.

"What, Pooquie?"

"You angry at me, huh?"

"Angry at you?"

"Yeah."

"Why would I be angry at you?"

"Cuz I ain't goin."

"Goin where?"

"*You* know."

"No, I am not angry at you over that. Why would I be? Why should I be?"

"Cuz you know you want me ta go."

He slid tha game under tha bed. He folded his arms across his chest. He tried ta smile, but it wasn't workin. "Yes. Yes, I do. I want you to go. But you can't. And I accept that." He pecked me on tha lips and moved up ta his side of tha bed.

I wasn't buyin none of it. I moved up ta my side. "Then why you angry at me?"

"I'm not."

"Then what's up wit' you?"

"Nothing."

"C'mon, Baby, you can't fool me."

"I can't?"

"No, you can't. You bailin on me. I know somethin's wrong."

He just looked at me. "It…it's nothing, Pooquie."

"That ain't true, Baby, and you know it. C'mon. Tell me."

He sighed. He found his spot on my chest. I held him.

"I'm...a little scared, Pooquie."

"A little scared?" I chuckled. "Baby, how you gonna be a *little* scared?"

"Well...I don't know. I just am."

"About what?"

"About the reunion."

"What about it, Baby?"

"I...I...I'm gonna feel funny, that's all."

"Whatcha mean?"

"Well...what am I gonna say to people? That I've only held *one* full-time job since graduating, that I quit that job, that I'm suing my former employer, and that I'm currently unemployed with *no* prospects?"

"You ain't unemployed, Baby."

"I am too, Pooquie."

"No, you ain't. You doin a lota work fuh folks."

"Don't you mean I work *for* a lot of folks?"

"So what if you ain't got no nine-ta-five? You earnin a livin, and you doin what you like ta do. I mean, how many of them folks can say they went ta tha Grammys? That they did stories on Whitney, Toni, Tevin, and Aretha? You gonna be doin Q&As wit' Gladys and Anita soon. And how about that background work you doin? You got *two* careers, Baby."

"I do that just for fun, Pooquie. I don't wanna be a professional singer."

"Baby, anytime you singin wit' L.V., you a professional. You got what it takes ta go solo."

"You think so?"

"I *know* so."

"Well, thanks, Pooquie. But that has never been a dream of mine. I didn't leave that school with dreams of hitting number one on the charts. I left that school as a writer for the newspaper, the literary magazine, and an editor of the yearbook. And I was the valedictorian. They're gonna expect me to come in there and announce I am a senior editor at *Newsweek* or something. And anybody can name-drop. Half the time folks think you lyin, anyway. When you go to these types of things, you have to have somethin to really brag about."

"You can brag about me."

He looked up at me. He smiled. I did too. I kissed him.

"You can't be nobody but you, Baby. And that's jood enuff."

"I...I know, but...you know...sometimes...I think it's all a mistake."

"What?"

"Taking them to court."

"It ain't, Baby. You can't let them mutha-fuckas get away wit' what they did. If you do, they gonna keep on doin it."

He sighed. "Yeah. I guess you right."

"You know I am."

"I…I just feel like…like…"

"You don't belong no place, huh?"

"Yeah. How you guess?"

"Cuz I been there, *too* many fuckin times, Baby, be*lieve* me."

"That's why the birthday party meant so much to me. Yeah, it reminded me I was gettin older, but that I still belong, that I am a part of something."

"Baby, how long you been feelin like this?"

"Uh, I don't know…a few months."

"*A few months?* Why you ain't tell me?"

"I…I guess I thought that keeping myself busy with you…and Junior…and the work I got…it would…it would help keep my mind off feelin…depressed."

"*Depressed?* Baby, how you gonna be walkin around here all this time depressed and not let me know? I thought you was enjoyin yo' break from tha daily bump 'n' grind."

"Well, I was, at first. It was great setting my own hours, doing what *I* wanted to do, not havin somebody lookin over my shoulder. But lately…I don't know. I guess its novelty has worn off."

"I just can't believe you ain't tell me."

"I'm sorry, Pooquie."

"You *better* be."

"I better be?"

"*Hell*-fuckin-yeah. Whatever you goin thru, I go thru too. You don't hafta keep shit like this ta yo'self. That's why I'm here. That's why Li'l Brotha Man is here."

"Yes, you're right."

"I know I am. You better not *ever* do that again, you hear?"

"Yes. Yes, I hear you."

"A'ight, then. And don't worry, Baby. You gonna kick *Your World*'s ass, you gonna get a better job, and you gonna do *real* jood at that reunion."

"It…it's just hard not to worry, Pooquie."

"Try."

"OK, OK…I will."

"Jood. And if I ain't never tell you befo', I'm proud of you."

"You are?"

"*Hell,* yeah. L'il Brotha Man is too. You somethin ta be proud of, Baby."

"Thanks, Pooquie."

We kissed. We breathed tagetha.

"Little Bit?"

"Yes?"

"I wish I could go wit' you." And I really did.

He sighed. "I know, Pooquie. I know. But you will be there with me in spirit. Junior will too."

"Uh...will you-know-*who* know we there wit' you?"

He giggled. He squeezed me tight. "Hmmm, don't you worry. He will."

REWIND '91

Yo, man...that was good. That was real *good. I ain't cum like that since...since...*last nite! *Just jokin wit'cha, just jokin. It coulda been even better if you ain't fight me and shit...yeah, fight me. It's like, you ain't wanna be on tha bottom. Ev'ry time I had you down in a good position, I start bumpin 'n' you start movin, and we start gettin a serious buzz on, our dicks just wagin war like two swords and shit, you disturb tha groove, rollin us over so you can be on top. Man, what's* up *wit' that? We coulda had a whole lot mo' fun if you ain't wanna play ring around tha rosy and shit. I mean, all that pushin 'n' pullin was kinda fun. I like ta wrestle a nigga, see if he can handle me. But when I just knew tha station was right, you had ta go 'n' change tha channel....*

Yeah, yeah, I know: you don't go that way. She-it, *I don't either. I wish you had told me that befo' we came all tha way tha fuck up here and shit.* Day-am, *I was just* ready *ta tap that ass! I don't know why you ain't think I wasn't gonna want some. I mean, I was all over that shit at tha party—and tha shit is somethin ta be* all *over! Sara Lee ain't* never *bake no cakes like that! Brotha, you got one of them suicide booties, tha kind ya just wanna stick yo' whole mutha-fuckin head* all *tha way up in and risk yo' life bein smothered ta death and shit, tryin ta get all that juice outa there.* All big, round, smooth, tight...*day-am, Big Bob gettin hard just* thinkin *'bout it! I could tell ain't nobody ever lick yo' split befo'. Wit' all that squirmin 'n' squealin, I could only get me a little taste. But yo, that booty was rootie, tootie, fresh,* and *fruity! Man, you sure you don't wanna gimme just a little? I ain't gotta stick it all tha way in. Just tha head, and I be good to go, Joe....* Man, it sure is a shay-hame, *you not lettin nobody go ta work up in* that. *Yo, you* ever *wanna give it up, you gotta let me have some. I just know that shit is gonna be worth tha wait....*

Nigga, what made you think I *was gonna give it up? Yo, there's some of us that* do *and some of us that get* done, *and I'm just one of them niggaz who do da doin, ya know what I'm sayin? Big Bob been leadin tha way, he always be gettin tha call, and I just go where he wanna go. And you know he was talkin* real *loud when you walked pass me tanite. I knew there wasn't no way I could pass you up. Yup, that ass was just callin.* Just *callin. No offense, brotha, but*

I still think it's a waste. I mean, tha way you was ruff-housin*? Man, if you ever give it up, whoever gets it tha first time is gonna be one lucky mutha-fucka. I like ta be a fly on tha fuckin wall ta see* that *shit.*

It's a shame you don't suck dick, neither. Man, them lips you got...them mutha-fuckas was just made *ta wrap around somethin like Big Bob. You sure you don't wanna try? Yo, I don't mind you experimentin on* me*! I betcha them mutha-fuckas is just so soft...huh?...nah, nah, brotha, I don't kiss no nigga on no lips. I don't go fuh that. I save that shit fuh tha ladies. I mean, I ain't never kiss no nigga, but I just know it ain't tha same, ya know? You do that shit? Man, I tell ya, I just don't think that shit is right. I mean, if that's yo' thang, hey, do whatcha wanna do, like tha Isleys say. But I think some things you ain't s'pose ta be doin wit' no nigga, and* that's *one of 'em.*

But one thing? Niggaz sho' can suck dick better than tha ladies! I don't know, but tha ladies, they always complainin and shit: 'it's too fuckin long,' 'it's too fuckin big,' 'go slow,' 'not too fast'...yeah? See, you know what I'm sayin. Tha brothas, they don't need no fuckin coachin, and I ain't gotta do nuthin but lay back, sit back, stand back, and let 'em swallow *back. Suck it up, suck it in, suck it* down, *like a vacuum cleaner, ya know, gettin that serious Hoover action goin on, pullin on my fuckin* kidneys *and shit. And look, Ma, no hands! Yo, I'm like, if you gonna suck dick,* suck dick—*don't be lettin yo' hands do tha work fuh ya. Anytime you gotta use ya hands ta do tha job yo' mouth is s'pose ta be doin, you ain't got no bizness suckin dick, and that's how them ladies is. I guess that's just a parta them bein ladies. They ain't s'pose ta know. But tha brothas? Ain't* no *question. Ain't no mutha-fuckin question they know how ta blow, and they tha only ones that get tha chance ta blow Big Bob. Yeah, a few times when I was* really *hard up, I let some white boys do it, but they ain't know what tha* fuck *they was doin. They was just* too *mutha-fuckin happy ta have a Big Bob ta play wit'. They just couldn't get over how big he was. You know, a vision in* mutha-fuckin *3D, a double digit dick in* full *niggafied effect. I know they wished* they *had it like that. But my dick ain't no mutha-fuckin toy, you know what I'm sayin? And them mutha-fuckas ain't had tha equipment ta work it like it's s'pose ta be worked. I mean, they* knew *how ta take it—they just couldn't get enuff of Big Bob bobbin in 'n' out up 'n' down all around, wantin me ta fuck 'em all nite long—but they ain't got no lips ta warm you up, and that's where it's gotta start. And hey, we just got tha lips fuh it, ya know what I'm sayin? And man,* you *got 'em. I'm tellin ya, you ever wanna find out what it's like, you just call me. Don't lose my number, a'ight? I don't care if I'm at work and shit, I leave tha fuckin* job *ta get me some....*

Big Bob, he still ain't satisfied...nah, man, nah, don't even sweat it. Things ain't go like I wanted, but it was cool. I'm gonna see if I can find somethin ta get up in between. I'm goin ta this place called Harry's. You know it? It's down in Faggotville...you know, tha West Village...you ain't never been down there?

Well, it really ain't no place ta go ta. I hate goin down there, but sometimes, when Big Bob get like this and I can't find nobody noplace else and them five fingers just ain't gonna do it, I take that trek...man, ain't nuthin but a whole lota fuckin sissies there. But some of 'em ain't that bad. Ha, I met a few MDs and shit, corporate niggaz, lettin 'em spend them dead presidents on me—and I ain't talkin 'bout no Washington, Lincoln, Hamilton, or Jackson. Yo, man, a big blue-Black nigga like you, you be snatched up like that. They go fuh men like us. Yo, when ya can't be it ya try ta have it, and they ain't it so they gotta find tha real thang. If you ain't got nowhere ta go, you can come wit' me. I can't promise ya no ride home, cuz I know I'm gonna be leavin wit' somethin. But you ain't gonna be leavin by yo'self, no way.... Yeah, man, it's free. She-it, you know it is, cuz I ain't payin fuh no puswah.... Puswah? It's just my name fuh boy pussy. You know, niggaz who give it up. Them sissies think they got pussies, any-ol'-way...yeah, pus-wah. Tha shit is funny, ain't it? Ha, funny...like them. I ain't funny, I just mess around, ya know what I'm sayin? And some of them bitches can't handle it. They be gettin an attitude if you say you ain't like them, like somebody would wanna be like them. You know, 'Whatcha mean, you ain't gay? Then whatcha doin up in here?' You just gotta blow 'em tha fuck off. They leave you alone once they know you punch tha shit outa 'em. I letcha know which bitches ta stay away from.

But tha aggravation is worth it, man, cuz I got some of my best puswah up in tha place.... Nah, man, it ain't nuthin but a little hole in tha wall and shit, can't nuthin but sixty, seventy niggaz fit up in there at one time. They got a little jukebox and shit. Them bitches be tryin ta sing, but I fix that shit when I plug in some Public Enemy or NWA. They just freak tha fuck out, just lookin 'round wonderin who put that shit on.... Nah, man, it ain't owned by no brothas. You cray-zee? Them crackers ain't gonna let us own shit down there. We can't even lay a fuckin claim ta tha dirt you kick up walkin in tha place. But it's a cute spot. She-it, it's really tha only spot you can go ta where you ain't gotta pay ta get in and you know you ain't gonna leave wit'out somethin.

You 'bout ready? Yeah, it's like 2:30, and they close up at like 3:45...nah, man, you ain't gonna need no ID. That mutha-fucka at tha do' gonna take one look at you and he not only gonna let yo' ass in, he gonna give you his callin card and make sure you get a free drink and shit. Yo, man, what's yo' name again?... Raheim? How you spell that?... Oh, yeah? Man, you a fuckin Muslim? Nah? Ha, a'ight. Sound like a fuckin he-man and shit. Them bitches gonna love that, and they gonna love yo' ass. Just stay away from my picks, a'ight, and there ain't gonna be no static....

AN END WIT' A BEGINNIN

I regretted this day comin.

Angel said he woulda stepped tha minute tha contract was signed. But Little Bit said I was makin my move at tha right time. He ain't want me gettin a big head, thinkin I can just sit back cuz it looked like I got it made.

But I wasn't goin out like that. I stuck around cuz it was hard fuh me ta let go. Fuh tha first time in my life I had a job I loved, and I ain't wanna leave it. Wit' all them other jobs, I was just earnin a paycheck, mostly fuh my Li'l Brotha Man. Fuh six years, I been workin around tha clock just ta make sure he taken care of. But this tha only paycheck I was proud of cashin. It wasn't about tha money; it was about me. I ain't had ta drag myself outa bed or force myself ta hop no train ta punch no clock, cuz I couldn't wait ta hit tha road.

People always ask me, "Why would you *want* to be a bike messenger?" I'm like, "*Why not?*" Some folks just don't get it: some of us stakin out tha streets cuz we wanna do it—not cuz we hafta, not cuz we ain't got no choice, not cuz we too *stoo*pid and we can't find nuthin else. Two fellas workin at Mel's, Corey 'n' Vernon, both got MBAs, but they soon found out that that corporate thang wasn't fuh them. They was makin most bank, but they was miserable. Corey, one of tha whitest white boys I ever seen (yeah, like chalk), said he was so stressed out he started doin coke. Vernon, a brotha from Boston, got tired of fightin tha white boys and almost had a nervous breakdown and shit. Fuh them, tha money wasn't buyin happiness.

But Mel don't play wit' tha pay, any-ol'-way. I started at twelve-fifty and got up ta seventeen an hour. Mel can come high like that cuz he been around thirty years and got himself a jood rep in tha city, servin a lota them big law firms. They been lookin out fuh him, so he can really look out fuh us. He makes sure we got helmets and pads (things I almost never use), gloves fuh ev'ry season, goggles fuh tha snow, sweats fuh tha cold, trenches fuh tha rain, sunglasses and caps fuh tha sun, and Deer Park fuh tha thirst. And while we ain't got no health plan wit' Blue Cross, he kicks out a healthy five grand ev'ry year fuh us all, an emergency pot just in case we need it.

Yeah, Mel, he always gotcha back.

My last day at Mel's wasn't no exception. You know Tha Kid was his fav'rite, so he had ta send me off like I was tha don and shit. He closed up shop at one so he could take me out fuh what ended up bein a three-hour lunch. And not only was he treatin all tha fellas, he was payin ev'rybody (includin me) fuh a full day's work (we was a rainbow coalition and shit—three white boys, three brothas, two Puerto Ricans, one Asian, and one Indian). But *I* got tha *real* bonus: five crisp $100 bills, plus a plaque wishin me jood luck and thankin me fuh bein such "a jood employee" (and he spelled *jood* right).

It ain't really hit me till I was on my way Uptown that I wasn't gonna be gettin up on Monday at six. It was like a part of me was gonna be missin. I ain't really see till then—I mean, I ain't never hang out wit' none of them fellas—but it felt like I was leavin a family.

My real family was waitin fuh me when I got home.

"Daddy, Daddy, Daddy!" Li'l Brotha Man pulled me inta tha apartment.

I took off my knapsack. "Yo, my man, what's up?"

He kept tuggin on my sleeve. "It's Grammy, it's Grammy."

"Hunh?"

"Something's wrong with Grammy."

"What's wrong?"

"I think she in shock."

I grinned. "In *shock*? What do that mean?"

"That's what you feel when something surprises you."

"Yeah?"

"Uh-huh."

"You learn that in school?"

"No. Mommy told me."

"Uh-huh. And how you know Grammy is in shock?"

"Because she looks just like Mommy looked when you told her that Uncle D went to heaven."

Day-am, he so sharp it's scary.

He brought me ta Moms's room. "Grammy is in there. She won't come out. She says she doesn't feel well. I asked her if she wanted some chocolate milk—that always makes me feel better—but she said no."

"A'ight, man. I'll see what's wrong. Jood lookin out. Now, go in tha livin room."

"OK." He ran off.

I knocked. "Ma? Ma, you a'ight?"

"Uh…come in, baby."

I stepped in. She was standin near her window. She looked like she was cryin.

I walked toward her. "What's up, Ma?"

"Close the door."

I did. Uh-oh. This must be some heavy shit.

"Sit down, Raheim."

"Ma—"

"Please, please…just sit."

I did. She joined me. She took my hands. Tha look on her face. Tha way she trembled. Her red eyes. Tha way we was, it…it was like…like déjà vu. Like we was here befo'.

We was.

Moms *couldn't* believe it. I ain't *wanna* believe it. And Little Bit ain't know *what* ta believe.

"He's *back?*" he asked fuh the third time.

"Yeah."

"Did you see him?"

"*Hell* no. Moms talked ta him."

"How did she know it was him?"

"She said she know his voice anywhere. She freakin out. That mutha-fucka talked ta Li'l Brotha Man."

"He did?"

"Yeah."

"Does Junior know who he is?"

"Nah, he don't know. He told Li'l Brotha Man that he a old friend of his grandma. That mutha-fucka. I told Moms I don't want Li'l Brotha Man knowin nuthin."

"Well, does your father—"

"Don't call him that."

"What?"

"He *ain't* my father, cuz he ain't never been around, he ain't never been there fuh me. So he ain't *nuthin* ta me."

"OK, OK."

"I want that mutha-fucka ta just go away."

"Well, then, tell him to."

"Baby, I don't wanna speak ta him. I don't wanna *see* him. *Day-am,* why he hafta just come out tha fuckin blue and shit?"

"I don't know, Pooquie...but there's only one way to find out."

"But I don't *wanna* find out."

"Why?"

"Cuz, Baby, that mutha-fucka ain't worry about me all this fuckin time. Why should I wanna hear anything he gotta say?"

"Well, you've wanted to know for so long why he left, why he wasn't around.... This is your chance to find out."

"He ain't gonna say nuthin ta make it better."

"No, he never could, Pooquie, but you'll at least know why. Aren't you the least bit curious?"

I shrugged.

"I don't know, Pooquie...I just think you owe it to yourself."

"Whatcha talkin 'bout, Baby?"

"Pooquie...never mind."

"What, Baby?"

"Nothing."

"C'mon, Baby, tell me."

He sighed. "It's...my father...there are so many things I would love to tell him...to ask him...things I know only he could tell me."

"But yo' pops ain't walk out on you, Little Bit."

"I know, I know, but...well, this is gonna sound crazy, but...sometimes I wish he did."

"Hunh?"

"I do. Sometimes I wish he did just walk out."

"Why?"

"Well, if he did walk out, at least then I could've lived with the hope that he could walk back *in*, that he is somewhere out there.... But he's not coming back, and...and I'll never know."

A tear rolled outa his right eye down his cheek. I took him in my arms.

"Baby, you a'ight?"

"I—I'll be OK.... Pooquie, you have the chance to do something I wish I could, and...and I just don't want you to push it away."

"But Baby, how about what he did ta my moms, and—"

He pulled me closer. "This is not about your mother, Pooquie; this is about *you*. If *you* don't want to give him a chance to be in your life because of what he did, then so be it. No one says you have to do that. But you've been carrying around so much the past sixteen years. Don't you think it's time you were able to let it out?"

We just looked at each other. I guess he was waitin fuh me ta answer. I just shrugged again.

He sighed. "Nothing says you have to love him, and nothing says you have to like him. If you hate him, so be it; and if that's what you want to tell him, do it. But it's *your* chance, Pooquie. It's your chance to say and ask everything you've wanted to. And...and I wish I had it."

He buried his face in my chest. I could feel his tears fallin on my shirt. Nah, I ain't mind. I hate it when he cries, but I love ta hold him when he does.

Ain't this somethin—he wish he could talk ta his pops, and I wish mine would go back ta where he came from. I wish I coulda brought his pops back so Little Bit could talk ta him. But just like Little Bit said, he would have somethin ta say ta him. I ain't got *shit* ta say ta that mutha-fucka, cuz there ain't *nuthin* ta say. If anything, he need ta be fucked up fuh even callin us up. Uh-huh, he bold, but he be one *stoo*pid mutha-fucka if he show his face around me. I do a D-Day on his ass. Yeah, I hate him. I *hate* his sorry ass, and I got ev'ry right ta.

And I ain't gotta see or talk ta him fuh him ta know it.

SECRET LOVERS

"Ma, I can't believe you *talkin* ta this nigga!"

It had been over two weeks since she dropped that nuclear megaton bomb on me. We hadn't touched it at all, but this was settin it off. I couldn't believe what I was seein on that little blackboard, shaped like a heart, on tha fridge; Li'l Brotha Man gave it ta her fuh Mother's Day. They had ta be *his* digits: Moms said he was livin in Jersey City, and we ain't never known anybody wit' a 201 area code.

She crossed her arms. She shook her head. She sighed. "OK, OK. We both knew it was comin. Sit."

We both did, at tha dinin room table.

"First, for the one-millionth time: I do not like you usin that word to describe *anybody*. Secondly, you need to stop walkin around here pretendin like nothing's goin on and that nothing's wrong. And *please* do not say there ain't nothin goin on and there ain't nothin wrong. The sooner you admit there is, the better. And third, you came out of *my* womb, OK, so don't fall up in this house thinkin you can question *me*."

I plopped my Gatorade down on tha table. "C'mon, Ma. Why would you wanna have anything ta do wit' him? All that sufferin he put you thru, all them changes—"

"Huh? Child, you don't know me as well as you think. This ain't one of them last-mama-on-the-couch plays, OK? You'd think I was walkin around this house the past seventeen years wearin a black veil and recitin Bible verses."

"Ma, you know what I mean."

"I'm sure I do...but why don't you tell me."

"I...I saw you, Ma. I felt it. It's...it's like, he leaves us, flat-out leaves us. How you just gonna fuhget that?"

"Who says I forgot? I'm willing to forgive, but I can't forget." She smiled. "Humph, thanks, Aretha. I tell ya, she and Randy could always come through for me."

"So, you fuhgive him?"

"Yes. I forgave him, years ago."

"Why?"

"Because my life had to go on. And my life *did* go on."

"But…you was all by yo'self—"

"I was *never* by myself. I always had *you*. I always had *me*."

"Nah, nah, that ain't what I'm talkin about…what I mean is…you know…you…you ain't had nobody."

"Oh…you mean, I wasn't gettin none?"

I choked on my Gatorade.

She giggled. "Uh-huh, *that* was what you meant."

I coughed. "Day-am, Ma, you ain't had ta put it like that."

She grinned. "Well, I *was* trying to put it tastefully."

"I just ain't talkin about *that*…I mean, I know there was times when…when—"

"—being with you or being with myself wasn't enough, right?"

"Yeah."

"Well, you're right. It wasn't enough sometimes."

"It…it's like you was cheated outa havin somebody."

Her eyebrows raised. "Excuse me?"

"You know, Ma…just havin somebody in yo' life. Just ta be wit', ta be around."

"You mean, to hold my hand and make me feel jood?"

"Yeah."

"Uh, what makes you think there *wasn't* somebody?"

Jood thing I ain't had nuthin in my mouth, cuz I woulda choked again.

"Just because you never saw another man come through this apartment doesn't mean there wasn't one in my life."

Yeah, I was gaggin. *"Huh?"*

"Uh, what part of that statement did you *not* understand?"

My hands went up. "Ma, don't *even*—"

She leaned forward. "—go there? See, I can be like Mavis: I'll *take* you there *and* bring you back."

We laughed.

I frowned. "But…if you had somebody, why you ain't tell me?"

"Because there was nothing to tell you."

"Huh?"

"There was nothing to tell you."

"But if you was seein somebody, how come I couldn't know?"

"Because it was none of your business."

"None of my—"

"—business, yes. I certainly didn't need your permission. But I didn't want to introduce any man into your life that you could become attached to. I was afraid."

"Afraid?"

"Yeah. What if you got close to him and things didn't work out between us? I'd rather you not meet any man I dated thinking he might be your next daddy than take that chance. As long as you knew it was you and me, I knew things would be OK."

"But...but I thought you was so unhappy."

She shook her head. "Once again, did I act like Juanita Moore in *Imitation of Life,* all resigned and reserved because of life's struggles and heartaches?"

"No."

"Then why would you feel that?"

"Cuz...cuz...I guess I saw ev'rybody else's moms wit' somebody."

She frowned. "Humph, most of those women were better off by themselves."

I nodded. "Yeah."

"I had a...what would I call him?...a special friend."

"Uh...how long was y'all tagetha?"

"Well...I guess you're old enough to know. We started seeing each other when you were ten. And we stopped...almost four years ago."

"Why y'all stop?"

"Because, son, all jood things must come to an end. Besides, he couldn't help but break it off."

"Why?"

"He died."

"Oh."

"You wanna see a picture of him?"

I shrugged. She got up. She grabbed our photo album. She opened it. She pulled out a grainy black-and-white picture. Tha brotha in it was tall, not really slim but not exactly stocky. He was light skin, had short curly brown hair and a recedin hairline—tha only thing that gave away his age. He wore a dark blue two-piece suit and these thick black-frame glasses. He looked like one of the Temptations. I turned it over. It said, *To Grace: Thanks for a second chance at love. Kendrick.*

She sat back down. "He's not much to look at—"

She read my mind.

"—but I could look at him for hours. He had...I don't know...I guess they call it charisma."

I gave it back. "You miss him?"

She placed it on tha table. She looked at it. She smiled. "Yes. Yes, I do, very much."

"Did you love him?"

"Yes, I did. I still do."

"But you musta been hurtin a lot, Ma, when he died. I mean, y'all was seein each other fuh eight years."

"Yeah...yeah, I was."

"I...I don't understand. I mean, if he was that special, he coulda been special ta me, too."

"Baby, you're right. You just *don't* understand. Or maybe you do and you just don't wanna see it."

"Whatcha mean?"

"You're not going to let just anybody you date meet Junior, right?"

"Nah."

"And if and when that time comes that you meet someone really special, you want to be sure, right?"

Well, I know I done met that person, but she ain't gotta know...or do she already? I just nodded yeah.

"But there is one major difference between you and Junior: he has *both* parents in his life. I didn't feel I should try to fill that space with someone else. Kendrick...oh...I haven't said his name aloud in over a year...."

I took her hand in mine. She smiled.

"Kendrick felt it was best, just like me, to leave things the way they were. He felt that there could be only one man of this house, only one man *in* this house with me. His coming in...it would've only threatened things."

"But if you loved him, Ma, I could have too. We coulda made room fuh him."

"Baby, I know you mean that when you say it, but think about it. You're twelve, thirteen years old, actin like and *lookin* like a man, and here comes this strange man claimin a place in your mother's heart and your home. You think it would have been easy to make room for him *now*, but it would have been a very different story back then. Besides, Kendrick didn't want another wife and I didn't want another husband. Humph, I guess to you he would've seemed ancient."

"How old was he?"

"Well, I was twenty-eight and he was forty-four when we first...met. But we didn't become involved until two years after that."

"How y'all hook up?"

"We hooked up...well, he would always be riding the train I took in the morning. And if I got on and he was sitting, he'd give me his seat. He was such a gentleman. He would always smile, tip his hat, and wish me a good day. It went on like that for a year. Then, one day, I forgot to wear my wedding ring. He let me sit, but this time he didn't just tip his hat and smile. He bent down and said, 'Did you finally get a divorce, or did you leave your ring and your husband at home?' " She giggled. She sighed. "He was a funny one."

"So, it started then?"

"No. I allowed him to court me for a year before we actually became…a couple."

"But…how was you able ta keep him a secret all this time?"

"Well, I'm jood at keepin a secret…unlike you."

"Me?"

"Yes, you. You always wear them all over your face."

Uh-oh, maybe she *do* know. "I do?"

"Yes, you do. Just like…you know who."

I frowned.

"Remember those weekends you stayed with D.C. and Francie because I was working double and triple shifts?"

"Yeah?"

"I was spending that time with him at his apartment here in the city or his home in Philly."

"He had two places?"

"Yes. He made his money in real estate and lived a very comfortable life. He could have easily had someone drive him to work every day. But, like he said: 'Never let anyone drive you where you want to go in life, 'cause they'll never get there when you want to.' He lived life in a simple way."

I sat back, slumped in tha chair. "I…I just can't believe you kept it from me."

She leaned forward, caressin my hands. "Baby…I didn't want to risk you getting hurt. I was taking a big chance myself. I just wanted to protect you. I'm sorry if it hurts you. I did what I thought was best for all of us." She sighed real heavy. "Kendrick made me so happy. He helped me be strong. He brought me through that rough time. And that wasn't easy for him, because he could see I still loved your father."

"Why you callin him that?"

"Now, I'm *not* going to go there, 'cause that's another show, Oprah. But I don't want you to think that I kept him from you, because I really didn't. I *did* share what I had with Kendrick with you…you just never really knew it."

"Whatcha mean?"

"He had faith in me…he had faith in us. And that gave me more faith in myself…and in me *and* you. And, of course, there are the gifts he gave you."

"Gifts?"

"Yes. The clothes, the comic books, the art equipment, that stereo mixing system, those tickets to see the Bulls play the Knicks, that autographed basketball from Michael Jordan."

"He...he gave me all *that*?"

"Yes, he did. And he bought clothes and toys for Junior."

"Oh...I ain't even get ta thank him."

"You did, baby, every time I told him how much you enjoyed what he gave you. And I never asked him to give you or Junior—any of us— anything. He wanted to."

"Uh...you been wit' somebody since he died?"

"You just a nosy child, ain't you?" She smirked.

I grinned.

She shook her head. "No, not really."

" 'No, not really?' "

"Yes. There've been one or two, but...let's just say that they were strictly around for maintenance purposes only."

I blushed.

She grinned. "Humph, just because *he* died doesn't mean *I* did."

"But if you had somethin so special wit' him, why would you want *him* back?" I groaned.

"Who *says* I do? You just don't know what you're talkin about. All you know are appearances. What you think is, what things *look* like to you. He may not be my husband by law, or by God, *or* by you, but he once was. And even though I'm sure I know the reasons, I deserve to hear from his own mouth why he decided not to be anymore."

"But Ma—"

"Don't, OK? *Don't.* You may not like it; that's your prerogative. But I need to face the man I loved."

"*Loved?*"

"Yes, *loved*. Past tense."

"But he don't deserve ta even explain it, Ma. You don't owe him nuthin—"

"I owe *myself* this." She frowned. "What are *you* afraid of?"

"Hunh?"

"You heard me. You don't want to face this? Fine." She walked over. She hugged me. She kissed my forehead. "You can go on trippin about it, but I can't wait to thank him."

"*Thank* him?"

"Yes, thank him. He walked out, no question. But he left me with the greatest gift: you."

REWIND '93

"...The End."

"Thanks, Mitch-hull."

"You're welcome. Did you like the story?"

"Yes, I did."

"I'm glad."

"I heard it before."

"You did?"

"Uh-huh."

"Well, you should've told me. I could've told you another one."

"That's OK. I like the way you told it."

"Thank you. Well, it's time to go to sleep."

"Aw, do I have to?"

"Yes, you have to. You should've been asleep by now. It's already way past your bedtime."

"OK."

"Now, let's get you under—"

"Mitch-hull, I have to say my prayers first."

"Oh, uh, OK."

"Now I lay me down to sleep, I pray the Lord my soul to keep. If I should die before I wake, I pray the Lord my soul to take. God bless my mommy, and my daddy, and my grammies, and my uncle D, and my aunt Lay-tee-sha, and Precious, and my aunt Francie, and my uncle Angel, and my aunt May-ree-sol, and Anjelica...and Mitch-hull. Amen."

"Good."

"Mitch-hull, it's not good. It's jood."

"Oh, yeah, I forgot. Sorry."

"That's OK."

"Now, are you going to be all right? It's not cold in here, is it?"

"No. I'm wearing my Ninja Turtle jammies. They always keep me warm."

"OK."

"Mitch-hull?"

"Yes?"

"My mommy said to thank you for letting me stay the weekend with you."

"You're welcome. I hope you have a good...I'm sorry, a jood time."

"I think I will."

"Do you want this light on?"

"No. You can turn it off."

"OK. Good-night, Junior."

"Mitch-hull, I told you, it's jood!"

"Oh, yes, sorry. Jood-night."

"Jood-night. Sleep tight. Don't let the bedbugs bite! Ha-ha-ha-ha!"

"Now, that is funny. Where did you learn that?"

"From my daddy... Is he asleep?"

"I don't know. I think he's taking a shower."

"If he's still awake, tell him I said jood-night."

"I will. See you in the morning."

"OK."

I DO U...U DO ME?

"Little Bit?"

"Yeah?"

"What's up wit' that?"

"What's up with what?"

"I want some."

"Come on, Raheim, I don't feel like it."

"Huh?"

"I don't feel like it. I just want to go to sleep now."

"That ain't fair."

"What ain't fair?"

"That you get some and I don't."

"That I get some and you *don't*? Raheim, what are you talking about?"

"You got some, now you don't wanna gimme mine."

"Wait, OK. First off, I didn't *get* mine. I made love to you. Secondly,
what I have that you claim is yours doesn't belong *to* you. You're not
just gonna get it because you want it. And third, nothing says that every
time we do it, both of us will make love to the other."

"Why not?"

"'Cause it's not always gonna be like that."

"Why not?"

"*Because* it doesn't have to be."

"That ain't fair, Baby."

"Raheim, are you keeping score or something? Is this a game where
you show me yours and I *have* to show you mine? I do you so you *have*
to do me?"

"Nah, nah, nah, it ain't nuthin like that."

"Well then, tell me: *what* isn't fair about this?"

"Baby, it's like...we ain't finished. I'm just gettin started, and you just
wanna end it."

"Raheim, there are gonna be times when one of us won't want to.
Like last night. I wanted to take the Pooquie plunge, but you didn't

want me to. I didn't get all bent out of shape about it. Now the tables are turned. What makes it so different now?"

"It just ain't fair, Baby. You do whatcha wanna do ta me and then just turn yo' back—"

"Ex*cuse* me? I didn't force you to do anything you didn't want to, Raheim. You begged me for it, remember?"

"I ain't beg you fuh *nuthin.*"

"Oh, *no*? Then what do you call 'Please, just a little bit, Little Bit, *pleeze*'?"

"That ain't no beggin."

"It ain't, hunh? Funny…that's what *you* call it when I wanna give it to *you.*"

"Don't *even* go there, Baby."

"Raheim, the world is not going to end if I don't *give* you some, is it?"

"It's like you…you takin advantage of me."

"*Taking advantage of you?* Raheim, you're being silly—"

"I *ain't* bein silly!"

"Look, Raheim, it's obvious that we see this differently. I'm sorry you do. I don't know why you have a hang-up about this—"

"I ain't *got* no *fuckin* hang-up."

"Well, it seems like it to me. Look, you don't have to be…you don't have to pout about it.… You know, you look so cute when you do that, just like Junior. Oh, come on, Pooquie. Talk to me…Pooquie?"

"*Don't* fuckin touch me!"

"Come on, now, don't be like that."

"*Get off!*"

"All right, all right, fine. I won't touch you, I'll get off you. But you…where are you going? Raheim? OK, OK, fine, just run away, like you always do when you can't have your way."

Slam!

"*And don't think I'm gonna run after you. I'm going to sleep. Good-night!*"

COMIN 2 A HEAD

Tha shit really hit tha fan when me 'n' Li'l Brotha Man was eatin some of my Baby's famous sweet-potato pie (Moms can't touch him there; I guess he can make it like that cuz, like my man Domino say, he tasty like that). Just like his daddy, Li'l Brotha Man wanted another slice. Little Bit took our plates and went in tha kitchen.

"You'd think I'd know by now that you two can't just have one slice," Little Bit said, gettin tha pie out tha fridge.

"You *should* know that by now, Mitch-hull," agreed Li'l Brotha Man.

"Thank you, Junior." Little Bit winked and smiled at me.

"Daddy, watch this." Li'l Brotha Man started blowin bubbles in his chocolate milk. He knew I ain't like that.

"What you think you doin?" I asked.

"Watch, Daddy, watch."

I tapped his arm. "Li'l Brotha Man, stop."

"Daddy, I'm trying to show you a trick I learned in school."

"What I say?"

"But Daddy—"

I grabbed him by tha arm, pullin him out his seat, shakin him. His glass and straw fell on tha table, and so did tha chocolate milk. "What tha *fuck* I say about doin that shit?" I started spankin him.

I ain't realize what I was doin until I heard Li'l Brotha Man 'n' Little Bit screamin fuh me ta stop. I did.

I let go of his arm. He grabbed it, runnin ta Little Bit, flyin inta his arms, cryin.

Aw, *shit*. I *really* fucked up.

But then I made things worse: I got up and walked out. That was a *stoo*pid-ass thing ta do, too. But I just couldn't believe what I just did, and I ain't know what ta say or do.

I came back when I knew Li'l Brotha Man would be sleep. But I ain't count on findin Little Bit waitin fuh me outside, sittin on tha stoop.

He looked at his watch. "It's about time."

I came inside tha gate. "Whatcha doin out here?"

"What *you* think?"

I sat down a few steps below him. "What about Li'l—"

"He's asleep. The reason, I'm sure, why you've come back now."

Uh-huh, he knows me.

I sighed. "Uh…how he doin?"

He sighed too. "He…hurts. But I'm sure the emotional pain is worse than the physical."

I looked down.

"You shouldn't have left, Raheim."

"I…I know."

"You say that a lot. But sometimes I think even when you *do* know, you don't care."

"I do, too."

"Then why did you leave?"

I stood up. I shrugged. "Cuz I…I…"

He stood too. "He wanted his father. You hurt him, and only you could make him feel better. I can't be his daddy."

"You *ain't* his daddy."

"I'm *not?* You forced me to be just that tonight."

I ain't say nuthin, cuz he was right.

He crossed his arms. "I'm not gonna ask you what's wrong, because I know what it is."

I looked at him, then looked away.

"Well, stop takin it out on *us,* OK? You been walkin around for the past few weeks groanin and grumblin, actin like the whole world is against you. You got a problem, deal with it. *Face* it. Don't make it everybody else's."

He turned and went upstairs. I followed him.

Standin in tha hall, he pulled me ta him. "He's in our bed. You stay with him. I'll sleep out here tonight." He kissed me, and I watched him go in tha livin room.

I'm so fuckin lucky ta have him.

I walked inta our room. I kicked off my shoes, slid off my jeans, pulled off my shirt, and climbed inta tha bed, scoopin Li'l Brotha Man up in my arms. He woke up, rubbin his eyes. Thanks ta tha streetlights comin in tha room, I could tell they was red and puffy.

I rubbed his face. I tried ta smile. "Hey, Li'l Brotha Man."

"Hi, Daddy." His voice was really low. He was talkin thru his throat, like he was hoarse.

"Uh, how ya doin?"

He shrugged. "OK."

"Uh...I'm sorry, my man. I was punishin you fuh somethin I ain't want ya doin...and I took somethin else out on ya. I shouldn'ta done that. I ain't never gonna do it again. I'm sorry I hurt ya.... I hurt me, too, doin that ta you.... I love you, Li'l Brotha Man. Do ya still love me?"

He looked in my eyes. He seemed kinda confused, but he nodded yes.

"Uh...can ya fuhgive me?"

He nodded yes again.

"Can I have a big hug?"

Yes, again.

He put his arms around my neck, squeezin me tight. It felt so jood. I kissed his forehead. "Let's go ta sleep, a'ight?"

"OK."

He found his fav'rite spot, layin his head on my chest. I wrapped him up.

He tried ta get his little arms around me, squeezin me as tight as he could. "Jood-night, Daddy."

I sighed. "Jood-nite, Li'l Brotha Man."

He was fast asleep, snorin up a storm, when my tears started fallin.

REWIND '93

"It's about Uncle D."
"What about him, Daddy?"
"He got shot."
"He got…shot?"
"Yeah."
"With a gun?"
"Yeah."
"Is he hurt real bad?"
"He…he gone, Li'l Brotha Man. He dead."
"Dead?"
"Yeah."
"You mean…he in heaven?"
"Yeah."
"Like Nanny and Grampy?"
"Yeah."
"Who shot him, Daddy?"
"This guy me 'n' Uncle D grew up wit'."
"You grew up with him?"
"Yeah. We lived in tha same neighborhood and went ta school tagetha."
"Why did he do it, Daddy?"
"I…I don't know."
"Oh…"
"We gonna bury him on Wednesday."
"Bury him?"
"Yeah. When you bury somebody, you take 'em ta tha cemetery."
"A cemetery?"
"Yeah."
"Um…is that the place where they have, uh, a head-stone?"
"Yeah."
"We see them sometimes when we ride in the car."
"Yeah. There's gonna be a funeral, too."

"I know what that is."

"Oh, yeah?"

"Yes. Grammy told me what it is. That's when the family and the friends say good-bye to, uh, the person who went to heaven."

"Right."

"Is Grammy going?"

"No, my man. She don't like funerals."

"Is Mommy going?"

"Yeah. Me 'n' mommy goin. Do you wanna go?"

"Um, yes. I think so."

"You sure?"

"Uh-huh. I wanna say good-bye."

"Now, you ain't never seen nobody in a casket. You might get scared. I know they scare me."

"A cas-ket?"

"Yeah. That's what they lay tha dead person in."

"Oh. I won't be scared."

"You ain't?"

"No. And you don't have to be scared, Daddy. I can hold your hand if you want me to."

"You will?"

"Yes."

"Thanks."

"You're welcome. Daddy?"

"Yeah?"

"What will he wear in the cas-ket?"

"A suit."

"Will his eyes be open?"

"No, they gonna be closed."

"Like...he asleep?"

"Yeah."

"Can I touch him?"

"Yeah, you can. You can touch him. You can kiss him good-bye if ya wanna."

"I can?"

"Yeah."

"Will he feel it?"

"Yeah, Li'l Brotha Man. He will."

"I think I wanna do it."

"A'ight."

"Daddy?"

"Yeah?"

"*Why did he have to…go to heaven?*"

"*I don't know, my man…I don't know.*"

"*I wish he didn't have to go.*"

"*Me too.*"

"*I hope he's OK.*"

"*Me too.*"

"*Daddy?*"

"*Yeah?*"

"*Am I gonna go to heaven?*"

"*Uh…uh…yeah…yeah, you will, Li'l Brotha Man, but not now. A long time from now. Not till you real old.*"

"*Are you gonna go to heaven?*"

"*Yeah. But not until I'm real old too.*"

"*You promise?*"

"*Uh…uh…I…I can't promise ya that, Li'l Brotha Man.*"

"*Why not, Daddy?*"

"*Cuz…cuz I don't wanna go till I'm real old, but…I can't control what's gonna happen in tha future.… If I could, Uncle D still be here wit' us…you understand?*"

"*I…I think so.*"

"*But as long as I can help it, I'm always gonna be here wit' you. I ain't goin nowhere. Believe that. A'ight?*"

"*OK.*"

"*Can I have a hug?*"

He gave me a big one.

"*Daddy?*"

"*Yeah?*"

"*I miss Uncle D.*"

"*I do too, Li'l Brotha Man. I do too.*"

MOMENT OF TRUTH

"I'm glad you called me."

If I was gonna do this, I had ta be comf'table, I had ta be someplace where, if I felt like it, I could tell him ta get tha fuck out. I ain't even hafta ask Little Bit; he said I could talk ta him at our place. I know I'm callin it *our* place when it's really Little Bit's, but I *feel* like it's my place too. I couldn't talk ta him at my house—meanin tha scene of tha crime. That would mean we on common ground, and there ain't no way we could be. That shit would be just too fuckin spooky. And I ain't wanna go nowhere he wanted, cuz I ain't want *him* ta be comf'table. He ain't got no right ta be. And even in my 'n' Little Bit's space, I was gonna make sure of that: I wasn't offerin him nuthin ta drink, not even a seat.

He checked out tha livin room. "This is a nice place you got."

He ain't hafta know it wasn't mine. "Yeah, I know."

"So, son—"

Son. I *hated* tha way that shit sound. He ain't had no right callin me that. "*Don't* call me that."

He put his hands in his pockets. He nodded. He sighed. "So, uh…how long have you lived—"

"Man, just cut tha bullshit, a'ight? You ain't come here ta talk about where I live. We s'pose ta be talkin about where you *ain't* been livin tha past seventeen *fuckin* years."

He rubbed his chin. "Yeah, yeah…you right. That's what we are here to talk about." He looked at me. "I know you got a lot to ask and a lot to tell me, so go on. I'm listenin."

I just glared at him. "Nah. See, you wrong. I ain't really got shit ta say *to* you, cuz there ain't nuthin ta say. But I only got one thing ta ask."

He nodded. "All right. What is it?"

"Why?"

"Why?"

"Yeah, why you here?"

"I'm here because you wanted to see me."

"You know what tha fuck I'm sayin. Why you come *back* here?"

"You really want to know?"

I threw up my hands. "I'm askin tha question."

"This ain't gonna be easy...." He sighed. "I'm here because... because it was time."

"It was time? Time fuh *what?*"

"It was time for me to...face myself."

"Face yo'self? What tha *fuck* you talkin about?"

He sighed again. "It was time for me to face what I had created, what I left behind. You."

"Ah, yeah. And how about tha *wife* you left behind?"

"That's somethin you don't have to worry about."

"*Say what?* Who tha *fuck* you think been livin wit' her all this time?"

"She and I can handle that, all right? The short answer for you: what I couldn't do I knew she could do—without me."

"Man, she couldn't be no man of tha house and shit. That was *yo'* job. And you ain't had no right just passin it off on her. I don't call that bein no man."

"You don't?"

"*Hell*-fuckin-no. All you did was step. That don't make you nuthin but a *punk.*"

He shrugged. "If that's what I am to you, fine. But I know I made the right choice. The proof is right in front of me that I did."

"Yeah, just talk that shit now, a'ight, bein we was able ta make it wit'out yo' ass bein around."

"That's right, you all did. But I *was* around."

"*Hunh?*"

"I left behind the one thing I knew Grace could count on."

"Man, you ain't makin no fuckin sense."

"I would always be on her case over the way she was with you. I'd tell her, 'You gonna make him a mama's boy, woman.' You probably don't remember—"

I do....

"Grace, leave the boy be."

"What you mean, 'leave him be'?"

"What I just say? You always smotherin him."

"Well, he is my baby."

"He ain't no baby, woman, he a boy, a growin boy who don't need to be up under his mama's titties all the time."

"Errol! *That's a terrible thing to say—*"

"*Well, sometimes the truth ain't nice. You keep it up, he gonna grow up to be a punk—*"

"*A punk?*"

"*Yeah, a punk.*"

"*And what is that supposed to mean?*"

"*What I just say. Damn, you got a hearin problem? A punk, a sissy, a faggot, a girl.*"

"*Showing my son how much I love him and letting him see that there is nothin wrong with showin his love for me ain't gonna make him none of those things.*"

"*Yeah, well, we see what happens when he start wantin to play with dolls and jumpin rope and wantin to get with other boys....*"

...but he ain't gotta know.

He shook his head. "—but she didn't stop. And you just clung to her. I finally saw that what you two had...you both had that strength. And you got that strength from her, not me. And I wanted that strength, that closeness from her, but she couldn't give it to me 'cause it wasn't in me to accept it. I was walkin around all the time feelin sorry for my damn self. I couldn't take care of my own fuckin family, and I blamed every damn body...including your mother and you."

"Me?"

"Yeah. I would look at you two, knowing that you're both mine, all I got, and be so proud. But sometimes...I was jealous of my own child. I was jealous of my own family. And I couldn't be a father to you and a husband to her, feelin that way...and that's why I left. I knew your mother would take care of you and you would take care of her. I knew your mother would be better off without me. And you would too."

"Man, how you sound? You expect me ta be*lieve* that shit? How would you know what tha fuck is best fuh anybody? How *you* know we was better off wit'out you?"

"I know 'cause, like I said before, I was around. I saw it with my own eyes."

"Hunh?"

"Yeah, I saw it all. You think I could just walk away and forget about you two? I watched your mother. Yeah, she was hurt I left. It hurt me like hell to see her those first few days, those first few months. Her face, the way she walked.... But I think even she knew that that was the way it had to be. She struggled, workin and raisin you, but she did it all—and she didn't have me standin in her way.

"And you. I saw you grow up. I saw you get your first bike—"

"Boy, what you think you doin?"

"Hunh?"

"Don't 'hunh' me! I bought that bike with training wheels for you to ride with 'em, not take 'em off."

"Ma, I don't need them wheels. I can ride it without them."

"How you know? You don't even know how to ride a bike."

"C'mon, Ma, I can do it."

"All right. But if you fall flat on your face, don't come cryin to me."

He laughed. "You *did* fall flat on your face and tried not to cry about it, but there were some tears. But you got back up, again and again and again, till you was ridin it, scraped knees and bruised arms and dirt on the face and everything."

I ain't believe it. "Nah, Moms musta told you—"

"And I saw when you and Derrick took Crystal and Laticia to their prom—"

"Yo, Brotha Man, hurry up, tha limo is here!"

"Good evening, Raheim."

"Hey, Miss J."

"My, my, my, don't you look nice in that tux. You got a hot date?"

"Yeah, uh, me 'n' D.C., we takin our ladies ta their prom. But we may never get there if this slow-ass nigga don't hurry up. Oh, uh, sorry, Miss J."

"That's all right, son."

"A'ight, a'ight, man, I'm here."

"It's about...man, fix yo' tie...and where's Laticia's corsage?"

"Hunh?"

"You ain't get one, did ya?"

"I knew there was somethin I fuhgot. Ah, shit! Uh, sorry, Miss Jones."

"Quite all right, son."

"Day-am, Brotha Man, now we gotta make a detour and get her one."

"Why? She don't need it, cuz she got me."

"Uh-huh, well, that ain't what she gonna think or say when she see me pin one on Sunshine. Now, we gotta find someplace open that sells 'em. That's mo' money we gotta spend burnin up gas."

"You know, boys, Mr. Wilson may have some—"

"That's right. Yo, run on down there, man."

"Run? Brotha, we got wheels. We can ride."

"Man, tha time we wastin standin here talkin about it, you coulda been gone and back by now. Go get it while I call and let 'em know we leavin."

"A'ight. I'm outy."

"Thanks Miss J."

"You're welcome. And you both have a good time."

"We will."

"—I saw when you brought Raheim the III home—"

"Yo, Raheim, is that yo' kid, man? Let me see him, Brotha."

"Day-am, nigga, let me get out tha fuckin cab first, a'ight? And don't be gettin so fuckin close, you don't need ta be breathin on him."

"Raheim, don't be nasty."

"Sunshine, I ain't bein nasty. You think this nigga would get tha bag from you."

"Uh, I'm sorry. Ya want me ta carry that fuh ya?"

"No, D.C., I have it, thank you. It's just baby formula and diapers. It's not heavy."

"Let him carry it, Sunshine."

"Will you just stop bein so jumpy and please hold that baby right? You gonna drop him."

"Yo, I got him, don't worry. I ain't gonna drop my Li'l Brotha Man."

"Yo' who?"

"My Li'l Brotha Man."

"Yo, I thought you was gonna give him yo' name?"

"I did."

"So why ya call him that?"

"Cuz it's just my own special name fuh him."

"Why?"

"Cuz that's who he is."

"But yo, how about me, Brotha?"

"What about you?"

"I thought I was yo' Brotha Man?"

"Yeah, man. You just ain't tha only one no mo', a'ight? Now, will you get out tha way so we can go upstairs? Tha least you can do is open tha fuckin do' fuh us."

"A'ight, man, a'ight. You got it."

"—and I saw when you all buried Derrick—"

"Ma, you need anything?"

"No, baby. It's been a long day. I just want to go to bed. And I know you need to too."

"Nah...I just wanna walk some."

"Baby, ain't no use in you wanderin these streets. Whatever you lookin for you ain't gonna find out here. Come on upstairs. I'll fix you a hot-oil bath so you can relax."

"Nah, nah, Ma, I'll be a'ight."

"OK. Are you coming back tonight?"

"I...if you don't hear my key in tha next hour, nah, I ain't."

"OK.... Baby?"

"Yeah, Ma?"

"D.C. would have been proud of you today. And he wants to be proud of you always. And I am proud of you."

"Thanks, Ma."

"I love you, baby."

"I love you too."

I was seriously buggin out. It's like, my mouth was open but wasn't nuthin comin out. Tha mutha-fucka just told me my whole life story and shit. "Man, you...you lyin...you ain't see none of that shit."

"How much you wanna bet? I can tell you the exact dates, the days of the week, the times, and the weather. I was there."

"But you *wasn't* there."

"Yeah, I know. I couldn't be there the way you wanted me to or the way Grace wanted me to, but I was there in the only way I *could* be."

"Man, you could too, you just ain't wanna—"

"Man, will you quit tellin me what the *fuck* I felt and what the *fuck* I shoulda done?! Until you in *my* position, until you walk in *my* shoes, you can't say what the *fuck* you would do or say. You don't know every damn thing. You wanted to hear the story, I'm tellin it, so just *fuckin* listen."

Somethin had changed in him. It was like he was really cryin out fuh me ta listen. His voice really didn't get loud. It was in his eyes. And fuh tha first time, I felt like I had ta *really* listen ta him. Somehow, my feet took two steps back, and I landed in a chair. He looked down at me, and I paid attention, not exactly lookin him in tha eye.

He put his palms tagetha and pointed his hands at me. "You need-ed someone to look up to, and I'd rather you hated me for *not* bein in your life than hate me for bein in your life and not bein able to show you the way 'cause I didn't know the way myself." He backed up. "So...do you hate me?"

"What tha fuck *you* think?"

"I don't know what to think...that's why I'm askin."

"Yeah," I blurted out, sayin it like I meant it.

But he wasn't havin it. He grinned. "Both you and your mother...y'all needed someone to believe in. But how could y'all believe in somebody who ain't believe in himself?"

I stood up. "So, whatcha sayin, now you believe in yo'self, you got yo' shit tagetha, and you wanna come back?"

He laughed. "Hmmm…hearin somebody else sayin it, it's funny. It's like a joke. You know, like somethin you'd hear on Oprah: 'I believe in myself.' 'I found myself.' But yeah, it's true."

"*Yeah-mutha-fuckin-right!* And we just s'pose ta let you back in and just fuhget about ev'rything cuz you *found* yo'self? Mutha-fucka, you found yo'self too *fuckin* late."

"Son, I—"

"And I *told* you not ta call me that! I *ain't* yo' son. What's a son ta you? *Nuthin!* See, I know. I know what it's like ta *have* a son. My Li'l Brotha Man, he my all, he my heart, and I could *never* leave him. I can call him my son cuz he is. But I ain't *never* been that ta you."

He sighed real heavy. "All right, all right…you *ain't* my son. But let me tell you somethin: no matter *what* you do, no matter *where* you go, no matter *who* you become in this life, you gonna be takin *my* blood with ya. That's *my* blood in you. That's *my* blood in *your* son. *My* blood…and ain't nothin *ever* gonna change that."

I turned my back on him.

"Raheim…you can hate me if you want, I can't stop you. And I don't expect you to understand me or what I did right now—or ever. It took me all these years to understand *myself.* And you and your mother…y'all can't just let me back in, I know that. I can't walk into somethin that ain't there. There ain't no space there for me."

"Uh-huh, if you really believed that shit you wouldn'ta come back."

"Well, I believe that, and it's because I believe that that I *did* come back. I don't expect you or your mother to forget or forgive me, and I can't expect to be a husband to her or a father to you.…"

When he said that, my whole body just jerked. He musta saw it, cuz he stopped talkin. He was quiet; I guess he was kinda bothered by my reaction. I ain't give a shit. But then his hand touched my shoulder.

"*Man, don't fuckin touch me!*" I yelled. I really wanted ta punch tha shit outa him. But ain't no way I could go on like that. I wasn't gonna give him tha satisfaction of knowin he got me so fuckin worked up.

He lifted his hands as if ta say, *I give up.* "I…I would love to be a part of your lives because now…now I'm ready to be."

"Ya know, I'm just so mutha-fuckin happy fuh yo' ass. You ready, and cuz you ready that means ev'rybody else gotta be, right?"

"No, that's not what I'm sayin. I just want you to know that I am sorry for what I did because of how it made you feel. But I'm *not* sorry I did what I did, because it had to be this way. You asked why I came back. I came back because I don't want you or your mother to hate me: it takes too much out of ya to do that. It drains…your spirit. I know. I spent so much time hatin myself for who I wasn't and then hatin myself for what

I put you two through.... It ain't fair to you or your mother that y'all had to carry that anger, all that hurt around about me, and I didn't want y'all goin through the rest of your lives thinkin it was somethin you said, somethin you did...somethin you ain't say *or* do. I think I owed you both that...and Li'l Brotha Man, too."

That's when I saw red. "Nah, nah, mutha-fucka, you can just fuh*get* that. You think I'm gonna let you do ta him whatcha did ta me?"

"I would never do that—"

"Talk is cheap, mutha-fucka, and that's all you seem ta have goin fuh you. Li'l Brotha Man is mine. Ya hear me? *Mine.* And you ain't gonna have *no* fuckin parta him. You think you so *fuckin* slick, callin tha house and talkin ta him, and talkin all that shit ta Moms. That shit might work on her, but it ain't gonna work on me. You...I'm tired of listenin ta yo' bullshit. I ain't got nuthin else ta say ta you." I headed fuh tha do'.

I know he wanted ta say somethin, but what could he say? He just walked behind me. I opened tha do' fuh him and stepped outa tha way. I looked at the ceilin. He just looked at me. He walked out, and I slammed tha do' behind him. I stomped inta tha bedroom and fell on tha bed on my back. My heart was beatin so fast, it seemed like my breathin couldn't keep up wit' it. I closed my eyes, but that didn't stop tha tears from comin out.

"So, how do you feel?"

"I...I don't know, Baby."

"Do you feel better?"

"No."

"Um...are you sorry you did it?"

I shrugged. He rubbed my face. I squeezed him real tight.

"Uh...he asked me if I hated him."

"What did you say?"

"Whatcha think, Baby?" I snapped.

"I don't know, Pooquie, that's why I asked."

"Sorry."

"That's OK."

"I told him I did."

"Do you?"

"I...I know I did. But...but..."

"You don't have to hate him, Pooquie."

"I do too."

"No, you don't. Why do you?"

"Cuz of what he did, Baby. I could never stop hatin him fuh that."

"But you just said that you *use* to."

"I…I just hafta."

"No, you don't."

"I do too."

"Why?"

"Cuz…cuz I…"

"Pooquie, you hated him, but you got past it. That isn't a bad thing. You don't have to hate him, because this is not about getting even. You might have felt some of that hate seeing him, but just because he reappears, that doesn't mean you have to start hating him all over again."

"Baby, you…you just don't understand."

"I know, Pooquie. But I'm trying to."

"I…I…"

"Tell me. You can tell me."

"I…I always felt it was his fault."

"What was his fault?"

"That…that…I'm this way."

"What way?"

"*You* know."

"No, I don't."

"You do."

"Maybe I do, maybe I don't. What way, Pooquie?"

I broke away from him and got up from tha couch. "You know, Baby, *day*-am, why I gotta—"

"—say it? Because you *don't*. You never do."

He sat and waited.

"A'ight, a'ight…that I'm…that I'm a *faggot*, a'ight? And it's all be-cuz of *him*."

He got up from tha couch. He stood in front of me. "Pooquie, you're not a faggot."

"That's what it comes down ta, don't it?"

"No, it doesn't."

I put my hands in my pockets. I sighed. "He wasn't there, Baby…. Maybe if he was…I wouldn'ta turned out like this."

"Pooquie, how can you think that?"

"That's how it…it happens."

"It doesn't just *happen*, Pooquie."

"It do too, Little Bit."

"You did not *become* gay because your father wasn't in your life."

"How you know, Little Bit?"

He smiled. "Well, I think I should know something about this subject."

"Yeah. *You* ain't grow up wit' yo' pops, and look."

"Pooquie, I did not become gay because my father was not in my life."

"How *you* know?"

"I think I would know. Besides, if what you said was true, then why isn't my brother gay?"

Jood question. I ain't have no answer.

He put his arms around my waist. "Why, Pooquie...how did you come to believe a thing like that?"

"All of us, Baby...all of us ain't had our pops at home when we was growin up...me, Brotha Man, Angel, Rockhead, Smooth...and look..."

"Pooquie, being gay is not something you *become*. If sexuality were airborne, then we all could just become gay, straight, bi, whatever we wanted at any given moment."

"But, Baby—"

"Gene is right: you just love doin da butt, don't you?"

I smiled. It was tha first time I did all day.

He frowned. "Let me ask you a question. Do you think being in Junior's life means he will *not* be homosexual?"

"*Hunh?*"

"You heard."

"Li'l Brotha Man *ain't* gonna be that way."

"How do *you* know?"

"Cuz I—"

"'Cause you know, right? You *don't*. Whoever he is he will be because it is a part of who he is. It isn't something you or anybody else can control. And *it* is a part of you. It's always been there."

"No, it ain't."

"Yes, it has—"

I broke away. "*No, it ain't!* How tha *fuck* you gonna tell me what I been feelin? *I* know what I been feelin. *You* don't know. You don't know. You don't know...."

My hands started shakin.

"Pooquie, what is it? What's wrong?"

I wanted ta open my mouth, but it wouldn't open. My whole body just started shakin. It was like somethin was tryin ta get out. Somethin was tryin ta get out. And it did.

"*Rrraaauuuggghhh!*"

I fell ta my knees. Tha tears was just comin outa me like a ocean. I don't know what I was sayin, but I remember Little Bit sayin "It's OK, it's OK" and cradlin and rockin me.

I woke up tha next mornin, on tha carpet, in his arms.

TAKE A CHILL PILL

I never thought I'd be tha one ta say ta Little Bit, "I need some space." But I did just that.

I ain't know exactly why I needed it; I couldn't really say what it was I had ta check. But whatever it was, it came outa me like a...like a... day-am, I can't even describe *how* it came out. Ain't no words fuh it. All I know is, my world ain't my world no mo'. My world ain't been turned upside down, like when Li'l Brotha Man was born. It ain't been turned inside out, like when me 'n' Little Bit got back tagetha. It's just been *turned*.

And that shit is scary.

I ain't do nuthin but lay around tha house, just starin. I wasn't thinkin about nuthin. Can yo' mind really go blank? That's what it seemed like. It's like...there was no questions in my mind, cuz there ain't no mo' questions. Ya know, you searchin 'n' searchin 'n' searchin, tryin ta figure out tha punch line. You finally get tha answer—an answer you might not be cool wit'—and you left wit' nuthin. My mind been on a trip, and now that trip is...over?

Uh-huh, and *that* shit is scary too.

Moms knew ta just leave me alone; she just shook her head, sayin, "There he goes again, Moody's Mood." Little Bit called a few times— yeah, just ta hear my voice (I love it when he sings that song by Oleta) and just ta say "I love you" (that's one tune by Stevie I hate). He knew if I needed him, I would let him know.

My break doin nuthin was broke when Sunshine came by tha house ta go over tha plans fuh Li'l Brotha Man's birthday–graduation party. She was just goin on about Li'l Brotha Man gettin inta that academy, how it's such a jood opp, and how we got so much work ta do befo' school starts ta get him ready. Then...

"Uh, your mother told me."

"Told you what?"

"About your father."

"Who?"

"Your father."

"*Who?*"

She sucked her teeth. She sighed real heavy. "Why do you wanna play that game?"

"I ain't playin *shit.*"

"She said you met him, that you two talked."

"She say a lota things she shouldn't."

"What did he say?"

"Nuthin you need ta know."

"Hunh?"

"You heard."

"Well, I do need to know, and I wanna talk about it."

"Ain't nuthin ta talk about."

"Yes, there is. We are talking about our son's grandfather."

"Look, just drop it, a'ight?"

"No, I *don't* wanna just drop it. I believe I have something to say about it."

"You got somethin ta say about it. *You* got somethin ta say about it? What tha fuck *you* got ta say about bein left behind by yo' own blood? What tha fuck *you* got ta say about havin ta be there fuh yo' moms when she cryin her eyes out and shit?"

She leaned back in her chair. She folded her arms across her chest.

I leaned back, lettin my palms fall on my thighs. "Come on. I'm waitin ta hear what *you* got ta say."

She sighed. She looked down.

I leaned forward. I put my hand ta my ear. "What's that I hear? What's that? Nuthin?" I nodded. "Uh-huh. I *thought* so." I put my arms on tha table.

She leaned up. She grabbed my right hand. She squeezed it. "OK. I don't have anything to say about that. But what I do have to say is that Junior deserves to have both a father *and* a grandfather. And if he finds out one day that his grandfather came back and his daddy kept him from him, what do you think *he's* going to say?"

"He ain't gonna say nuthin, cuz he ain't gonna find out."

"He's not? Don't count on it."

"You ain't tellin him a *God*-day-am thang."

"*Don't* curse at me, and don't *fuckin* tell me what to do, OK?"

Wham! Now, this was wild: Sunshine almost never curse. I knew she musta been too thru wit' me. I coulda called her out about cursin at me, but…as many times I done it ta her? She deserved that one. I did too.

"I won't have to tell him anything. He knows you. He'll know some-thing is up, because it is not going to go away. And it's like my mother always says: Everything in the dark comes to the light."

"Some things need ta *stay* in the dark."

"Why?"

"Cuz, Sunshine, he don't *need* that mutha-fucka. You want him ta hurt Li'l Brotha Man tha way he hurt me?"

"I don't think he came back to hurt Junior, or your mother, or you."

"How *you* know? You don't know him—"

"And neither do *you,* and that's my point. You're not protecting Junior from him by keeping them apart, you're just trying to punish him. And you might think you're protecting yourself, but you're gonna end up punishing yourself, just like you always do."

"Huh?"

"You can't go on keepin secrets like this, Raheim. They eat at you, they haunt you. I should know."

"How *you* know?"

"How do I know? How could I *not* know? Everything you've done, everything you've said in the seven years I've known you…it's all been influenced by him in one way or another. He may not have been *in* your life the past seventeen years, but he's always been there."

I looked down.

"You've tried to erase him. But not even naming our son Junior can do it. And every time I see you *with* Junior…I can see it in your eyes. I know you are trying to give him what you never had. But you can only give Junior what *he* needs. You can't relive what never was through someone else. Your being a jood father doesn't make everything even."

I took my hand away. I leaned back.

"Not only is it not fair to Junior to keep his grandfather away from him, it's also unfair to you."

I pointed at myself. *"Me?"*

"Yes, *you.* He might not ever feel like a father to you or be like a father to you. But the one thing he *can* do is bring you closer to being at peace. You can't keep walkin around with those demons, measuring your life, your relationship with Junior, against him."

I looked down. I closed my eyes. She got up, stood behind me, and started massagin my shoulders.

"Don't you wanna get rid of all this?"

My eyes popped open. "All what?"

"All *this?*" She ground her hands inta me. "I've felt it all this time. It's never gone away. It's time to let it go."

I lifted my head. I sat up and sat back. She kept on.

I sighed. "Y'all seem ta know so fuckin much, huh?"

"Who is y'all?"

"You. Moms. Li—" Ah, *shit.* I had ta catch myself. "Mitch." Day-am, that sounded so funny comin outa my mouth. I can count tha number of times I said his name.

"We can't help *but* know. You're such an open book."

I laughed. "I am?"

"Yeah."

"What that mean?"

"It means you try to hide, you try to disguise, but you don't do a jood job. You wanna be figured out. You wanna be *read.*"

"I do?"

"Yes. You're still a mystery, still trying to be a mystery to me, your mother, Junior, everybody, even yourself. But ya know what?"

"What?"

Her arms draped my chest, and she kissed me on my right cheek. "It's time the mystery was solved."

REWIND '93

"*Why him?*"

"*Why* not *him?*"

"*Well, I hardly know him.*"

"*I know him.*"

"*You hardly know him too. I mean, you said you met this past summer. A few months is not a long time.*"

"*It's enuff time ta know he's tha one.*"

"*I...I just think it should be a family member.*"

"*Brotha Man wasn't blood.*"

"*No, he wasn't, but he was like family. I was thinking about Geoff.*"

"*Nah, nah, Sunshine, fuh*get *that.*"

"*What do you have against Geoff?*"

"*I ain't got nuthin against him. I just don't like him.*"

"*Why? He's never done anything to you.*"

"*What tha fuck he know about kids? He don't have any.*"

"*Mitchell doesn't have any.*"

"*No, he don't, but kids don't run 'n' hide when he around like they do wit' Jeff. Li'l Brotha Man don't like him.*"

"*That's not true.*"

"*It is too, Sunshine. He a fake, he a* flake, *and Li'l Brotha Man can see it. Ev'ry time he come home fuh Christmas, he always showin pictures of them dead-head surfer boys from Beverly Hills he be hangin wit' and some white girl he bonin. Ha, he'd* hafta *be bonin a white girl, cuz ain't no sista stoo*pid enuff *ta sleep wit' his wanna-be-white ass.*"

"*Raheim, he isn't a wanna-be because he is half white.*"

"*Uh-huh, and* that's *why he so mixed up. I wouldn't have no problem wit' him if he would just accept all of who he is, not just* half. *And he* know *his moms ain't spell his name like that on his birth certificate.*"

"*Well, he's my cousin, and I love him.*"

"*Ain't nobody stoppin you from lovin that mutha-fucka. That don't mean I gotta.*"

"*Geoff* wants *to be his godfather; he's always wanted to be. And I've practically promised him he can be.*"

"*So, unpromise him. And what tha fuck you doin, tellin somebody they can be somethin ta* my *son wit'out askin me first?*"

"*I just love the way he becomes* your *son when there is a decision to be made about him. And I obviously ain't the only one promisin folks things.*"

"*Mitchell don't even know about this.*"

"*Well, how do you know he* wants *to be Junior's godfather?*"

"*He already* act *like it. From tha first time they met, they been like* that. *All Li'l Brotha Man been talkin 'bout fuh tha past three months is Mitch-hull this 'n' Mitch-hull that. You heard him yo'self. I'm tellin ya, he jood people, Sunshine.*"

"*Well, I don't know. I just don't feel right saying someone can be his guardian but they are a total stranger...to me. I'd feel better about it if I got to know him.*"

"*Fine. I ain't got no problem wit' that.*"

"*OK, OK. I'm not makin any promises, but I'll give him a chance. Give me his number.*"

"*Huh?*"

"*Give me Mitchell's number so we can talk.*"

"*Uh...uh...y'all can't.*"

"*Why not?*"

"*Cuz he...he been outa tha city...doin some assignment fuh his job.*"

"*He's* still *away? Junior told me a few weeks back that he was.*"

"*Yeah. He just got it like that. That's how me 'n' Li'l Brotha Man got on tha cover of his magazine.*"

"*Hmmm, that was a really nice cover.... Junior does miss him.*"

"*I know.*"

"*Well, when will he be back?*"

"*Uh, next week, on Columbus Day.*"

"*OK. Hmmm, now I have to figure out what I'm gonna tell Geoff.*"

"*That's simple: just tell him tha* Blacker *man won.*"

"*Raheim!*"

"*But let me ask Mitchell if he wanna do it first, befo' you be quizzin him and shit.*"

"*I won't be quizzin him.*"

"*You will too.*"

"*I won't.*"

"*A'ight, a'ight, we see....*"

TELL ME SOMETHIN JOOD

"What tha fuck he mean, I'm handsome, but I ain't no Brad Pitt?"

Me 'n' Little Bit was talkin on tha phone about a news story about me. Almost three months after meetin tha press, I finally got some play. Yeah, they flashed my face on E! and BET. And there had been like a dozen or so articles; Little Bit got 'em hangin up on tha fridge. They all say All-American is startin a new campaign. They all say it's targetin "the urban market." They say tha ad is a lota things: "provocative," "striking," "powerful," "abrasive," "sexy," "contemporary," "revolutionary," "hot," "eye-opening." Some ran it, so folks could see it fuh themselves.

But I did all that Q&A fuh nuthin, cuz ain't none of them muthafuckas even mention me. Can ya be*lieve* that shit? Like, who tha fuck they think *made* tha ad? Uh-huh, Tha Kid was just too Black and too strong fuh 'em.

But they couldn't dismiss Tha Kid no mo'. Folks been caught stealin tha ad from subway stations and bus stops here in York Township, in La-La Land, and other cities. All-American's stock done gone up, sales done jumped thru tha fuckin roof (which ain't sayin shit since most folk still don't know they exist), and they about ta release tha ad as a poster. How about that: *me,* hangin up on people's walls and shit. And I ain't believe it, but there it was on tha page, in black 'n' white: All-American was chargin twenty bills a pop. I'm like, *Say what?* I just knew *that* musta been a misprint, that somebody was miscalculatin. But then Tommy Boy said it was true and that they already got like 20,000 calls. Yo, if ev'ry single call adds up ta just one sale, I'm gonna be collectin a phat forty g's, G.

But all this hype over tha ad been happenin under my nose. I mean, ain't nobody been runnin up ta me askin fuh no autograph. I know there been times when folks recognized me, but they just stared. I could tell what they was thinkin: *He looks like him, but that* can't *be him. Ain't no way he'd be a messenger.* Now that I think of it, I wasn't seein tha ad no fuckin place when I was still makin my rounds (now I know why). And I been layin low since leavin Mel's, any-ol'-way. I ain't even leave tha house ta talk ta tha brotha from the Associated Press.

So I was happy about finally gettin my name in print and gettin quoted. But that Pitt bullshit irked tha fuck outa me.

It irked Little Bit too. "What does *he* know, Pooquie? He wouldn't know what beauty in color looks like. And his opinion is really suspect if he thinks Brad Pitt is not only good-lookin but better-lookin than you. He's probably still angry because you brushed him off when he asked about representing you."

"He did?"

"Yeah, at the launch. He had his business card in his hand, holdin it out as he approached you. When he pressed you to set a lunch date with him and you told him no thanks, he had that look that said, 'How *dare* you turn *me* down!' Don't you remember?"

Oh yeah…I did. "You mean that roly-poly mutha-fucka wit' tha fucked-up toupee?"

He giggled. "Mmm-hmmm. Believe me, if you were his client, he would have said you were the *new* Brad Pitt."

"Why he even gotta compare me ta somebody, any-ol'-way?"

"Because they *always* have to. We just can't be us. We have to be held up to *their* standard. But you got your own standard. *We* got our own standard, and they can't touch it."

"Ha, ya know it, Baby."

"It's a jood story, though. And when AP does a story, the majors usually pick up on it right away. It looks like we did a very smart thing bringing Babyface in when we did."

"Yeah. If he ain't get them ta change none of that shit, I wouldn't be gettin a piece of that new pie."

"And if that poster moves the way they think it will, who knows, there could be a postcard, maybe even a greeting card."

"A *greetin* card?"

"Yeah. Just like Babyface said, they're gonna make as much money off of this deal as they can. So those modeling agencies should be banging on your door any minute now."

"Ha, yeah, like them white talent scouts and college coaches trekkin ta tha hood, promisin hoop dreams and shit. Can't none of 'em be trusted, any-ol'-way."

"Well, you're gonna have to get some sort of rep."

"Why can't *you* do it, Baby?"

"Pooquie, we already talked about this—"

"I know, but you be jood at it."

"I don't know the first thing about the business. You need someone who does. And besides, I have a career, remember? It may be in flux right now, but it's still there."

"You still worried about that?"

"No, no, I'm not worried. Just…antsy."

"Don't be, Baby. Somethin's gonna find you."

"Somethin's gonna find me?"

"Yeah. You too jood ta hafta go out and find somethin. Just like all that freelance you got, yo' next full-time gig is gonna find you."

I could feel him smilin.

"Thanks, Pooquie."

"You welcome."

"What I *can* do for you is some research, and see about a Black agent."

"That would be jood."

"And while I'm at it, I'll ask Babyface about a Black entertainment lawyer and B.D. about a Black accountant. I think he has one. You'll need them all to keep an eye on All-American."

"Thanks, Baby."

"Anytime, Pooquie. Anytime."

"Little Bit?"

"Yes?"

"I miss you much."

"I miss you much too. It's only been eight days, but it feels like eight months."

"Tell me about it."

"You ain't been lettin nobody get up in my stuff, have you?"

He got me. "Huh?"

"You heard. We know how you can be. You don't get none in like a week—no, let's make that six days—and you *really* start to itchin."

He got me ta smile this time, but I brushed it off. "Why you even wanna try and go there, Baby?"

"*Try* and go there? Have you forgotten that I *live* there?" He giggled. "But, seriously…are you doin OK?"

I sighed. "Yeah…as OK as I can be doin."

"I'm sure you're doin much better than you think."

"I hope you right."

"You know I am."

I looked at tha time. "Oh, Baby, I gotta go. Li'l Brotha Man, he gettin out early."

"Is it his last day?"

"Yeah. They had a party."

"Well, kiss him for me. And here's one for you."

Puck, Smack, Slurp, Pop.

My shit jumped. *"Day-*am, Baby. I felt *that.*"

He giggled. "Well, that was the idea. I'll speak to you later. Love you."

"Love you, too. Peayce."

LONGEST DAY OF MY LIFE

"Aw, Daddy, do I have to?"

"Yeah, you hafta. This yo' graduation. You wanna look jood, right?"

"Yes."

"Well, then..."

"But it's so *hot*, Daddy."

"I know, I know, but you can take it off when it's all over, a'ight?"

"OK. But don't make it tight, Daddy."

"I ain't."

When I was done, I smiled. "You look jooda than me."

"I do?"

"Yeah, you do."

"Thank you." He smiled.

Tha phone rang. He ran and picked it up.

"Hell-oh?... Hi, Mitch-hull!... I'm doing jood, how are you?... That's jood.... Huh?... Uh-huh... Yes, I still know it by heart.... Are you gonna come?... Jood!... Uh-huh... Daddy is right here...he just put my tie on for me.... Uh-huh... I think so.... OK... Thank you... OK, I'll see you later...here's Daddy. 'Bye."

He turned ta me. "Daddy, it's Mitch-hull."

I got up from tha sofa. I took it. "Thanks, man."

"You're welcome." He smiled.

I did too. "Go and see if Moms is ready, a'ight?"

"OK." And off he went.

"Hey," I mumbled.

"Well, hello, good morning, and happy birthday to you."

"Thanks," I sighed.

"Boy, I can tell you're glad to hear from me."

I leaned against tha fridge. "Ain't you callin just a little late?"

"Am I?"

"Yeah, and you know it."

"Pooquie, it was after midnight when I got in."

"So? I told you I was gonna be up—"

"And I told you I don't make it a habit of callin people's houses after ten o'clock."

"I said I was gonna be puttin up tha balloons and fixin up tha house and shit. I wanted ta talk ta you."

"Well, you must not have wanted to talk to me *that* bad. You coulda called me."

"I know, but I ain't know when you was gettin in. I ain't wanna keep gettin tha machine. When you get in?"

"At around two."

"You have a jood time?"

"Yes."

"How ya speech go?"

"I wouldn't exactly call it a speech. I just said a few words."

"You was representin tha whole class, Baby. That's a big deal."

"Well, it went fine."

"Was he there?"

"You know he was."

"And?"

"And what?"

"Did he want some?"

"Well, that's puttin it rather bluntly."

"You asked."

He sighed. "Yes, he did. And I told him my man wouldn't appreciate him hittin on me. And then I showed him my picture of you and Junior." That was one of my birthday gifts ta him, and ya just know he started cryin after he unwrapped that giant 16-by-22 print. Ev'rybody at tha party fell in love wit' Li'l Brotha Man (B.D. and Lynette said they wanted ta adopt him; I gave 'em both a wallet-size photo instead).

I guess that coach could see we was a package deal too. I grinned. "What he say?"

"That we make one cute family. And that you are lucky to have me."

Yeah, I am.

"So, how was the boys' night out?" he asked.

"We had a jood time."

"What did you two do?"

"He ain't wanna do nuthin special. We hit Mickey D's and had Big Macs. Then we came back here and made a big bowl of popcorn and watched *Aladdin*. He just loves that movie. I sketched a few things, and he colored them in. We did one of you."

"Y'all did?"

"Yeah. And he gave me my present."

"What did he give you?"

"This gold chain wit' a charm that says #1 DADDY."

"That's really nice."

"Yeah. How come you still home?"

"I'm about to leave. It's not gonna take me long. I wanted to find out if there was something you all needed or wanted me to bring."

I chuckled. "I don't know about nobody else, but I know whatcha can bring *me*!"

"Oh, no, I am not *even* goin to take *that* trip this morning, because I do not have time to pack a bag, OK?"

"You ain't gonna *need* no luggage, Baby!"

"Uh-huh. *Any*way, I just don't like showin up at a party empty-handed, even if it's for a child."

"I can't think of nuthin, Baby."

"All right. I just want to make a jood impression."

"On who?"

"Who you think? My mother-in-law."

I did a double take. *"Huh?"*

"You heard. I want her to like me just as much as mine likes you."

"Baby, tha way Li'l Brotha Man talk about you, she like you already."

"Well, I hope she doesn't change her mind after she meets me."

"She ain't."

"OK. I'll be waiting outside the church."

"Cool. We see you there."

"Pooquie?"

"Yeah?"

"I love you."

"I love you too, Baby." I hung up tha phone and made my way ta tha bedrooms. "C'mon, y'all, let's be out. I don't wanna be sittin in no Jim Crow seats!"

Just like he said he would, Little Bit was there when we pulled up. I let Li'l Brotha Man, Moms, Sunshine, and her moms, Gloria, out so I could find a parkin space. I was lucky enuff ta catch a brotha pullin out just a block away. I could tell by tha look on Little Bit's face that he wanted ta jump in tha car wit' me—he ain't wanna be left by himself wit' Moms 'n' Sunshine. But when I got back, they already found seats up front, and it looked like Moms 'n' Sunshine was fightin over Little Bit's attention. I sat down next ta Sunshine on tha end of tha row, and she ain't even notice I was there till tha organ started chimin. I had tapped Little Bit on his shoulder as they talked; I winked at him and when he winked back, I knew he was a'ight. But wit' my arm around Sunshine and Little Bit holdin her hand...this was just *too* mutha-fuckin close fuh comfort, ya know what I'm sayin?

There was only thirty students graduatin, but you'd think there was hundreds gettin diplomas wit' all them folks up in tha church. Ev'ry inch of ev'ry pew was filled. But these days, anytime somebody movin ta tha next level, even if it's just ta tha first grade, it's time ta celebrate. That's why they had tha ceremony in tha church, which is across tha street from tha school. Havin somethin like this in some gymnasium or auditorium just ain't tha move. And Li'l Brotha Man was right: it was hot as a mutha-fucka outside, but it was cool inside, thanks ta them fans blowin ev'rywhere. I had one sittin right in fronta me, so I was jood-2go.

I was so fuckin glad it started at twelve sharp and that it ain't last long. We was outa there in a hour. That's one thing I hate about goin ta church: you don't never know when you gonna be comin out. Don't let them church queens get happy (uh-huh, there's no sissies like church sissies like no sissies I know, ya know?) or let them church ladies get ta testifyin that "Can't nobody do me like Jesus" or "Jesus is the only man I need" (uh-huh, and that's cuz no other man wants 'em or would wanna do 'em, right?). A service that's s'pose ta be an hour be stretchin ta two or even three. And I'm usually asleep five minutes after sittin down, any-ol'-way.

But ain't no way I was gonna be snorin today. It was my job ta get it all on videotape, and I got tha lens in position as soon as Li'l Brotha Man and his posse started marchin, girls down one middle aisle swayin, boys down my side struttin. They was in line by height, so Li'l Brotha Man was bringin up tha rear. He was all teeth when he was about ta pass us, wavin 'n' tossin tha tassel on his cap (like their gowns, it was purple). He took his seat wit' ev'rybody else in tha choir stand.

I wasn't int'rested in no preacher prayin, nobody singin (even tho' a sista tore up "A Dream With Your Name on It" by Jennifer Holliday) or no principal or teacher braggin about their class. I just couldn't wait ta see my man bein brought on as valedictorian, gettin his award and takin his bow. Sunshine, who started cryin as soon as tha thing started, really got ta boo-hooin when his name was called. Between wipin her tears and blowin her nose, all she could say was, "Oh, my *baby*." Yeah, I couldn't talk: I was sheddin a few myself, not ta mention yellin shit like, "A'ight, Li'l Brotha Man. That's *my* son." I could tell he was ner-vous; as tha applause died down, he just froze. When he saw me nod at him, he looked straight ahead and said his speech, which Little Bit helped him write:

"On behalf of my class, I want to thank our principal, Mister Price, our teacher, Misses Scott, and our parents for making this a special day for us all. We hope we made you proud today and hope we keep making you proud tomorrow. Thank you."

Man, you'd think he just scored a three-pointer wit' zero seconds left on tha clock tha way them folks started whistlin 'n' shoutin "Amen." I looked at Moms—she was just smilin, rockin 'n' noddin her head. She ain't had ta say nuthin. Her tears said it all, too.

"Oh, my *ba*-by!!" cried Sunshine fuh tha umpteenth time as Li'l Brotha Man flew inta her arms when it was all over.

When she stopped huggin tha life outa him, he was able ta finally say, "How did I do, Mommy?"

She kissed him on his nose. "You did very, *very* jood."

"You sure did," agreed Little Bit.

"Thank you, Mitch-hull."

"What else could he be but very, very jood?" said Moms, holdin out her arms. They hugged. Then he hugged his Grammy Gloria. Then Little Bit, who was clickin his own camera, tweaked his nose, and they hugged.

Then it was my turn. Little Bit took tha video camera. I got down on one knee. We hugged. I kissed him.

"Did I do jood, Daddy?"

"You did *better* than jood."

"*Better* than jood?"

"Yeah."

"How can something be *better* than jood?"

"I don't know, my man, but it was. Was you nervous?"

"Uh-huh. I almost forgot what I was gonna say!"

Ev'rybody laughed.

He nodded. "But I remembered."

"I know. And ya know somethin?"

"What?"

"I'm proud of you."

"Thanks, Daddy."

His eyes twinkled. We smiled. We hugged again.

"Daddy, don't cry." He wiped my tears.

"I can't help it. This tha best birthday present I *ever* got."

"It is?"

"Yeah. But I ain't tha one havin tha party. So let's get on home, a'ight?"

"OK. Um, Daddy?"

"Yeah?"

"Can I take off my tie now, *pleeze?*" He went fuh it.

I chuckled. "Hold up, hold up, man. You can take it off after we get some shots outside. A'ight?"

"OK."

I picked him up, wit' Sunshine leadin tha applause, and we headed fuh tha heat.

We all trekked back ta my house fuh Li'l Brotha Man's party at 2:30. It was a jood thing I already put up all them decorations, cuz folks started showin up at like 2:15. That was just enuff time fuh all of us ta catch our breath and fuh me 'n' Little Bit ta move tha furniture in tha livin room inta Moms's room. Moms was surprised Little Bit could handle such heavy stuff, but when he changed his clothes ta help, she saw where that strength came from. Little Bit been workin out wit' me, and I brought over my weights so he could pump it up durin tha day. He still slim, but he turnin inta a little mini muscle man—a step above tone but two below cut. He don't have a six-pack like Tha Kid, but he could soon. In a year or two, if he keep at it, he could be as thick as me. I told him his body could be better if he just worked on it. Now, when I'm wrestlin him down, tryin ta have my way, he can really put up a fight. He so jood at flippin me over, foldin me under, and lockin me up, he could prob'ly give Kenny Monday somethin ta fear on tha mat. And yeah, all that manhandlin turns me tha fuck on so much I want him ta turn me out (and he does). He lookin so jood now, I know I'm gonna hafta be wonderin which one of us folks are scopin out.

Like thirteen of Li'l Brotha Man's friends came, five from his class. Angel brought Anjelica, and Laticia dropped off Precious, who is lookin so much like Brotha Man it's scary. Just like last year, Li'l Brotha Man ran tha show. He decides what game they gonna play, when they gonna play it, how they gonna play it, and when it's over. Them kids just fall in line, obeyin his ev'ry command. And he already breakin tha girls' hearts: two of 'em looked like they was about ta fight over blindfoldin him fuh Pin the Tail on the Donkey.

I caught on tape another scene that really blew my mind: Moms, Sunshine, and Little Bit standin back, watchin it all, comparin notes and shit. I had 'em all wave and say hi. Seein them tagetha, I just couldn't believe how much they all "looked" alike. I mean, ev'ry one of 'em is a diff'rent shade of brown, and Little Bit don't be fillin in his clothes like Moms 'n' Sunshine. But there was just somethin about 'em all—I can't really say what it was—but whatever it was, I could see it in their eyes, in their faces, and it said ta me why Sunshine 'n' Little Bit are in my life. Could they see it too, lookin at each other? Tha way they got along, laughin and carryin on, I just knew they had ta.

When they started playin musical chairs, wit' Little Bit dee-jayin, our bell buzzed.

Moms inched her way by me. "I'll see who it is. Somebody sure is late."

A few minutes had passed when she came back.

"Excuse me, Spike Lee, but there's somebody at the door downstairs for you."

"Who is it, Ma?"

"Who do I look like, your receptionist? Go and see."

"I can't. I'm recordin history."

"I'll take over."

"You sure?"

"I think I know how to work a camera, OK? Go."

"A'ight. Don't miss nuthin."

"Don't worry, I won't."

I wasn't wastin no time waitin fuh no elevator, so I just jetted down tha stairs. I got ta tha lobby and stopped dead in my tracks comin out tha stairwell.

It was him.

The first time I ain't notice how much he looks like me. We was tha same height. He ain't have as much muscle as me, but he was bulk solid. He had a short fro and a goatee, both of 'em streaked wit' gray. Is this how I'm gonna look in twenty years?

"Uh...happy birthday."

I ain't say a word. I just frowned.

"Uh...I don't wanna interrupt. I know this is a great day for everybody. Li'l Brotha Man, he's made us all proud."

He smiled. I didn't.

"Uh, well, I just wanted to give...wanted Li'l Brotha Man to have this. A graduation and birthday gift." He handed me a small white envelope.

"He don't need nuthin from you."

He sighed. He frowned. "Let the boy have the gift. You don't have to tell him it's from me."

I looked at it. I looked at him. I took it. "Is that it?"

"No, no it's not—"

"Make it quick, a'ight? I'm busy."

"Raheim...I just want you to know—"

"Yeah?" I snapped.

"I...I know I hurt you. But I didn't hurt anybody more than myself."
He went in his shirt pocket. "I...uh...also have somethin for you."

"You can keep that, cuz there ain't nuthin I want from you."

"It ain't for me to keep. It doesn't belong to me. It belongs to you."
He held out a blue velvet ring box.

I stared at it. I started shakin.

I knew what was in it.

Knock, knock.

"Raheim?"

"Yeah?"

"Can I come in?"

I wiped my tears and cleared my throat. "Uh...yeah."

It was Little Bit. I was in my room, thinkin. He closed tha do'. He
smiled, lookin at my walls.

"Well...The City of New York, Department of Health, Certificate of
Birth...Raheim Errol Rivers Jr....June 5, 1988...5:10 A.M....hmmm...Li'l
Brotha Man at two weeks...he was such an adorable baby...Li'l Brotha
Man, one month...Li'l Brotha Man, six months...Li'l Brotha Man, one
year...two years... three...four...five..." He looked at me. "And soon to
be six." He sat next ta me on my bed. "You didn't tell me your room was
a shrine for Junior."

I nodded.

"So, where are you gonna put his diploma?"

I shrugged.

"I was expecting wall-to-wall Michael Jordan, not just two posters and
a Wheaties box." He laughed. "I guess Junior knows how his daddy
feels about him."

I sighed.

"He was asking for you. Well, everybody was wondering where you
disappeared to. The dance contest just ended; Junior and Bernadette
won. They make such a cute couple. It's about that time to cut the
cake. You know he wants to sit on his daddy's lap for that."

I looked down.

He grabbed my right hand. "What is it? Tell me."

I went in my shirt pocket. I took it out. I put it in his hand. He
looked at it. He looked at me.

"He gave it ta me...when I was like three...I remember."

Little Bit let 'em dangle. "Are they your baby rings?"

"Tha gold one is mine. Tha silver one is his. He put that necklace on me ev'ry nite…befo' I went ta sleep."

"He took it with him?"

"Yeah. Moms always said it was lost. But when she finally told me he was gone…I knew."

"Did he tell you why he took it?"

I took tha card out my pocket. I gave it ta him. It read,

> *Raheim,*
> *I know I took away so much.*
> *Maybe this is the only thing*
> *I can give back.*

I got up and walked over ta tha window. "Baby…I don't know what ta do."

"What do you mean?"

"I…I wanna…I wanna…" I turned around. "I wanna see, ya know…I wanna…find out…but I'm scared."

He walked over. He held me. "It's OK to be scared, Pooquie."

"And…I'm angry…and I'm…I don't know…kinda confused, ya know? And…and…uh…I…I just ain't sure, Baby."

He smiled. "And it's OK to be angry. And to be confused. And to be unsure. It's OK."

"I…I wanna be careful, ya know?"

"I know. None of those feelings are gonna go away overnight. But they can."

We tapped foreheads.

He frowned. "Does this mean you're gonna stop callin *me* Daddy?"

I blushed.

He grinned. "Happy birthday."

"You already told me."

"Yeah, I know. But I didn't get to *show* you."

He tongued me like tha world was gonna end—I swear, I felt that tickle all *down* my throat—and Tha Kid was enjoyin it.

"Pooquie?" he mouthed.

"Mmm," I groaned, goin fuh mine.

He giggled. "Uh, your son is waiting."

I stopped. I realized where we was. We was exchangin some serious looks all day. We both got pinches and brushes in when nobody was lookin, but we was never alone.

Yeah, Tha Kid was frustrated. "Day-am. It's been over a week, Baby."
"I know. But don't worry. Tonight, it's *definitely* on."

"C'mon, Li'l Brotha Man...I wanna talk ta ya."
"OK, Daddy."
I sat on my bed, puttin him on my left knee. "So, you have a jood time taday?"
"Yes! It was the *best* birthday and graduation party I ever had!"
I chuckled. "Oh, yeah?"
"Uh-huh."
"But this was yo' first graduation party. How can it be the best?"
"Be-cause..."
"Ha, be-cuz what?"
He clapped his hands, grinnin like cray-zee, them eyes just twinklin.
"Be-cause I loved all my presents."
"You did?"
"Uh-huh. I can't wait to ride my bike. Will you help me learn to ride, Daddy?"
"You know I will."
"And I had *two* cakes! They were *so* cho-co-latey, and *so* jood! And all my friends came...did you see Bernadette, Daddy?"
"Yeah, I did."
"I *told* you she was cute!"
"Yeah, she is, Li'l Brotha Man. You got jood taste, just like yo' daddy."
"And Mitch-hull came! I love the clothes he gave me. And I can't wait to read my books. I'm so happy he's my god-daddy."
"Yeah, I think he's happy about that too. Uh, listen, Li'l Brotha Man...I got somethin ta tell ya. I...I...I'm kinda scared ta tell ya."
"Why?"
"Cuz...it's a lot ta deal wit' and...I don't know if...if—"
"Remember what you said to me, Daddy?"
"What I say ta you?"
"You said I don't have to be scared to tell you something. So you don't have to be scared to tell me something."
I nudged his forehead wit' mine. I grinned. "Thanks, man."
He grinned too. "You're welcome."
I was searchin fuh tha right words; nuthin was comin. He started rubbin my hands, which were folded on his lap. He smiled. I did too.
"Remember when I said that...Grampy is...in heaven?"
"Uh-huh."

"Well…he ain't in heaven."

"He's not?"

"No, he ain't."

"Where is he?"

"He…he alive."

"Alive?"

"Yeah."

"You mean…he's not dead?"

"Yeah."

"How, Daddy? I thought you said when somebody dies, they don't come back?"

"Li'l Brotha Man…I told you he was in heaven cuz…cuz we…cuz I thought he was."

"Well, where was he, Daddy?"

"I don't know. Uh, he gave you tha tickets ta tha movie."

"You mean, to see *The Lion King* at Radio City?"

"Yeah. They was yo' present."

"You mean, I have a *grampy*? And he gave me a *present*?"

"Yeah."

"Joody, joody!"

"You happy about that?"

"Yes, I am! But, Daddy?"

"Yeah?"

"If Grampy is alive, why didn't he give me the present himself?"

"Cuz, uh…I ain't want him comin ta tha party."

"Why, Daddy?"

"Cuz…I…I don't like Grampy."

"You don't?"

"No."

"But why, Daddy? Aren't you supposed to?"

"Well, I guess most people would say yeah, but…sometimes things happen that make you not like somebody…that make you not love 'em…that might even make you hate 'em."

"Oh…uh, do you hate Grampy?"

"I don't know if I hate him right now, Li'l Brotha Man…but I know I did when I was young."

"But why?"

"Cuz…he…he walked out on me and Grammy."

"He walked out?"

"Yeah."

"You mean…he left you and Grammy?"

"Yeah, he did."

He looked down. He clasped his hands tagetha. Then he looked at me wit' them sad eyes.

"When did he do that?"

"When I was yo' age."

"Why did he do it, Daddy?"

"I'm still tryin ta find out. It's hard ta get thru."

He nodded. "He did a very bad thing."

"Yeah, he did. I still hurt, and I can feel it right here—" I put my right hand ta my heart; he put his left hand over it—"and that's why I ain't want him comin ta tha party."

"Oh."

"See...I ain't sure if I'm gonna let him see you...at least right now. There's things we gotta work out...it's gonna take time, cuz things...they still tense between us. Things just ain't gonna change like that. But this ain't got nuthin ta do wit' you. You not tha problem. You understand?"

"I think so."

"I just need you ta be patient wit' me, wit' us. A'ight?"

"Patient? What does that mean?"

"That means waitin fuh me, fuh us, ta do what we gotta do and say what we gotta say so things can get better. You think you can do that?"

"Yes, I think I can."

"Jood."

"Daddy?"

"Yeah?"

"Um...is that why you got upset and you spanked me?"

Uh-huh, just like a razor. That's my son.

I sighed. "Yeah, Li'l Brotha Man. I was upset about him comin back. Angry, kinda confused, and...not really sure about things. And I wasn't handlin anything tha right way. I'm sorry."

He rubbed my face. "That's OK. I forgive you. Do you feel better now?"

"Yeah, yeah, I do. Thanks ta you."

"Jood." He smiled, then he frowned. "Um, Daddy?"

"Yeah?"

"Um, are you...are you gonna leave me?"

"*Leave* you?"

"Uh-huh. Like Grampy left you and Grammy."

"No, Li'l Brotha Man. I ain't gonna leave you. I ain't *never* gonna walk out on you. Whenever you need me, I'm *always* gonna be there. Believe that. A'ight?"

"OK."

"Can I have a hug?"

"Of course, Daddy. You don't have to ask."

He squeezed me real tight. It felt so jood.

"You still love me?" I asked.

He laughed. "Of *course* I do, Daddy. You my Daddy. I'm *always* gonna love you."

"Promise?"

"Promise!" he saluted. "Do you still love me?"

I laughed. "You know it. I'm *always* gonna love you, too. You my Li'l Brotha Man."

"Daddy?"

"Yeah?"

"Um…you think you ever gonna love Grampy?"

"I don't know, man…I can't say."

"Um…I know he did a very bad thing, but…would you be mad if…if *I* love him?"

"Nah, nah, I wouldn't be mad. But you never even met him. What makes ya think you gonna love him?"

"I don't know. I…I just always wanted a grampy."

"Oh, yeah?"

"Uh-huh. Anjelica and Bernadette and Theresa and Terrence have grampies, and they say how much fun it is."

"Well, if y'all get ta meet, and if you end up likin him or lovin him, that's a'ight. I ain't gonna stop lovin you if you do. A'ight?"

"OK."

"Gimme a kiss."

He gave me a big one on my lips.

I stood up, and he held on to me as I carried him. "A'ight, let's go home."

"Daddy?"

"Yeah?"

"I hope you love Grampy one day."

"You do?"

"Yes."

"Why?"

"So we can be one big family!"

"Oh, yeah?"

"Uh-huh. Because then I'll have my mommy, my daddy, two grammies, *and* a grampy!… Ooh, ooh, I know what I can do, Daddy. I can pray about it."

"Oh, yeah?"

"Yes. That's what Grammy and Mommy say I should do when I want something really bad." He put his hands tagetha like he was gonna do it right there. "You think it can help, Daddy?"

I shrugged. "I don't know, Li'l Brotha Man. Maybe it can."

"Yo, Baby, what's this?"

I walked inta tha livin room, and there was a candle lit wit' two glasses and a bottle of bubbly sittin on tha coffee table.

He hugged me from behind. "Just a little something to celebrate everything."

"Ev'rything?"

"Yes. Junior. You. Us."

"Well, let's get ta toastin."

We sat on tha couch. He poured. I kicked off my sandals. We held up our glasses.

He smiled. "Here's to Li'l Brotha Man, who made us proud. Here's to you...happy birthday. May you have many more...with *me*."

I blushed.

"And here's to us, one year later. Happy early anniversary, Pooquie. I love you."

"I love you too. Happy anniversary, Baby."

We clinked. We looped arms. We sipped. We kissed.

He settled against my chest. I wrapped him up. He sighed real heavy. "Yeah?" I asked.

"Mmm...I still can't believe you came tonight."

I started ta get up. "Yo, you want me ta go—"

He held me back. "*Hell* no! I mean, you've had a pretty long weekend, and it's not over yet."

"I know. But ain't no way I could be someplace else tanite. We got some catchin up ta do."

"Yeah, we do."

Lip lock time.

"So, tell me what happened with Junior."

I sighed. "Uh...we talked."

"And?"

"And I told him what tha deal was."

"*And?*"

I shrugged. "He cool wit' it."

"Of course he is. He's Li'l Brotha Man. Whatever he can do to make his daddy happy, he's gonna do it."

"Yeah."

"I'm sure he loves the fact that he finally *has* a grampy, even if he hasn't met him yet."

"Yeah. He knows it's gonna be some time. He wanted ta know if he looks like his grampy."

"What did you tell him?"

I sighed. "I told him we both do."

He nodded. "What about your mother and Crystal?"

"What about 'em?"

He smacked me on my thighs. "*You* know what I'm asking. What did they have to say about *me*?"

I chuckled. "Baby, I told you you ain't had nuthin ta worry about."

"Uh-huh. *What* did they say?"

"They said they really like you. Moms said she glad I got a friend who don't wear his pants off his behind. And she's happy you wear a belt."

We laughed.

"And she 'n' Sunshine said Li'l Brotha Man is lucky ta have a god-daddy like you."

"They did?"

"Yeah. Ain't they tell you? All that talkin y'all did…"

"Did we make you nervous?"

"Nah, nah. I ain't had nuthin ta be nervous about."

"Uh-huh. Well, we *did* have a lot to talk about."

"Y'all did?"

"Yeah. We talked a lot about me, but we also talked about you."

"About me?"

"Yeah."

"*And?*"

"Well, Crystal agrees with me that you are stubborn. We also agree that it is an inherited trait."

I frowned.

"And your mother feels, like I, that it is time you got your GED."

"Yeah, yeah, I know. I been thinkin about it."

"According to her, that's *all* you been doin."

"I'm gonna do it."

"Uh-huh. *When?*"

"Startin next month."

He jerked his body around ta face me. "*Really?*"

"Yeah. I'm gonna have tha time."

"Does this mean you're gonna apply to college, too?"

"Can we just do one thing at a time? And don't be leavin no college catalogs around tha place, neither. One thing at a time. A'ight?"

"OK, OK."

"You gonna help me study?"

"Help you *study*? You a walkin almanac. You don't need my help."

"I will, too. I ain't been in no classroom in six years, Baby."

"I'm sure that won't matter. But if you need me, you know I'm here for you."

"Thanks, Baby."

"Anytime, Pooquie, anytime."

I squeezed him so tight I know I musta hurt him, but he ain't say nuthin. I think he needed it just as much as I did.

When I let him go, he went inside tha coffee table and came out wit' two cards and two jewelry boxes: one white, long and thin, tha other black, compact and square.

He handed me one of tha cards and tha thin box first. "Well, it's almost midnight. You have to open these first. Happy birthday."

"Thanks, Baby." Tha card was from Hallmark. A fine brotha was on tha front, and it said, TO MY MAN, ON HIS BIRTHDAY. Hmmm…I just know Hallmark ain't expect this card ta be given *by* a man *to* a man. It was really sappy 'n' sweet inside, but these kinda cards are s'pose ta be, right? Just like Li'l Brotha Man, I started gigglin and shakin tha box.

It was a gold link bracelet wit' POOQUIE engraved on it. It was so shiny, I thought I was gonna go blind lookin at it.

"*Day*-am, Baby. This is capital P-h-a-*t*."

"I thought you might like it. Can I put it on you?"

"Go 'head."

He roped it around my right wrist. It felt so cool. It was just tha right size.

I shook my hand, just gleamin over it. "Thanks, Baby. I ain't *never* get nuthin like this from somebody."

I laid a slammer-jammer on his lips.

He grinned. "*Well*. You are *most* welcome. I can't *wait* to see what I'll get after you open the other gift." He gave it ta me. "Happy early anniversary, Pooquie."

I knew he ain't get *this* card from no Hallmark: there was two naked brothas on tha front, holdin each other, just gazin in each other's eyes. They "looked" like us: one was brown and slim like him, tha other was taller and a diesel cut chocolate like me. Inside he wrote,

> *There's been joy and pain*
> *there's been laughter and tears*
> *They said it couldn't be done*
> *but we're celebrating one year*
> *Happy Anniversary, Pooquie*
> *4-Ever, 4-Always, My Love…*
> *Little Bit*

"That's beautiful, Baby." I grinned. He did too.

I opened tha box, and my eyes couldn't believe what they was seein—and neither could my mouth. I couldn't say nuthin. It just stayed open as I took out tha silver-plate key chain wit' POOQUIE on it. I tapped tha two gold keys, and they started danglin. I just sat there, watchin 'em.

He smiled. "One is for the doors downstairs, the other for the apartment. You won't need the bolt lock since we never use it."

I was still speechless. Now that *that* day had come, I ain't had shit ta say.

Little Bit grinned. "What's wrong, Pooquie—cat got ya tongue?"

We giggled.

"Uh, yeah, I...I guess. I guess I just don't have tha key ta yo' heart, hunh?"

"No, you don't."

Our lips did a slammer-jammer again. We snuggled.

He found his spot on my chest. He sighed. "Welcome home, Pooquie."

I grinned up a storm.

ABOUT THE AUTHOR

James Earl Hardy is the author of *B-Boy Blues*, praised as the first Africentric, gay, hip-hop love story. He has penned two nonfiction titles—a bio on Spike Lee and a portrait of Boyz II Men, both from Chelsea House's Black Achievement Series. He is featured in *Out With It: Gay and Straight Teens Write About Homosexuality*, *Out in All Directions: The Almanac of Lesbian and Gay America*, and *Shade: An Anthology of Fiction by Gay Men of African Descent*.

An honors graduate of the Columbia University School of Journalism, he is also a feature writer and entertainment critic. His work has earned him grants from the E. Y. Harburg Arts Foundation and the American Association of Sunday and Feature Editors; two Educational Press Association Writing Awards; a Columbia Press Association Feature Writing Citation; a *Village Voice* writing fellowship; and scholarships from the Paul Rapoport Memorial Foundation and the National and New York chapters of the Association of Black Journalists. He lives in New York City.